*A*t the twenty-five-yard line, I spun around, continuing to jog backward. Jude was still at the mouth of the tunnel, watching me with a grin, appearing as enamored by me as he had on the day he'd confessed his love. That look, more than any of the others, got to me in all the ways a guy's look was supposed to "get" to his girl.

I perused the stands one more time to make sure we were alone. It felt so damn open in here, which was unnerving, but how many times could a girl say she'd been with the number-one-ranked college quarterback in the nation right on the fifty-yard line?

Yeah, this was a once-in-a-lifetime deal, and I wasn't going to let it pass me by.

Inhaling a slow breath, I reached for the hem of my sweater and started sliding it up my stomach.

CRUSH

Nicole Williams

HARPER

An Imprint of HarperCollins*Publishers*

Crush
Copyright © 2013 by Nicole Williams
All rights reserved. Printed in the United States of America.
No part of this book may be used or reproduced in any manner whatsoever without written permission except in the case of brief quotations
embodied in critical articles and reviews. For information address
HarperCollins Children's Books, a division of HarperCollins Publishers,
10 East 53rd Street, New York, NY 10022.
www.epicreads.com

Library of Congress catalog card number: 2013934073
ISBN 978-0-06-226717-7 (pbk.)

Typography by Erin Fitzsimmons
13 14 15 16 17 LP/RRDH 10 9 8 7 6 5 4 3 2 1
❖
First Edition

For Eric, the man who I have loved, do love, and always will love. You believed in me from the start, even when I wasn't so sure. Here's to April 21, 2001, bruised shins, and going out on a limb . . . so glad you did.

ONE

*U*p, down. Round and around. Rinse and repeat. That was our pattern. That was our world.

With a guy like Jude Ryder at my side, the lows in life were lower and the highs were higher. This was our reality, our story . . . our *love* story. We fought; we made up. We messed up; we apologized. We lived; we learned. Jude and I had made a lot of mistakes in the history of our relationship, but one thing we always seemed to get right? Our all-consuming love for each other.

This was my life.

And you know what?

Life was pretty damn good.

Even despite the fact that I had no clue where I was.

"What are you up to?" I whispered back to Jude, continuing to let him lead me into the black hole.

"Something you'll love," he replied, squeezing my shoulders as he steered me along. My heels began to echo around me.

So we were in a tunnel, but what tunnel was totally beyond me, because Jude had made me close my eyes the moment I'd answered the door this evening. Other than driving around in his ancient rumble-wagon of a truck for the better part of a Friday date night, I'd lost my bearings in every way a girl could ever lose them.

Given the fact that Jude Ryder was my fiancé, my bearings had been a tad off-kilter for the past few years, but they were especially off the grid tonight.

Did this tunnel have an end? The longer we continued down it, the louder my footsteps echoed around us.

"Is whatever you're up to illegal?" I asked, not sure I really wanted to know.

"Is that a trick question?" he said, sounding amused.

"Is that a trick answer?"

He didn't respond immediately. Instead, I felt his mouth warm the skin at the base of my neck. One full breath out, and one full breath in, slow and deep and suffocating, before his lips grazed the heated patch of skin.

I tried not to react like his touch was hardwired to drive every bit of me crazy, but even after years together, Jude could still unravel me with one touch. My skin was pricking to life with tiny goose bumps that trailed down to my lower back when his mouth pulled away.

"There will most certainly be high points tonight that could be classified as illegal in every one of the Bible Belt states," he said, his voice low with desire. Not quite as rough as it got when he needed me right then and there; it was still restrained enough that I knew he wasn't going to throw me up against the nearest wall and start fisting up my skirt before we got a step farther. "Does that answer your question?"

"No," I said, trying to sound controlled. Trying to sound like he hadn't made my stomach clench with desire from one kiss. "It doesn't answer my question. So let's try this again . . ." I cleared my throat, reminding myself I was trying to sound unaffected. "In whatever never-ending hallway you're leading me down, toward whatever location you're aiming to wind up at, could either one of these trespasses be considered illegal if we were to be tried in court?"

He didn't make a noise, but I knew he was trying to contain a chuckle. One of those low, rumbling ones that vibrated through my body when he was pressed up against me. "Since you put it that way . . ." he started, stopping me suddenly. His hands left my shoulders and tapped my eyelids. "Yes. It could be. However," he said, "they'd have to catch us first. Open your eyes, babe."

I blinked my eyes a few times to make sure what I was seeing was real.

After another half dozen blinks, I could be reasonably certain that what my eyes were taking in was, in fact, real.

We were inside the Carrier Dome, just at the mouth of one of the tunnels. However, this was the dome like I'd never seen it in the past three years of attending almost every home game. At the center of the field, right at the fifty, a blanket was spread out, and what looked like a picnic basket rested in one corner. A smattering of white candles in clear jars were dotted around the blanket. It was still, silent, and peaceful.

Not the first three words you'd usually use to describe a college football arena.

And this wasn't the place a girl expected her fiancé would take her on a big surprise date he'd wanted her to get dressed up for.

I grinned.

Not what I'd expected, but exactly what I wanted.

"What do you think? This worth 'illegal'?" he asked, winding his arms around my waist and tucking his chin over my shoulder.

I couldn't take my eyes off the candlelit scene in front of me. A picnic on the fifty-yard line.

I knew it might not have ranked in the top-ten desired

dates for most girls, but it hit the number-one spot for this girl

"It's only illegal if we get caught," I answered, turning my head so he could see my smile, before breaking free of his arms and jogging over to the blanket.

This was the first time I'd been down on the field since Jude and I got engaged our freshman year of college, but it really did seem like it had been only a handful of days ago. I'd discovered another one of life's clichés by being with Jude: The happier you are in life, the faster it passes you by. Life was one sick bastard if happy people were repaid with a life that seemed short. Short life or long life, it didn't matter—I wasn't giving up Jude either way.

At the twenty-five-yard line, I spun around, continuing to jog backward. Jude was still at the mouth of the tunnel, watching me with a grin, appearing as enamored by me as he had on the day he'd confessed his love. That look, more than any of the others, got to me in all the ways a guy's look was supposed to "get" to his girl.

I perused the stands one more time to make sure we were alone. It felt so damn open in here, which was unnerving, but how many times could a girl say she'd been with the number-one-ranked college quarterback in the nation right on the fifty-yard line?

Yeah, this was a once-in-a-lifetime deal, and I wasn't

going to let it pass me by.

Inhaling a slow breath, I reached for the hem of my sweater and started sliding it up my stomach.

Jude's expression changed instantly. His forehead lined deeper and one corner of his mouth twitched.

Raising a brow, I lifted the rest of my sweater, tugging it over my head and dropping it onto the Astroturf. My adrenaline was pumping. The anticipation of having Jude with me set it off, and the thrill of being here was firing it to new heights.

Winding my arms behind my back, I unclasped my bra. It snapped free, sliding down my arms to join the sweater at my feet.

Jude wasn't looking at my face any longer.

Wetting his lips, he started toward me.

I started my backward journey again, flicking him a coy smile. I was going to have fun with him, draw this out. Get even with him for what he so often did to me.

He stopped as soon as I started moving away, staring at me like he knew exactly what game I was playing and he both loved and hated being a pawn in it.

Pausing just long enough to step out of my heels, I slid my thumbs under the waist of my skirt and lowered it down my hips, slowing just enough to gather the material of my panties with it. I let both skirt and underwear gather at my ankles.

Jude's eyes drifted lower, his chest rising and falling noticeably, even from where I stood thirty yards away from him. When his eyes did shift back to mine, they were dark with one thing.

Absolute need.

His body sprang to action as he burst onto the field after me, running at the same pace he did when he was playing a game. I turned and laughed with every step as I ran away from him.

It was a futile effort, running from Jude—both right now, and in life in general.

Jude always caught up with me. Sometimes he gave me a head start, but he never let me get too far.

This time, I barely made it ten yards before I felt his strong arms cinch around me. A shout of surprise punctuated my laughter as he pulled me hard against him. Not only had he managed to cover thirty yards in the time it had taken me to sprint less than a third of that, he'd removed his shirt in the process. The heat coming off his chest warmed my back, and the movement of his muscles against me as he breathed in and out warmed everything else.

"Going somewhere?" he said, nudging at my neck until I

gave him better access to it.

"Anywhere," I answered, letting my head fall back against him when his mouth smoothed down the arch of my neck. "As long as you're with me."

I felt his smile against my skin. His hands slid lower, pausing when they reached my hips. "How would you feel about 'anywhere' being on that blanket over there?"

Everything south of my navel tightened. "I'd say even if I wasn't so sure, you'd keep trying to persuade me," I said, gliding my hands down his forearms, pausing to weave my fingers through his where they still rested over my hips.

He pressed harder against my back. "You'd be right," he said, skimming our hands up my stomach as he steered us toward the blanket. Our hands didn't stop until they slid beneath one of my breasts, molding around it.

Nipping at the skin of my neck, he picked up his pace until we were weaving through the glowing candles. At the edge of the blanket, Jude spun me around. His mouth parted, as he sucked in streams of air in quick bursts. This was his tortured look. When he couldn't have me fast enough.

It was a look I tried to savor, because it never lasted long. I could only hold Jude off for so long before me, him, or both of us gave up trying to prolong the inevitable.

"Damn, Luce," he breathed, stroking my cheek with his hand. "You're so beautiful."

I smiled. Not so much at what he said, but at the way he said it. Jude conveyed his emotions and intentions in words and expressions that did unhealthy things to a girl's heart. "If you're trying to convince me with a little foreplay, I'll let you in on a secret," I said, winding my arms around the back of his neck. "You're going to get lucky no matter what you say or do, so you can save the sweet nothings for a time when you've pissed me off and are trying to get a little makeup sex."

He chuckled, his gray eyes darkening with every passing touch. "I don't seem to remember it requiring sweet nothings to ever get you—"

"Oh, shut up already," I interrupted, smirking up at him.

One corner of his mouth curved higher. "Why don't you make me?" he challenged, his gaze dropping to my lips.

Pressing harder into him, I let my fingers ski down the plane of his stomach, settling on the fly of his jeans. Tugging the button free, I slid my hand inside as my lips covered his mouth, a groan escaping it.

That shut him right up.

TWO

*J*ude's head reclined in my lap as he crunched into an apple and stared at the ceiling of the dome. He was still naked from the waist up, but his jeans hadn't made it all the way off. Apparently we hadn't been able to justify waiting the three seconds it would have taken to free him of them before we could get down to business.

We weren't big believers in delayed gratification.

I'd wrangled myself back into my sweater and skirt before we'd exchanged one hunger for another and dived into the picnic basket, although my panties and bra still littered the thirty-yard line.

"Tomorrow's the big day," he said around another bite of apple. The air smelled like the tangy sweetness of the fruit in his mouth. Not able to resist, I leaned down to kiss him, wanting to taste the aroma. It was even better combined with the taste of his mouth.

He was oozing that notorious Jude Ryder ego when I leaned back. He knew what he did to me. And he loved it.

I loved it too, although I didn't love how well *he* knew it.

"Tomorrow I could be a first-round draft pick, Luce," he continued, circling my ankle with his fingers. "We could be millionaires in twenty-four hours."

I had to force myself not to visibly wince. This talk—the draft, the money, the lifestyle—had been an area of contention this past year with the likelihood of Jude's being drafted into pro ball. I wasn't so sure how I felt about it, but Jude was sure enough for both of us.

Trouble was, his confidence wasn't rubbing off on me. If anything, the more confident he became, the less I felt. Money had the potential to change things. It had the potential to change people. I was worried about how all that money might change us. I loved him, and me, and us, just the way we were now.

Jude's being drafted his junior year of college was a one-in-a-million kind of an opportunity, the kind of thing college players would sell their souls to achieve. But it also meant he'd be dropping out of school. He'd made it this far; a part of me wanted to see him finish his degree—astound all those people back home who'd always pegged him as a high school dropout. Playing in the NFL had been a dream of Jude's forever. I couldn't postpone his dream any more than he could mine.

"From dining on peanut-butter sandwiches tonight to twenty-ounce, grade-A prime filet tomorrow night," he continued, his face almost glowing as his eyes drifted off to money-land. "We could get a new place, a new fancy-ass car. We could take a vacation to Hawaii. Fly first-class and shit. Think about it, Luce. Anything we want, we can have. Anytime we want it. No more scrambling around getting grease under our fingernails or waiting tables late at night to pay the electric bill." He paused, a contented smile settling deeper into his face. "We could have it all, baby."

I swallowed. "I thought we already did." My voice sounded sadder than I meant it to.

The skin between Jude's eyebrows puckered. "What do you mean?" he asked, his gaze zeroing in on me.

"I thought we already had it all," I repeated. "I've been on both sides of the money line, and the only thing it changes is your zip code. It can't make you happy if you weren't without it."

"Well, I've been on the losing side of the money game my whole life, and I know for a fact that money can make your life better if you can't even find enough quarters in the couch cushions to do a load of laundry at the local Suds N'

Wash." Dropping his apple to the side, he sat up and turned until he was facing me. The candlelight flickered around him, shadowing the crevasses of his muscles, highlighting the peaks of them, and made the sharp lines of his jaw even more defined. A man like Jude shouldn't be classified as beautiful, but in moments like this, he kind of was.

Jude Ryder. My beautiful fiancé.

He was waiting for me to respond.

"Okay, so money can make your life better if you're destitute," I said, prying my eyes from where they traced the grooves of his ab muscles. "But we're not destitute, Jude. We're college students with a roof over our heads, gasoline in our tanks, ramen noodles in our cupboards, and shirts on our backs. I couldn't imagine being any happier than I am right now, and if it was possible, money would certainly be the last thing on that list that could make me more so." I grabbed the plastic wineglass Jude had filled from a cheap bottle of sparkling wine and took a sip. It was delicious. I was as happy with a five-dollar bottle of sparkling wine from the drugstore as I would have been with the finest bottle of champagne money could buy.

"No, we're not destitute, but we're not thriving in the money department either, Luce," he said, grabbing my hand and pulling it into his lap. "And you're right that money couldn't make me happier than I am right now." He smiled so big it made the scar on his cheek pucker. "But it does mean I can finally be rid of my piece-of-shit truck and get a jacked-up, three-hundred-and-fifty-horsepower jet-black monster truck."

I rolled my eyes and shoved at him.

"And we can trade in that little go-kart of yours for a zippy convertible," he continued.

"I like my Mazda," I muttered, plucking a grape free from the vine and popping it into my mouth.

"And we can afford a house with a room for each day of the year, with so many maids and butlers you wouldn't have to lift a finger again. Unless it was to call for a fresh-squeezed orange juice." He was really on a roll, the words spilling out of his mouth as his eyes sparkled with the visions. My own eyes were narrowing as my stomach twisted.

"Money changes people, Jude," I whispered, staring into my cup.

We were silent as we let that settle between us.

"That's what you're worried about?" he said, his voice soft. "That the money will change you?"

I shook my head, focusing on the bubbles that crept up the sides of the cup. "No," I said, before looking into his eyes. "That it will change *you*."

His eyes narrowed for the shortest second before they widened with understanding. Winding an arm around my neck, he pulled me to him. "Come here," he whispered outside my ear, wrapping his other arm around my back. "The only thing that could change me is you, Luce," he said. "You, not anything else. Mountains of money included." I heard the grin in his voice. "No matter what happens tomorrow or how many millions they throw at me, I'm the same guy I am right now." He rubbed my back, pressing slow circles into my spine. "I'll just be picking you up in a truck you won't be embarrassed to be seen in."

"I've never been embarrassed to be seen with you," I said, letting him tuck my head under his chin. "Not even in that sorry excuse for scrap metal of a truck."

He barked out a laugh. "Good to know, Luce. Good to know."

THREE

"How are you *not* nervous?" I hissed over at Jude, where he stood casually leaning against a wall. We were in the infamous green room on the first night of the draft.

Reaching his hand out for mine, he lifted a shoulder. "The coaches already know who they're picking. There's nothing I can do now to change that." Once I grabbed his hand, he tugged me close and folded me tight against him. "However, I'm starting to get nervous you're about to pass out any second."

That wasn't so far off. I reminded myself to breathe. "As long as you keep holding on to me like this, at least I won't crack my head open if I do."

His arms fastened tighter around me before he started to sway in time to an imaginary beat. "You can dance in front of hundreds of people and not break a sweat," he said. The movement was relaxing me. "But your fiancé is waiting for the phone call to see which city he'll be moving to so he can kick some big-time football ass, and you're a thin line away from losing it." Pressing a kiss to my temple, he leaned his forehead into mine with a small shake of his head. "Just when I think I've got you all figured out, Lucy Larson."

My laugh sounded manic. Probably because that was how I felt. "I have to keep you on your toes somehow."

Jude's eyebrows moved against my forehead. "You excel at that, Luce."

That tone again. The undercurrent that revealed he was trying to say something else. There'd been an increasing amount of "undercurrent" the past few months.

"Meaning?" I asked, peaking my own brows so they were as high as his. I reminded myself we weren't alone, that we were surrounded by the best players in college football, along with their closest family and friends. This was neither the place nor the time to get into one of our spats.

"Meaning if you didn't keep me on my toes every second of every day, I'd have figured out a way to get you down the aisle by now," he said, and it all clicked into place. He was sulking because he didn't have me barefoot and pregnant in the kitchen yet.

Okay, so "barefoot and pregnant" might have been an

exaggeration, but there was no denying that Jude wanted me to be his wife the second after I'd agreed to marry him. He'd only been asking, begging, whining, and, as of late, sulking when I replied, "*Not yet.*"

It didn't have anything to do with my not wanting to marry him. Jude was going to be my husband. I was going to be Mrs. Jude Ryder one day.

I just wasn't ready for that day to be today. Or yesterday. Or tomorrow, for that matter. I wanted to finish school and have a few years of actual on-the-job dance experience before I became a Mrs. I didn't want to be known as the one girl in the history of the twenty-first century to have gone to school to get an MRS degree.

So my answer was, "Not yet."

But one day.

However, this wasn't what Jude liked to hear. So instead of arguing back with my list of valid reasons for postponing marriage, I redirected the conversation. I'd become a diversion ninja.

"And if I hadn't kept you on your toes the past three years, you wouldn't be about to be a first-round pick and to sign your life away for mountains of money," I replied, throwing his words back at him.

"Come on, Luce. I'm growing tired of the whole, stop, drop, and divert routine," he said, looking down at me, but still keeping me close. "Marriage isn't the end of the world."

"Then why do you keep acting like my not wanting to tie the knot tomorrow is?"

"Because your saying 'not now' *is* the end of the world," he said, fighting a smile. "Come on, baby. Marry me," he said, not like a question but like a command. I didn't reply, letting the seconds tick off in silence around us. "Marry me?" he repeated, this time as a plea. It crushed me a little bit every time, Jude pleading with me to marry him.

"I'm going to marry you," I answered.

He smirked at me. "When?"

I smirked back. "Soon."

"Can I get that in writing?" he asked. "Maybe a date, a time, and a location? You know, just so I can make sure to be there when the marrying mood strikes you?" He looked away, the lightness in his eyes shadowing.

Dammit. We'd officially crossed from his being marginally upset to full-on hurt. I hated that Jude felt this way, but I couldn't cave. I couldn't get married because I felt guilty. That would be a marriage doomed to failure, and when I said, "*I do*," it was going to be a onetime deal.

"Jude Ryder," I said, tilting his chin until he was looking at me. "Are you having an insecure moment? I thought you were immune to those." I tried on a smile, but it felt superficial. "Are you worried I'm not going to marry you?"

Even my light tone sounded artificial, too saccharine to be believable.

Leaning the back of his head into the wall, he lifted his face toward the ceiling. He couldn't look at me, or didn't want to, but his arms never loosened their hold. And I knew, no matter what was said or done, they never would. That was one of the many reasons I loved this man.

"I'm starting to worry," he said finally, shifting his gaze around the room, pretending he was interested in the handful of players pacing the room like caged lions, and their respective entourages of family and friends attempting, and failing, to calm them.

"Jude," I said, pulling his chin back to me. "Jude, look at me." I waited for him to turn to me. I caught a glimpse of just how vulnerable Jude Ryder was. How very terrified he was of one day being abandoned by the person he loved most. How the ghosts of his past—his mother leaving and his father being imprisoned—had been resurrected by my indecision. Seeing him this way almost had me running off to the nearest wedding chapel.

Almost.

I had to bite my tongue to keep from saying the words I knew would have soothed his pain instantly. I carefully thought of new ones I hoped would appease him. "I'm marrying you one day. One day sooner rather than later," I began, holding his gaze, not even allowing myself a blink that would break the contact. "There's never been a question that I'm yours. Yeah, we're not husband and wife yet, but I'm yours. And you're mine. Does a new title and a piece of paper really matter that much?" I already knew Jude's answer to this.

"Yes," he said, his jaw clenching as his eyes flashed. "Shit, yes, it does, Luce."

I flinched from the intensity of his tone.

"I want you in every way a person can be with another. *Every* way," he said, his voice low. "I want you as my wife. My. Wife," he repeated, as Territorial Jude burst free of his cage.

Territorial Jude had a way of bringing out Temperamental Lucy.

"And then what? I get a new apron and spatula every Christmas and you pee on my leg every day before going to work, to mark your territory?" I snapped back, aware there were others around us within hearing distance, but not caring at this point.

"Dammit, Luce," Jude seethed, working his tongue into his cheek. "Don't you do that crazy Luce thing and twist my words all the hell up. If I wanted some submissive, respectful little housewife I sure as shit wouldn't have fallen in love with you." He was a few notches below a shout, but I knew that wouldn't last, since I was planning to respond with a few choice four-letter words, followed by telling him to stick his head where the sun didn't shine.

And then his cell phone rang.

A silence fell over the room. Our argument was over as quickly as it had started. Sliding his phone from his pocket, Jude glanced at me. His eyes were wide with excitement, sparkling with anticipation. This was the call he'd waited for, for the better part of three years. He'd left his heart and sweat and blood on the field after every game in his college career, and now those sacrifices were about to be paid back in spades.

Or dollar bills.

He flashed me a quick smile and drew me closer with the arm he still had wound around me. His eyes flickered to his phone. They widened further.

"San Diego," he whispered, examining the screen again. His smile split his face in half. Leaning his head back, he hooted with all his might, filling the silent room with celebration.

I nodded my head in encouragement, mustering up a smile for him. This was what he wanted; this team was his first choice. He deserved this. He needed my support.

Answering the call, he held it to his ear. "Sir, you just drafted yourself the hardest-working son of a bitch you'll ever come across."

My mouth dropped, but only a little. I'd learned years ago that when it came to Jude, he never said or did what was expected.

The caller on the other end said something, earning a few laughs from Jude. "I'm going to win you some championships, sir," he said, beaming into the phone. "Thank you for taking a chance on me."

Other than Jude's voice and my heart beating out of my chest, the room was still. Everyone had stopped pacing and turned to watch us. Most of the players looked happy for him, nodding their heads in acknowledgment, although a few were wearing sour expressions, no doubt confused as to why Jude Ryder had gotten the call before they had.

I could give them an answer: It was because Jude was the top-rated college quarterback in the nation and he believed in teamwork, unlike a growing number of showboaters who thought football was a one-man sport.

Ending the call, Jude's face was blank with shock; then it quickly morphed to the most exhilarated I'd ever seen it. Hanging his head back, Jude opened his mouth and let out a coyote call at rafter-shaking volume.

The room erupted with cheers, but even with dozens of other shouts, Jude's hollers still owned the room. I couldn't help it: Seeing him like this, overcome with excitement, I had to join in. Not even all my apprehension and anxiety could dim my joy in this moment.

Leaning my own head back, I screamed right along with him and threw my arms into the air. He'd done it. He hadn't only done it; he'd been a first-round draft pick. From troubled repeat felon to one of the most sought after and, although he hadn't told me the number yet, probably one of the highest-paid football players in the country.

This was the stuff American dreams were made of, and I got to experience it at his side.

Lifting me into the air like I was nothing more substantial than a football, Jude spun me around.

"We did it, Luce," he yelled up at me, his scar pinched deep into his cheek from the smile he wore. "We really did it."

And this was where Jude and I had different opinions. I thought we'd been doing it, doing great, all along. But I returned his smile and nodded my head. "Yeah, baby," I said. "We did it."

FOUR

We were at the airport having another gut-wrenching good-bye. Cue the déjà vu fairy.

At least this one didn't consist of Jude busting through security wearing a hospital gown, although I was crying right now about as hard as I had then.

"Why are you crying, Luce?" Jude whispered into my ear, clutching me like he was afraid to let me go.

I cinched my arms tighter around him, sniffling into his wet shirt. Not damp, not even tearstained, it was totally drenched on one side. "I've got something in my eye."

"There's my tough girl," he said, the smile apparent in his voice.

I felt anything but tough right now, anything but strong, but if it was easier for him to believe I was, then I could play along. "You're gonna miss your flight," I said, swallowing around the lump that was lodged midway down my throat.

"There's another one," he said. "Training doesn't start until tomorrow, so it doesn't matter what time I get in tonight." He wasn't being flippant. Jude wouldn't have any problem missing his flight and snagging a later one if it meant staying like this a little while longer.

But if he got in late tonight, he'd be beat tomorrow morning for his first practice, and he needed to be at his best. San Diego had to know from day one that they'd made the right decision. First impressions were everything and second impressions meant nothing.

"No," I said, making myself lift my head from his chest, "you can't miss your flight. So you'd better get going." I swatted his backside and looked up into his face.

His forehead was lined when he looked back at me.

"Yeah, I know. I'm one ugly crier," I admitted, pasting on a smile.

"I can't leave you like this," he said, swiping a tear with his thumb. "I've walked away from you too many times when I shouldn't have. When you needed me. I won't do it again."

These weren't just words to him. Jude never said or did anything as a mere formality. He was dead serious that he was not leaving, flight or no flight, with me in my current state of blubbering mess. I needed to be strong for him, like he had for me countless times before.

Blinking my eyes, I swiped them with the end of my sweater sleeve. Forcing my mouth into what felt like a convincing smile, I met his stare. The corners of his eyes were creased with concern, the rest of his expression a rung below tortured. This should have been a celebration moment, but I'd bulldozed right through it, thanks to my tears.

Our lives were about to change, to take a one-eighty, and while every other human being who walked the earth would have considered a seven-figure contract playing for one of the top teams in the league to be the best kind of one-eighty a couple could make, I felt the opposite. Money and fame did things to people. Transformed them. And while I had complete faith in Jude, I had no faith in the world he was about to be thrust into.

Football players as a species attracted women. Quarterbacks who made millions playing Sunday-night football were swarmed by any and every brand of fantasy female created. Jude was leaving for California, the mecca for beautiful girls, and the last image he'd have of me was a red-faced Lucy with her bed hair tied back in a ponytail, sporting pajamas, since we'd slept in and nearly missed the flight.

Speaking of flights . . . Jude needed to get his butt

through security in about two minutes.

"Go on. I'm fine." He made a face. "Better than fine," I clarified, smirking up at him. "Go kick some big-time ass. Show them what a bunch of overpaid, talentless pansies they are." Lifting up on my toes, I pressed my lips into his. Hunger for more Jude overwhelmed me, as it always did when we kissed.

Four years together, and I still felt every kiss all the way down to my toes. He had a gift, and I wasn't shy about accepting it.

"Two weeks before I get to see you again," he said against my mouth, dropping his hands to my hips. "Better make it a good one. A really good one."

My smile curved against his mouth. *Better make it a good one* had been our go-to farewell for the past four years whenever we'd had to say good-bye for any amount of time. It was a bittersweet moment, but one I never let pass me by without giving it my all.

This time, especially, was no exception.

Running my fingers down his neck, I pulled him closer. "*You'd* better make it a good one."

"Yes, ma'am," he said, cupping my backside and lifting me into the air. I wrapped my legs around his waist, and our mouths moved against each other in ways that should have been reserved for the bedroom, not surrounded by the masses making their way through the airport.

What was the big taboo against public displays of affection, anyway? It wasn't like we were forcing anyone to watch.

Jude shifted so he could hold me up with one arm while the other ran up the back of my neck. Kneading the base of it, he pulled me closer. Our lips crushed harder into each other. Parting his mouth, my tongue slipped in, tasting him. Exploring him. Claiming him.

Jude's fingers curled deeper into my backside as we continued kissing, his low groan swallowed up by the chorus of cheers that erupted around us. The young male TSA agents hooted the loudest, although a stream of servicemen in fatigues weren't about to be left out of the catcalling contest.

Jude's hand left my neck and extended behind me. From the chuckles that followed the cheering, I could imagine what signal he was giving everyone.

"Horny bastards," he mumbled against my mouth, putting me back down. As of late, Jude had been less and less of a PDA man, whereas I'd take whatever I could get. Wherever it might be. He said it had something to do with him not being okay with a bunch of guys jerking off to his fiancée's face later that night.

He glared at the loudest of the hooting offenders, then looked back at me. Just imagining him walking away from me, I could feel the damn tears returning.

"I wish I could go with you," I whispered, before I knew what I was saying.

His eyebrows touched the sky. "You can, you know," he said quickly, already setting his sights on the ticket counter.

"I've got a couple weeks of school to finish," I offered just as quickly, turning his head before he started making his way to the counter.

"Then come the day school is over," he said. "I'll send you a ticket and you can spend the summer at the beach while I work my ass off on the field."

"Exactly. You'll be so busy with training, I'd never see you."

"But at least I'd be able to crawl into bed with you every night," he said, setting me back down on the ground. Oddly enough, my feet on firm ground felt less natural than when they were wrapped around Jude.

"And fall into a coma after your daily doubles," I argued.

One corner of his mouth curled. "I might be bushed every night, but I'd never be too tired for *that*." I sighed in exasperation. "You'd just have to be the one on top."

I shoved him, earning nothing more than a laugh.

"Getting my ass beat on the field by day, enjoying a round of cowgirl-style sex by night." His eyes darkened. "Sounds like my kind of summer."

I glowered at him, not impressively, but it was a wonder I could look at his beautiful face with anything but awe, even now.

"Come on," he said. "Come with me." I was already opening my mouth to object when he cut me off. "Once you finish classes."

"I'm taking a summer class, Jude," I said, looking away. I might have forgotten to mention that.

"What?!" He gasped. "When did you decide to do this?" He looked equally pissed and hurt.

"When I decided I wanted to be the best damn dancer I could be," I snapped right back.

Jude paused before answering. "Skip it," he said at last. "You don't need to go to school. You can just dance."

I could feel the tips of my ears starting to heat with the blood pumping through me. "Without a degree, I'd be lucky to be dancing across a community theater stage as an understudy," I said, each word an emotional tidal wave. "I need to do this. I need to blaze my own path just like you have yours."

"Yeah, but my path's making us millions, so why don't

you cross over to mine?" he said without a sliver of remorse.

"It's not about money, Jude," I said, a notch below a shout. Why was he not getting this? Money was money, nothing else, nothing more.

He shifted, looking like he wanted to rub his temples in frustration. "Then what's it about?" he asked. "Because you've admitted it's not about the money. It's not about me. It's not about marriage." His voice was rising. "Then what the hell is this whole 'blaze my own path without you' shit about, Luce? Because I thought we were a team now. I thought we made decisions that were the best for us as a couple."

I opened my mouth to reply back with something, but it would have been a lie. When I failed at everything else, when the shit was really hitting the fan, I made it a priority never to lie to Jude. I bit my lip while I stalled for an answer. Jude's shoulders slumped as the rest of his body loosened. "Come on, baby, What's it about?"

Shaking my head, I sank a few more teeth into my lip. "I'm not sure," I admitted, and while I knew it was a suck-ass answer, at least it was the truth. I wasn't sure why it was so important for me to make my own way in the world, but it was.

I didn't think Jude could look any more frustrated. Clearing his throat, he cupped my elbow and pulled me close again. "Marry me, Luce," he whispered, his eyes begging mine to meet them.

Dammit. He wasn't doing this again. He knew my weakness for him ran deep, and coupled with that pleading tone and those tortured eyes, he did one hell of a demolition job on my resolution.

"I will," I said, still refusing to look him in the eyes.

He didn't let the air settle with my words. "Right now?" So much hope it was sacred. And I was going to kill it with a swift slit to the throat.

"Right later," I whispered, forming a half smile that was more frown than grin.

He was silent for what felt like an hour, like he was waiting for me to take it back, or processing the words and the meaning behind them. Finally, he sighed—long, deep, and one that pricked new tears to life in my eyes.

"Love you, Luce," he said, pressing a kiss into my forehead. "You change your mind, you know where to find me. I'll marry you in the middle of the night in some crummy wedding chapel in Vegas if that's the only option we have. Whatever you want, whenever you want it. I'll be there." Burying his face in my hair, he inhaled deeply before turning and walking up to the security gates.

My throat was too tight to let words slip through, and my eyes were so glazed over with tears that I saw nothing but a tall shadow walking away from me. Two seconds had gone by since his last touch, and my body was already quaking with withdrawal.

It was going to be a long two weeks.

FIVE

wo weeks—*fourteen* days—hadn't just gone by slowly. It had been like living a year in hell every passing second. Jude had called every night, sounding as beat as you'd expect a rookie NFL player to sound after a grueling daily double in eighty-degree heat. I lived for those calls, but I kind of dreaded them, too, because I knew we'd be hanging up shortly after and the clock would reset until we got to talk again. Another twenty-three and a half hours on the clock, please.

I tried to keep busy, immersing myself in the last weeks of school, dancing late into the night for no audience, just an empty auditorium. I'd taken my last final yesterday and was feeling confident my junior year of college had been my most successful to date.

I'd spent the first part of the day picking up applications

in hopes that I could land a summer job that would work with my summer class. However, plenty of schools had already let out for summer, and it seemed the majority of jobs, or at least the good ones that didn't pay peanuts, had already been scooped up. I'd be lucky if I could swing a part-time gig waiting tables at a late-night café.

I'd take it. I wasn't picky, especially these days. I'd take whatever employment I could find, especially with Jude being gone the entire summer. I needed something—in fact, many things—to keep my mind off missing him.

And if that meant pouring coffee and slapping hash browns down on diner tables until I was blue in the face, I'd do just that.

After gathering a couple dozen applications, I'd stopped by a few specialty markets in search of just the right ingredients for tonight's dinner, because today was day number fourteen. Jude's much anticipated homecoming. Cue the hallelujah choir, because I'd been jiving and waving my hands at the heavens all day long. Jude's flight was coming in late, so it wasn't exactly "dinner," but I'd never known Jude Ryder to turn down a good meal no matter what time of day—or night—it was.

In the years since starting college, I'd learned to cook. Well, *kind of* learned to cook. Not out of curiosity, but out of necessity. Cafeteria food was the last resort, especially after dining on my dad's culinary masterpieces for years. In fact, I was fairly certain the number one ingredient in cafeteria pasta was cardboard.

The other option was eating out every night, which, with an appetite like Jude's around, was impossible on a college student's nonwages. So I learned how to cook. Nothing fancy, but good, nutritious home cooking.

Tonight's menu consisted of roast chicken, garlic mashed potatoes, and roasted green beans—a Jude Ryder favorite. Like the weekends during the school year and the last two summers, I'd moved into Jude's and my apartment in White Plains. This year, though, I was planning on living in it during senior year and using public transportation to get to the city. I was done living in dorms. Done.

The apartment was a notch or two above being deemed condemnable, but God, I loved it. It was ours. Where we could be together. Where we'd formed more memories than most couples do in a lifetime. It was home, and I was happy to be here for another summer.

I would have been happier if Jude was here, too. But tonight I'd have him for almost twenty-four hours, because he had one rare day off of training and had to be back by Monday morning. So as soon as he walked through that door, I wasn't going to fixate on the fact that he'd be leaving in less than twenty hours. I was going to live each moment like it was a year. I was going to make time my bitch, pay it back for what it had done to me the past two weeks.

I checked the time on the new iPhone Jude had sent me last week, the first of what he said would be many sweet gifts. After warning him he'd better not start treating me like some expensive mistress he had stuffed across the country, I'd thanked him profusely and given him a few dozen air kisses through my sweet new phone.

"Crap!" I shrieked when my hand accidentally grazed the casserole dish holding the green beans that had just been baking at three hundred and fifty degrees for more than an hour. I was about to run the burn under water when the time registered in my brain.

"Double crap!" Jude was going to be here any minute and I wasn't ready. Tonight I wanted everything to be perfect. Normally I would have picked him up at the airport, but then I couldn't have surprised him with what I'd been cooking up the past few days.

He'd sounded hurt when I'd first told him he'd have to catch a cab because I was planning something. But when I repeated I was *planning something*, with just the right amount of inflection, I could feel his classic smile coming through the phone.

Blanketing my hands with oven mitts, I rushed the beans to our dining table. It was nothing more than a six-foot-long plastic craft table surrounded by a menagerie of mismatched chairs, but when you covered it with a nice tablecloth, it classed it up a rung so we looked less like poor college students and more like fresh graduates with their first paying jobs.

Dropping the dish on the table, I heard footsteps striding up the stairwell. Thundering footsteps. The walls were *that* thin and Jude's footsteps were *that* loud.

Loosening the knot of my bathrobe, I let it slide off my arms and chucked it onto the couch. After double-checking that the candles were lit, the table set, and the music playing at just the right volume in the background, I plopped down into my chair. The chair was chilly, running cool from my spine down to my backside. A metal folding chair probably wasn't the best seating option for a girl who was naked.

Well, naked except for the suede turquoise pumps that I'd chosen to match the tie I had loosely tied around my neck. A tie that had SAN DIEGO written above a yellow lightning bolt only a few dozen times.

Lounging back in the chair, I kicked my feet up on the table, crossing my ankles as I twirled the tie between my fingers. It was a very *Pretty Woman* moment. In fact, that movie, which had been replaying every night on TV, had been my inspiration.

The steps were getting louder, only a few strides from

our door. I sucked in a breath, trying to calm myself, as I was now reaching heights of epic overanticipation. Other than the time we'd split back in high school, this was the longest we'd gone without seeing each other. It should have been considered a form of torture to be separated from a guy like Jude Ryder for two weeks.

Bamboo shoots up fingernails was child's play in comparison to what I'd experienced.

Giving my hair a tease, I watched the door without blinking, waiting for the footsteps to pause at the front door . . . then, as they continued on down the hall, waiting for them to turn around and come back.

I waited a minute, long after the footsteps had disappeared into an apartment. Okay, false alarm. But he'd be here soon. Maybe he'd been held up at the airport, or maybe traffic was nasty tonight. Or maybe . . .

Nope, I wasn't going to let myself go there. He was coming. He'd be here. Nothing could stop Jude from what he wanted, least of all the NFL.

And that was when my phone chimed, causing me to jump. I still wasn't used to the ring of my new phone. Fumbling to grab it, I smiled when Jude's picture popped up.

"Where are you?" I said as soon as I picked up. "I've got one hell of a surprise waiting for you."

He was silent for a couple seconds, and then he sighed.

My heart sank. "You're not coming. Are you?" I tried to keep from sounding as disappointed as I felt.

Another sigh. "I'm so sorry, Luce. Coach decided to dish out a mandatory extra training session for the rookies late this afternoon, and he's called an early morning session tomorrow, too." His voice was labored, like he'd been sprinting, plus there was a ruckus in the background. "I tried texting you in between practices to let you know, but it looks like it didn't go through."

Nope. Definitely didn't.

"Where are you?" I asked, uncrossing my ankles and putting my feet on the floor. No sense in keeping a pose if he wasn't showing up to enjoy the view.

"In the locker room. I called you the second I got in here after finishing up practice for the day," he said, trying to talk over the voices of fifty of his teammates. "Can you hear me all right?"

"Yeah, I can hear you," I said, but he didn't wait for my answer.

"Hey, guys!" Jude hollered, the words muffled from what I guessed was his hand over the phone's mouthpiece. "Would you mind turning it down a notch? I've got my girl on the phone!"

Hollering requests at his teammates might not have been

the best way to forge relationships as the rookie on the team, but after an initial chorus of *oohs* and loud air kisses echoing around the locker room, the background noises dimmed.

Amazing. Two weeks on the team and he'd already managed to command the respect of his teammates. Not that I needed another affirmation, but Jude had indeed found his calling in life.

"Luce, is that better?"

"Yeah," I said, frowning at the table and all the food I'd spent half the day preparing, "that's great."

"I'm sorry, baby. I'm so, so sorry. You can't imagine how bad I need to see you right now," he said with such inflection, I could feel his pain. It was the same pain of separation coursing through me right now. "I need my Luce fix. *Bad.*"

I bit my cheek; I wasn't going to cry over this. "I need my Jude fix bad, too," I said. "So, when's it looking like we'll be able to see each other?" If he said another two weeks, I wasn't sure how I'd hold on to my sanity.

"Can you fly out next Thursday?" He didn't wait for my response. "I've got a light day Friday and only a half day on Saturday. We could spend every minute I'm not on the field together. I promise. Will you come?" Why he was pleading with me, I didn't know. I needed to see him as much as it sounded like he needed to see me.

"Of course I'll come. I'll book my flight tonight."

"Already done," he said. "I'll email you the flight infor mation later."

Of course he'd done it. "That confident I'd say yes?"

I could feel his smirk coming through the phone. "I was that confident I could persuade you, no matter what your answer was."

Even though he wasn't here to see it, I smirked right back at him. "You're not on the field anymore, Ryder. Don't forget to leave your ego there."

He chuckled that low, rumbling laugh of his. "You of all people ought to know this ego goes with me wherever I go, Luce."

"A girl can dream," was my reply.

That earned another laugh from him. "So . . ." he said, his voice going soft, "what are you wearing right now?"

If only he knew, he'd be racing to the airport and chartering the first flight out.

I looked down at my body. Not a whole hell of a lot.

"Something."

"Something?" he said, sounding offended. "How is *something* supposed to get a man through another long week away from his girl?"

"Use your imagination," I suggested, twirling the tie as I hatched a plan.

"I'm fresh out of imagination," he said around a groan. "I

need details. *Detailed* details." His voice got quiet again, like he was afraid one of his teammates might be eavesdropping. "For starters, how about the color, material, and style of the panties you're wearing."

Heat crept up my body. It was a welcome friend. "That might be hard to *detail*," I said, lowering my voice, "since I'm not wearing any."

"What?!" Jude's voice burst through the phone. I held it away from my ear in case another shout was on its way. When he spoke again, it was in a controlled, breathy voice. "Are you serious, Luce?"

"Don't you wish you could be here to find out?" I teased, which was promptly followed by another groan.

"I didn't think I could feel worse about not making it tonight, but I should have known," he said. "What else are you or are you not wearing?" was the next question.

I grinned. It was nice to know I could drive him mad from across the country after he'd just endured a good ten hours of training. I scanned my body again. Shoes? A tie? And then I realized that a picture was worth a thousand words.

"It's kind of hard to describe," I began. "Why don't I snap a photo and I'll send it to you."

"I like that plan." Sounded like he had a devilish grin on.

So did I. "Okay, I'm going to hang up and then I'll text

you the picture. Sound good?"

"Sounds . . . great," he said.

As soon as I ended the call, I kicked my heels back up on the table. Adjusting the tie so it wound down the center of my chest, I bent my arm over my head and grabbed the top of the chair. Sampling a few expressions on the camera screen, I settled for the one I figured Jude would like the best: a soft smile topped by expectant eyes. Snapping the picture, I double-checked to make sure he'd get the what-I-was-or-wasn't-wearing picture. The *whole* picture.

Yeah, it was hot.

Typing in a quick message that read, WISH YOU HERE HERE, I hit send before I could talk myself out of it. The message delivery button pinged, and I'd barely had a chance to sink my teeth into my lower lip when my phone rang.

Jude's picture popped up on the screen again. That was fast.

I let it ring a few more times before answering.

"So," I answered, "what do you think of the tie?"

His breath was racing again. "What tie?"

I laughed; he sounded serious.

"Oh, you mean the tie that's buried between that beautiful chest of yours?" His voice was nothing more than a whisper. "If I wasn't so seethingly jealous of it, I might actually like it."

I ran my fingers down it again. "Well, I got it for you, so I'll make sure to bring it next week. I know you've got a total of one tie to your name, so now you'll have two."

"And the first thing I'm going to do is tie you up with it and screw you until we're both blue in the face."

Yeah, I felt those words all the way down to my naughty parts.

"Jude," I warned, "it might not be the best time to be discussing bondage and screwing when you're surrounded by your teammates. They're going to think we've got some kind of pervy thing going on."

"Would they be wrong?" There was a degree of teasing in his voice, but only a fraction of one.

"Yes," I emphasized, "they would be. We don't do whips, chains, or whatever other things are out there. I'm a sex purist."

"Did you just use the words *sex* and *purist* in the same sentence?" he said, sounding offended.

"That would be an affirmative," I replied, taking a sip of water to cool myself down.

"Please, Luce, for the love of all my manly pride and ego—please don't ever use the words *sex purist* to describe what we have again. I mean, what's next? Are you going to be comparing us to vanilla ice cream?"

"No," I said, finding it amusing that he was so insulted.

When it came to what Jude and I did between the sheets, or straddling the recliner, or up against the wall, or bent over the hood of his truck, et cetera, et cetera, et cetera, there was no room for complaint. But I had to have a little fun with him. "I'd say our sex life was more in line with *French vanilla*, if I had to assign it a flavor."

"That's it," he said, determination blossoming in his voice. "I'm introducing you to French vanilla's naughty cousin, rocky road." The background noise suddenly began to fade as I could hear the echo of his cleats jogging down a hall.

"Ryder, what crazy-ass scheme are you up to now?" Did I even want to know? One of the many things I loved about Jude was his ability to keep me in suspense. He was the definition of spontaneous, and I'd surrendered to it somewhere along the way.

"French vanilla," he repeated, sounding offended as he continued his jog. "I'm insulted."

"Jude, come on," I said, shaking my head. "Have you ever heard me complain? Because a whisper of a complaint has never even crossed my mind when it comes to you and me and—"

"Our French vanilla sex," he interrupted.

I covered my mouth to contain my laugh. "What are you up to? The suspense is killing me."

"I already told you," he answered, as the clopping of his cleats stopped. "I'm introducing you to French vanilla's badass cousin." A shrill creak dimmed into a low moan—it was a sound I was familiar with.

"What are you doing out in your truck?" I asked, leaning forward in my seat. This conversation had taken a turn from the devastating to the intriguing in two minutes flat. "You are not planning on driving across the country in that beater, are you? Because you might think that piecer has another hundred thousand miles in it, but you'll be stranded before you cross the California state line."

He huffed. Jude took serious offense when anyone tried to take a crack at the second love of his life: his rust bucket of a truck that was so worn with age you couldn't tell what its original make and model had been. Jude may have wanted a fancy new truck *someday,* but this one would always hold a special place in his heart.

"No, as much as I'd love to break every speed and traffic law in existence to give you a firsthand introduction to rocky road, you're just going to have to wait until next Thursday for that."

I needed another sip of water. "You know what they say? The key to happiness is having something to look forward to," I said, taking another long drink for good measure.

"*I'll* show you something to look forward to." Jude

had mastered the art of inflection; these words were no exception.

Screw the drinking—I was going to have to douse myself with water if he kept up that kind of talk. "Even more to look forward to."

"I'm going to hang up, Luce, and call you right back," he said. "Okay?"

"Oh-kay?"

The line went dead and, before I could wonder what he was up to now, my phone was ringing again. Instead of Jude's picture that normally popped up whenever he called, the phone displayed me in real time, requesting a Face Time call.

The pieces of the what-was-he-up-to puzzle were starting to come together.

Accepting the Face Time request, I stared at myself on the screen a few more seconds before I disappeared and someone I enjoyed staring at much more appeared. I adjusted the phone so he had only a neck-up view.

His infamous smirk fell into place immediately. "Hey, Luce."

"Hey, Jude," I replied, cocking a brow. Seeing him made my heart as happy as it made it ache. I wanted to be able to reach through that phone and touch him and have his hands on me. It seemed like an eternity since we'd been together.

The day the cell phone manufacturers figured out a way to program a teleportation or virtual reality option into these so-called smart phones would be the day I'd call them "smart."

"Nice jersey," I said, appraising him. His skin had darkened in the Southern California sun, and his hair that he normally kept short had grown a bit longer and a shade lighter. His gray eyes were metallic tonight, somewhere between silver and pewter. A sheen of sweat dotted his face, dirt streaked his neck, and his shoulder pads made him appear even more superhuman in size than he normally did.

"Nice face," he said, his smirk growing more pronounced.

"I know how much you love it," I replied, "so I wanted to give you a close-up."

"Baby, that face is so damn beautiful a man could die happy looking into it, but you can't do this to me when I know what's on display below it." The skin between his brows lined as his eyes narrowed. Jude's tortured face was almost as sexy as that smirk of his.

"You mean this display?" I said, tilting the phone so it ran down my body. Slowly. I watched Jude's face shift from tortured, to expectant, to excited, ending at ravenous.

He stayed quiet, nothing but the heaviness of his breath exchanging with mine.

"Damn," he breathed when I made the round trip, ending back at my face.

I smiled shyly at him. I don't know what it was—Jude had seen me naked more than I'd seen myself, but something about sharing it over the phone, when there was no way for him to touch me, made the experience about ten times more intimate.

"You're a lucky bastard," I quoted back his favorite saying.

"Don't I know it," he said, licking his lips. "Do you have something you can use to prop your phone up with?" he asked, adjusting his and doing the same, I guessed.

"Maybe?"

"Luce," he said, exasperated.

"Fine," I relented, grabbing the champagne bottle and sliding it across the table. Propping my phone against it, I adjusted it so he had a view of everything. "I improvised and utilized the champagne we were supposed to be celebrating with tonight as my hands-free device. Happy now?"

"Happy always," he said, shifting on the seat of his truck. "Because you're going to need your hands free for what we're about to do."

I choked on the sip of water I was taking. Another puzzle piece slid into place.

"What the hell are you talking about, Ryder?" I said after clearing my throat. "And what the hell are you doing shifting all the hell around?" His head disappeared from the screen as he lifted himself. His hands slid down his sides, pulling on the seam of his football spandex.

"Taking my pants off," he said matter-of-factly. No shame—not even a hint.

His torso lowered right before I caught the X-rated version of this video. "Why?" I said, my voice cracking.

His lips parted, revealing a smile that made my thighs clench. "Because I'm about to give French vanilla a run for its damn money."

Shit. He was crazy. Loco crazy.

"I like French vanilla," I replied, my voice so shaky you would have thought I was a virgin on prom night.

"If you like French vanilla, Luce, I can guarantee you're going to love this."

Double shit.

"I'm going to love what?" I cursed myself. Why did I ask myself questions to which I already knew the answer?

"Touching yourself for me," he replied, his voice so deep it was dark.

Triple shit all the way to infinity.

"I'm not doing that," I said firmly. Skanky girls had phone sex. I certainly didn't. I'd do anything for Jude, with

perhaps this one exception

"Yes, you are," he said, his confidence the total opposite of what I was feeling. "Just pretend it's my hand on you."

"I wouldn't have to pretend if you were here like you were supposed to be," I said, peaking both brows.

"You're all kinds of moody tonight, Luce," he said. "An orgasm will take care of that." He interrupted me before I could argue back. "You know it will. Come on, baby. For me?"

And then he gave me the look—*the* look. The one where his eyes went all soft and light. In the battle that was man versus woman, this look should not be allowed.

I caved every damn time. This time included.

"Fine," I sighed. "For you."

His smile exploded for one moment, right before it dropped with desire. "Who's a lucky bastard?" he said rhetorically, pointing a finger at himself. "That's right. This guy."

I laughed, relaxing now that I'd accepted what detour this night was taking. In fact, I wasn't only relaxing, I was getting excited.

I needed another drink of water, but I'd emptied my glass pre–phone sex talk. Biting my lip, I felt my face heat. How did one go about this? I didn't have a manual. If I had a glass of champagne in me I would have felt more uninhibited.

Gauging the widening of Jude's pupils, I guessed there wasn't time for that.

"So . . ." I began, "when do we get started?"

I would have made the worst paid phone sex professional ever. My parents would have been proud.

A corner of Jude's mouth lifted. "I already am, Luce."

Damn, knowing Jude was touching himself right now made my body spiral out of control in a familiar way. It wouldn't take much "touching" to get me the rest of the way there.

"I suppose that dumb smile on your face should have given that away," I said, sliding my hand into place.

"There's my girl," he said, his voice husky.

My eyes closed at first, as my body rushed from my touch.

"What in the hell are we doing?" I said, my own voice raspy.

"Doing the best we can with what we've been given tonight, Luce," was his immediate answer.

"And giving French vanilla a run for its money," I added, gliding my other hand up my stomach before giving the tie a suggestive tug.

"Shit," Jude breathed, the muscles in his shoulders picking up speed.

Dropping my head back, I started kneading my breast,

rolling the nipple between my fingers.

"Holy shit." Jude's eyes couldn't have gotten any wider. "We *are* putting French vanilla in its goddamned place, baby."

If it wasn't for his confidence, combined with the way I'd already started on this train, I would have been trying to talk myself out of this whole thing. But I was too far gone to hit the brakes.

"What are you imagining right now?" I asked, staring into his eyes, pretending it was his hands working over me.

"With the view I've got right now?" he said, winking. "Who needs to imagine? This right here, a beautiful woman touching herself the way you are, is the American dream, Luce."

His words sent another pulse of pleasure to my body. "Let's just say you were here tonight . . ." I began. "And you'd just walked into the apartment. What would you have done?"

"Are you wanting me to talk dirty to you, Luce?" he asked with a smirk. "Because all you ever have to do is say the word and I will happily say filthy, filthy things to you."

"The word," I teased.

"If I wasn't about to come, I'd be lecturing you about your backward progress in the comedy department."

"Wait for me," I said, sinking my teeth into my lower lip.

That always drove him crazy.

"Always, Luce," he said. "Always."

"Okay, so I just walked through the door," he began, his shoulders slowing. "And there you are, naked except for that fine-ass tie around your neck, touching yourself and looking at me with those screw-me eyes."

One of Jude's many gifts of his lady-killer DNA was his voice. It was deep enough to make a woman's insides vibrate, but still clear enough to cut right through her. However, whenever we were intimate, that voice of his went as deep as it would go, vibrating in all the right places.

"I'd be across that room in two seconds flat, and have you up against the nearest wall two seconds after that," he said, the muscles of his neck popping to the surface. He was forcing himself to hold off.

He wouldn't have to for much longer.

"I'd slide that tie from your neck, hold your wrists behind your back, and cinch them together so tightly I could do whatever I wanted to do to you, however I wanted to do it."

"Oh, God." I sighed, kicking my leg up on the table to give myself better access.

"Then, in the time it would take you to wrap your legs around me, I'd have my zipper down and my mouth on yours. And then, baby," he said, his own head rocking back, "I wouldn't give it to you until you came and got it."

At this pace, with those kinds of words, I wasn't going to make it much longer.

"So, my wrists tied behind me, my legs tied around you, I'd lower myself over you, teasing you until *I* made *you* come and get it." Had those words just come out of my mouth? At this point in fast-approaching ecstasy, I couldn't be sure.

"And you'd be so ready for me, I'd bury myself so deep inside you I could come right then," he continued, groaning through the end. "But then you'd start moving, doing that little hip swivel thing you know drives me nuts, and then—"

"Like the two-pump chump you are not," I interrupted, feeling my climax building, "but like the sexual goddess I am, I'd whisper a few dirty words in your ear at the same time I tighten around you, and you'd come so hard you'd put me over the edge."

"Oh, God," he moaned, his face lining. "I can't wait, Luce. I'm going to come hard," he said, his eyes staying on me. "And I'm going to imagine it's you I'm six inches deep in when I do."

That was all I needed. The final push before I followed him.

My body tightened as much as it could before it let go, and then I was shaking from the intensity of my orgasm ripping through me. "Jude." I sighed again and again as he did the same with my name, paired with a couple other four-letter words.

As the last ripples of pleasure were going through my body, I rested my leg back down on the floor. My lower half was trembling and my breath was ragged at best.

"I might have been wrong, Luce," Jude said after both of us started breathing normally again.

Adjusting myself in the chair, I gave him a postorgasm smile. "Wrong about what?"

"Your dancing being the damn most beautiful thing I've ever seen."

My smile went a notch higher. "Oh, yeah?"

"Oh. Yeah," he emphasized. "Because what I just had the pleasure of watching for the past five minutes was on a whole other playing field."

I laughed. The expression on his face was that serious. "And I want to say kudos to you for improvising and managing to turn a sucky night into something . . . not so sucky."

He leaned forward. "Kudos to you, Luce," he said with a wink.

I flushed more than I already was. I was a physical wreck. The good kind of wreck. My inner thighs were still shaking, my left nipple was sore from the pain I'd unleashed on it, and my neck felt sore from all the rocking and tossing around.

"So," I said, "same time tomorrow night?" I was partially kidding, but mostly serious.

Jude's eyebrow lifted. "Who says we need to wait until tomorrow night for a repeat?" he said, leaning back against the truck's seat again. "I've got all night, Luce."

Grabbing the phone, I started for the bedroom. I was going to get comfortable for this round. "Me too."

SIX

'd slept in. I knew this because I awoke with that panicky feeling, consulting my phone for the time. Instead of showing me that, though, the picture on my phone was of Jude's room. The Face Time count was still going, in the six-digit realm.

Crashing my head back down on my pillow, I exhaled. For the first time since last September, it seemed, it was acceptable for me to sleep in. I didn't have an early class to be at, or a rehearsal to squeeze in before breakfast. Other than my summer class, my schedule was open to fill as I chose.

Turning on my side, I stared at his room. He must have left his phone behind so I could wake up to this. It was a small gesture that felt kind of grand.

The team had put him in a hotel during preseason

training until he found something more permanent, which I guess some players complained about due to the lack of space. From the looks of it, Jude's hotel room was almost as big as our apartment. Plus, it was about five times as nice and a tenth as old.

Following round two last night, Jude suggested we keep the Face Time on so we could fall asleep together. Well, it was more of a demand, but it was one I was eager to go along with. By the time he'd driven back to his room, I'd almost fallen asleep, tired from the day of running around, the double feature of orgasms, and arguing with him about how expensive his phone bill would be if we did this whole Face Time thing all night, every night, like he wanted.

He said he didn't give a damn about the bill, or the money; he cared about watching me fall asleep every night. Yeah, I melted and caved right then.

Curling around my pillow, I stared at his empty bed. His sheets were twisted, the blankets kicked down to the foot of the bed, and the pillows were stacked into a leaning tower. Jude had never been a good sleeper, never sleeping longer than a couple hours at a time before something jerked him awake. He'd always played it off as being a borderline insomniac, but I knew why he'd burst awake, swallowing a scream, his body covered in a sheen of sweat. Jude had nightmares. The same kind I did—his just came from a different point of view. He was on one side of the gun and the man that had killed my brother, and I was on the other.

The weekends we shared in the same bed, he said he slept better, but knowing how many times he jerked awake in the middle of the night when I was next to him, I hated to think of what his nights were like when I wasn't beside him.

Jude had an early practice this morning. And a late practice. Just like every day. In fact, if he wasn't on the field, he was in one of three places: at the hotel restaurant shoveling food into his mouth, sitting in the oversize chair talking on the phone with me, or trying and failing to sleep in the bed I was staring at. His life was busy, his hours filled with places to be and people to interact with.

My days felt the opposite.

With Jude gone, I had dance, night class, and a few friends who were, most of the time, too busy with their own lives to carve out time to hang with me. It had been months since I'd seen Holly, Jude's oldest friend; something about a full-time job, living across the country, and having an almost four-year-old to keep up with had a way of keeping a girl busy. When Indie, my old dorm roommate, wasn't beating off stockbrokers and ER docs in one of the clubs she frequented in the city, she was down in Miami dancing until sunset, beating away the Latin men she had a secret soft spot for. Thomas, my dance partner, bartended nights in the city and had been having girl troubles with the dancer he'd been dating for a year. What he called girl troubles, the rest of the world called cheating. Thomas liked to believe the best in everyone, God love him, and that was an honorable quality to have—when you weren't dating a girl who believed sleeping with a slew of other guys behind her boyfriend's back was acceptable.

After I grabbed my phone off its stand, it took me a few seconds before I was able to hit end. I had a window to Jude's room and I didn't want to close it. But life had to go on; I couldn't stay tucked under my covers all day staring at an unmade bed on the other side of the country. I had to get up, go through a routine, and do my best to pretend my heart hadn't flown to San Diego with him. This wasn't a foreign concept to me—fake it until you make it; I'd done it for five years following my brother's murder.

I knew this was different. Jude hadn't been killed in cold blood; I knew this. But my lungs felt like they'd collapse at every other breath, and the spot where my heart used to beat felt like it was a hollow void.

Not that I needed any more proof, but damn if I didn't love that man more than was healthy for me.

I typed a quick message, hit send, then made myself get out of bed. Shower or coffee first? After contemplating this for a good minute, I realized I was apparently incapable of making even the smallest decisions.

After a couple more minutes of indecision, I went with the coffee-first option. I had a handful of applications to fill out, not to mention a mess in the kitchen and dining room to clean up. Then I would shower, then off to the dance studio, then . . .

Oh, my God. I was going through my life like it was a step-by-step program. Not cool. To prove to myself I wasn't becoming a step-by-stepper, I took action. I showered first, then got to work on the job applications while I waited for the coffee to brew.

I'd gone through half a pot by the time I'd finished with the eighth and final application. Shaking my wrist, sure I was experiencing the early stages of carpal tunnel from that fill-in-the-blank marathon, I tossed a change of clothes into my dance bag and couldn't rush out of that apartment fast enough. Two weeks and I still hadn't adjusted to being alone in it.

I wasn't sure I ever would.

Two hours later, I'd handed off all eight applications. Half the places said the positions had already been filled—the other half said they'd take a peek and give me a call if they wanted to interview me. When I said I'd call next week to check in, I was promptly answered with some variation of the don't-call-us-we'll-call-you reply.

Outlook in the summer employment department wasn't looking good.

No Jude for another week. No job for who knew how long. No friends within a half-hour commute.

By the time I'd arrived at the studio, I was feeling every shade of sorry for myself. There was only one way to stop this train of self-pity in its tracks.

I had my pointes on and was ready to go in record time. I moved without the accompaniment of music, each movement an extension of what I was feeling. By the time I'd worked up a sweat, my pity party had come to a wrap. And by the time my toes started tingling, I'd built up enough positive endorphins to remind myself that life was pretty damn good.

Taking a water break, I checked my phone. I was checking for missed calls or texts, but the time caught my eye. My eyes bulged. I should have stopped being surprised how I could lose time when I danced the way I had been today, but losing four hours in the span of what seemed like a couple dances wasn't something I'd ever gotten used to.

The studio was quiet on weekend nights, and, other than the teenage employee obsessed by her phone, I was the last person in the place. After changing back into my shoes, I hurried to my car, rushing back to an empty apartment. I turned on every light, even the TV just to have a little background noise. Finishing cleaning up the mess from last night's botched dinner, I poured a bowl of granola cereal and curled up on the couch, my phone balanced on my lap. I tried not to check the phone screen every five seconds.

An hour later, the self-pity was starting to trickle back into my veins. Jude must have had a crazy-busy day of practice; he usually was able to shoot me a quick text or two throughout the day. But not today. I was resolved to not become one of those clingy girls who had to check in with her guy every hour, although tonight, I was getting dangerously close to jumping on that bandwagon.

After minutes of tapping my phone's screen, stalling, convincing myself not to call him, only to convince myself to call him the next second, the phone chimed.

I was so excited I nearly dropped it. I was in such a hurry, I didn't check the screen to see who was calling.

"I missed you so damn much today," I greeted Jude, my smile stretching into place.

Silence for one second on the other end. "I missed you so damn much, too?" was the uncertain reply. The *female* reply.

"Holly?"

"Most days," she answered.

"Oh," I said, trying not to sound upset. "Sorry. I thought you were Jude."

"Sorry to disappoint you, Lucy," she said, as little Jude

started talking up a storm in the background.

"No. I'm glad it's you," I said, telling a half-truth.

"Liar." She paused, hushing little Jude, and told him to go play with his blocks. "What? Did you and Jude have some sort of phone sex date tonight?"

I rolled my eyes. If only Holly knew. "How many times do I have to tell you that our sex life is none of your business?"

"You can tell me as many times as you want. I'm never going to stop sticking my nose in you and Jude's freaky business," she said. "I'm a single mom, Lucy. I have a better chance of dying in a plane crash than I do of getting laid again, so stop acting like such a prude and let me keep on living vicariously through you."

Another eye roll, but only because we were on the phone. Holly didn't tolerate eye rolling in her presence, especially if it was directed at her. "Go find another couple to live vicariously through. Jude and I are officially off-vicarious-limits."

"Repeating. I'm a single mom. The only thing that's more unlikely than getting laid is making friends with another couple I can live vicariously through." Jude went off like a siren again. She let him go this time. "And now I'm officially an unemployed single mom," she said with a sigh.

"What?" I said, sitting up on the couch. "You got

fired from the salon? You've been there for years. What happened?"

She cleared her throat. "I may or may not have 'accidentally' mixed up hair dyes. I 'might' have applied bright green hair color to a customer who also happened to be my brother's ex-girlfriend, who became an ex after screwing half the county's male population behind his back." I could hear the sly smile in Holly's voice. "It was a total coincidence."

"Of course it was," I deadpanned.

"Anyways, my boss said coincidence or not, a stylist mixing up platinum blond for neon green was a fireable offense."

"Please. Like every stylist doesn't have a similar story," I said. "At least your 'coincidence' came with a swift kick in the ass from karma to your cheating client."

Holly chuckled. "This is why I called you, Lucy. I know cheer isn't really your thing, but you always manage to cheer me up whenever I need it."

"Cheer aside," I said, "I'm glad I could help."

Holly replied back with something, but she was drowned out as little Jude beat on something that sounded like drums. Or cymbals. Or something that was up to the task of making my eardrums ring.

"So what are you going to do now?" I asked, after the musical explosion in the background ended.

Another sigh from Holly. "The only other 'salon' in this

town, and I use the word loosely, is Supercuts," she said, I could see her cringing. "And since I can't afford to have any pride when I've got milk and shoes to provide for a little man, I already stopped by to see if they were hiring. That would be a whole lotta nada."

This time, I sighed with her. "That sucks, Holly. You've worked so hard to be independent and provide for little Jude . . ."

"My mom was right all along. From the time I was a little girl she always told me I was destined for not-so-great things. She predicted I'd be knocked up and on food stamps before my nineteenth birthday." She paused, her voice lower than normal. "Knocked up before nineteen, food stamps a few years later. It feels supergreat knowing I've lived up to my mom's expectations."

"Oh, Hol," I began, feeling useless from all the way across the country. I wanted to give her a big hug, make her a cup of tea, and figure this thing out. If she was here, I could do more than offer empty words.

And that was when an answer of the genius quality came to me.

"Move in with me." The words were out a moment after the idea had popped in to my mind.

Holly was silent on the other end. So silent I had to check to make sure the call hadn't failed.

"What?" was her response.

"You heard me," I said in a hurry. I was getting more and more excited with the idea. "Pack up your stuff and fly out here. You can live with me rent free, and there are a ton of salons within walking distance where I'm sure you could work."

More silence. "And little Jude?"

It took me a few moments to figure out what she was asking. "And there's nothing little Jude can do to this place that could possibly leave it in worse condition than it already is." I was surprised, and a little hurt, that she thought she'd have to ask about little Jude. They were a package deal. I wouldn't invite one without the other.

"You'd do that?" she said, followed by a sniffle. If I didn't know better, I would have thought that stonewall Holly Reed was close to tears. "You'd really let a crazy, destructive caveman and me move in with you?"

"Hol," I said, "I've been sharing this place with a crazy, destructive caveman every weekend for three years, until he got himself drafted and moved across the country. I've got a caveman vacancy that needs to be filled ASAP."

The little caveman picked that time to scream, "I've got to go poo-poo, Mom!"

"You know how to go to the bathroom on your own," Holly replied.

"I can't get my pants off!" was little Jude's reply. "I need your help!"

"I'll be there in one minute!"

"See?" I said through my laughter. "He'll fill Jude's cave-man shoes perfectly."

"I love you so hard, Lucy," she said. "I don't know what I'd do without you and Jude."

"Please. You're the toughest girl I know. You're a fighter, Holly. You'd be just fine."

"Boy, have I got you fooled," she replied softly. So much like Jude. Long stretches of tough, interrupted by brief glimpses of vulnerability.

"You know, if you need any money to get you by . . ." I began, clearing my throat. "Your best friend just landed himself a pretty decent job, and I've got some money saved up, too. All you have to do is ask, Holly."

She was silent for a while. Then she sniffled again. "Love. You. So. Hard," she repeated. "And that's the nicest thing anyone's ever offered, but I can't take money from you guys, Lucy. I just can't. Okay?"

I didn't need an explanation. I got it.

"Okay," I said, realizing Holly was as much like me as she was like Jude.

"Mom!"

"Holy bloodcurdling scream, caveman," I said, making a

mental note to start baking brownies for my neighbors now so I'd be in their good graces when the shrieking little boy moved in.

"I gotta go. I've got thirty seconds before he craps his pants," she said, sounding like she was rushing across the room. "Call you tomorrow to work out the details?"

"Call me tonight after you put caveman to bed so you can be here tomorrow," I said, popping off the couch. I needed to start preparing for new housemates.

Holly chuckled. "Someone have a bad case of the lonelies?"

I blew out a breath. "The worst case."

"Don't worry. Soon you'll be done with school, married to one of the top-paid football players in the nation, and living in some house the size of this craptastic town."

That statement, minus the marrying Jude part, made my stomach queasy.

SEVEN

*E*ven though it felt like Wednesday night would never arrive, it was finally here. After a grueling afternoon session at the dance studio, I'd come back to the apartment and enjoyed tofu stir-fry for one. I was lonely. Morbidly so. I never thought I'd be the girl who couldn't stand to be alone, but this was the first time I'd lived on my own. Alone. *All* alone.

I was one of those girls.

However, tonight was the last night I'd have to spend all by my lonesome, because I would be with Jude tomorrow night through the weekend, and then Holly and little Jude were flying in Monday afternoon.

In the course of four days, Holly had managed to score a sweet deal on airline tickets, find someone to buy her trailer back home, get packed up, apply to every last one of the salons in White Plains, and start looking for child care for little Jude.

I took a while with the dinner dishes, deciding what to do with myself for the next couple of hours. It was too early to go to bed, I'd scrubbed and sanitized every surface in the apartment three times this past week, and we were smack into summer rerun season.

I was heading toward the bathroom to take a long bubble bath when a knock sounded at the door. I jumped—it had been a while since I'd had a visitor.

"Coming!" I called out as I headed to the door. I wasn't expecting anyone, and none of Jude's or my friends lived close enough to make the drive this late at night just to say hi.

"Come on already! Put a robe on, and get one of your asses to the door!" a familiar voice yelled on the other side of the door. "I'm developing crow's-feet out here."

I was smiling when I opened the door. "Hey, India."

"Hey, girl," she said, propping a hand on her hip. "What took you so long?" She peered over my shoulder.

"He's not here," I said. "But if he was you would have been waiting a lot longer than you were. A *lot* longer."

I matched my straight face to India's, waiting for one of us to crack. She did first.

The corner of her mouth moved. "There's my girl. Now

get your bony ass over here and give me some sugar."

Laughing, I wrapped my arms around her. She was in platforms, so she was freakishly tall—so tall her chin fit over my head.

"This is a surprise," I said, motioning her into the apartment.

India sauntered in, peeking into the bedroom like she didn't believe Jude wasn't in there. "A good or a bad surprise?"

"When it comes to you, Indie," I said, walking into the kitchen, "the best kind of surprise."

She winked. "Yeah. I'm pretty great, aren't I?"

"Like you and half the male population on the eastern seaboard aren't aware of that," I teased, filling the kettle with water. "You want some tea?"

"Only if you've got the kind I like." Dropping her purse on the dining table, she took a seat.

I rolled my eyes as I thumbed through my tea stash. "Will this do, Your Highness?" I asked, waving the packet in the air.

India inspected it before nodding. "Perfect."

I turned on a burner and set the kettle on it. "So predictable," I chided.

"Come on, Lucy. You know my rule. I take my tea the way I like my men."

"Dark and strong," I murmured, giving her a look.

"Yeah, well, at least I don't take my tea green and earthy like you," she shot back. "I mean, what does that say about Jude?"

"I sure have missed you, Indie," I said.

"Of course you have," she said, checking her phone. "What's not to miss?"

Indie and I could go another five rounds easy, but I had to get to bed sometime tonight, and, judging from the way she was dressed, she had plans to dance the night away at some club.

"Not to sound rude, because you know I love me a piece of the India pie, but what are you doing here?" I asked, dropping the teabags into a couple of cups. India was a big-city girl. She dodged being in the suburbs like it spelled social ruin.

She lifted a shoulder while texting a quick message. "My brother's up here for work, and one of his old college lacrosse teammates working for him is hot. And single. And Puerto Rican." She waggled her eyebrows at me, her eyes sparkling.

"Of course it would be a man who would lure you to the 'burbs. Not your roommate two years running and good friend." I tapped my finger on the counter, knowing it was useless to try to make India feel guilty. It wasn't in her DNA.

"Baby girl, no man or friend could get me to the 'burbs singlehandedly," she said, "but a smokin'-hot man *and* a snarky good friend could."

At least I was half the reason she was here.

"How long are you in town?" I asked, guessing she'd be on the red-eye back to Miami in the morning.

"A few weeks or so. Anton is managing a new call center branch here in town, and as the lowly second-born, my job is to stay out of the way and pretend to look busy." She made a whoop-dee-doo twirl with her finger.

"If you're going into the family biz, why are you majoring in music?" The teapot started whistling, so I turned off the burner and reached for a hot pad.

"I'm majoring in music because that's what I love. I'm going into the family biz because I actually want to make money," she said, huffing. "I figure if I do my time this summer and a year or two after I graduate, Mom and Dad will turn their heads while I live on music and my trust fund for a couple decades."

I poured the hot water into the cups. "And your first task in this new job is to go party the night away with a cute Puerto Rican?" I said, trying to hide my smile.

"What can I say? I'm living the dream." Her phone

pinged again. It was a noise that went hand in hand with India. Someone was always texting her, at any and all hours of the day.

I grabbed the cups and carried them over to the table.

"Hey, you wanna come with us tonight?" she said, glancing up from her phone. "It will just be me, Anton, and Ricky. We're going to the best club in town, apparently, which isn't saying much. I'll be surprised if they even have a bottle of Cristal for us to celebrate with."

"The horror," I deadpanned, setting her cup in front of her. "As madam requested. Dark, and strong enough to knock your panties right off."

Winking, India lifted her cup to her lips. "In that case, I'll have another."

"Thanks for the invite, and a night on the town is exactly what I need, but I'm flying out at the crack of dawn to see Jude," I said, taking a sip of my green tea.

"Where is the Jude man?"

"San Diego. He had to leave for preseason training a couple of weeks ago," I said.

Her eyebrows rose. "So if Jude's in San Diego, what in the hell are you doing here in this rat-infested hole?"

I stuck my tongue out at her, which earned another eye roll. "I've got a summer class I'm taking."

"Summer class? Pul-lease," she said, making a sound

with her lips. "You've got so many extra credits you could graduate a semester early if you wanted."

I made a mental note to not be so open with India when it came to any and all aspects of my life. She'd been born with a built-in BS detector.

"I'm looking for a job, too," I added, focusing on my teacup.

"Double pul-lease," she said, making that same sound with her mouth. "Why do you need some sucky minimum-wage job when your man's the newest member of the millionaires club?"

I sighed. Well, it was more like a groan. "Not you, too, India." I'd already had to put together a debate team–quality explanation for Jude; I wasn't looking forward to giving a repeat performance.

Setting down her cup, she studied my face for a moment. "Ah," she said at last, "I get it."

"You get what?" I replied, not really caring so long as I didn't have to explain what I didn't fully understand myself.

Grinning, she threw her hands in the air. "'All the women who are independent,'" she sang, swaying in time to the imaginary music.

I chuckled and joined in. "'Throw your hands up at me,'" I sang back, remembering why I was majoring in dance and not music. I couldn't carry a tune to save my soul.

"Is that what it has to do with?" she asked softly.

"Partly."

"And what's the other part?" she asked, grabbing hold of my hand.

"I'm still trying to figure that part out," I admitted. Contrary to what I'd thought, it felt good telling someone that I didn't have a clue why I needed to carve out my own way financially, that I just knew I had to.

"So, what sweet minimum-wage gig are you going to be slaving your summer away at?" she said before taking another drink.

I shrugged a shoulder. "I haven't found one. Yet." I was determined I would, though, and if I'd learned one thing in life, it was that Lucy Larson's stubborn resolve often got what it wanted.

India's face wrinkled before she put her phone up to her ear. "That's about to change," she said.

"Do I want to know?"

She held her cease-and-desist finger up as I heard someone answer on the other end. "I'm on my way," she barked.

Nice greeting.

"Well, Ricky's just going to have to wait a little longer," she cut in before the voice on the other end got more than a few words in. "And you're going to have to wait, too, big brother."

"Hey, Anton," I said, loud enough that he could hear me over India's voice.

"Yes, that was Lucy," she replied. "Yes, Lucy Larson, my old roommate."

"The one and only," I said, heading over to the stove to grab the teapot. India also drank her tea like she went through men: quickly and voraciously.

"Lucy lives here," India continued to explain. "No, obviously not year-round, dumb ass. The apartment here is her and her fiancé's little love shack they do naughty, naughty things in."

"India," I hissed, pouring more water into her cup, "control yourself."

"No, he's not here," India said, swatting my butt as I headed back from the kitchen. "He's got some sort of football training camp thingy."

"Thingy?" I called out.

She dismissed me with a wave. "I already asked her. She's got an early flight out in the morning, so she's taking a pass tonight."

"Next time," I called out again so Anton could hear me.

I had yet to meet India's older brother, but I'd been part of enough of these three-way conversations that I felt like I knew him. In a lot of ways, he reminded me of my brother. He was protective of India, checking in on her almost daily, had a killer sense of humor, and never seemed to run out of things to say. In a word, Anton was charismatic.

"Will you shut your mouth for two seconds so I can get to the reason I'm calling you?" India interrupted after a few moments.

Taking my seat again, I heard Anton reply, "Shutting mouth."

"Thank you," India said, settling into her chair. "Are you still looking for an administrative assistant?"

India waited for his answer.

"And how much were you planning on paying per hour?"

India's face squished when Anton answered. "Tell you what. You make that eighteen dollars an hour and I've got you the best damn administrative assistant you could ever dream to find.

"You'd want to interview her first?" she said, lifting her shoulders. "Okay. Interview her." Lifting the phone toward me, she pressed the speaker button.

"Hey again, Anton," I said, glaring at India for putting me on the spot. "Sorry my friend's such a lunatic."

"Lucy?" he replied, sounding as caught off guard as I was. "Don't worry about it. Sorry my sister's such a pushy maniac."

"No biggie. I'm used to it after three years," I replied, as I smiled innocently at her. She gave me the finger.

Anton laughed. His voice was so deep that when he laughed, it sounded like more of a rumble than a laugh. "So are you really looking for a job, or has India been eating too many 'special' brownies again?"

India glared at the phone.

"I'm really looking for a job," I said, feeling like I should let him off the hook by saying I wasn't interested in being an assistant, so he wouldn't feel obligated to give me the job, but I needed a job, and working for Indie's brother for the summer was better than about 99 percent of any other jobs I could find.

"Do you have any administrative experience?"

"No," I said, "but I'm a fast learner."

India shot me a thumbs-up.

"How many words per minute can you type?" Anton asked next, sounding every bit the professional businessman he'd become since graduating college a few years back.

I motioned to India, looking for help. She mouthed, "I don't know."

"Uh . . . *some*," I said, grimacing.

Anton was silent for a moment. Probably trying to figure out a way to let me down gently. "What's your proficiency with Microsoft Office Suite?"

"Well," I said, trying to keep a level voice. Might as well have a little fun with this impromptu interview. "I've danced lead in *The Nutcracker* three times."

India slapped her leg, rocking in her silent laughter. I swatted her, ready to burst into my own not-so-silent laughter when the sound of Anton choking on his own chuckles broke through the phone.

"Okay, Mr. Hotshot," I said, "I've never worked in an office setting before, and I don't know how many words I can type per minute or what my proficiency in Microsoft Office Suite is"—I made air quotes—"but I'm a hard worker. I'll be there on time, and won't leave until I've typed however many words you need me to. Okay?"

"Anything else?" Anton asked, partially composed.

"Yeah, one more thing. If you're looking for one of those smiling, coffee-fetching, vacant-eyed bimbo types for an assistant, I'm not your girl." This was positively the worst job interview in the history of interviews. Crash and burn, Lucy. Back to the want ads.

"Since I'm not big into bimbos," Anton said after a few seconds, "and I really hate coffee and smiling, I'd say you just landed yourself a job."

Say what?

I gawked at the phone, certain I hadn't heard what I thought I had.

India did a fist pump into the air as I remained silent.

"Can you start first thing tomorrow?" Anton was all business again.

I gave my head a swift shake. "I'm leaving tomorrow morning, but can be in at the crack of dawn Monday morning."

"Not even one day on the job and you're already requesting vacation days?" Anton teased. "What kind of employee did I just hire?"

Reality was finally starting to set in. I had a job. A sweet-paying job working for one of my best friend's brothers. "The kind of employee you thank your lucky stars for," I threw back, ready to hop out of my chair and bust a move.

"Lucy Larson, administrative assistant," Anton said. "I like the sound of that. See you Monday morning."

"First thing," I said. "Thank you, Anton. You won't regret it."

"No, Lucy," he replied, "I'm sure I won't."

You know that person who's the first out of her seat the instant the airplane comes to "a complete stop"? Yeah, that would be me.

I was the first person up and the first person off the plane that Thursday in San Diego. As I powered toward the baggage claim area, I had to remind myself to walk, not run. More than once I forgot.

I saw Jude before he saw me. He was spinning circles in place, and his eyes fell on me after a final revolution. His shoulders relaxed when he smiled. "Yo, Lu-cy!" he shouted—*Rocky*-style—above the noise in the airport, breaking into a run my way.

I didn't care that we were catching the attention of everyone within hearing and seeing distance; nor did I care about the show we'd be giving them soon. The only thing I cared about was the guy running at breakneck speed and getting his arms around me.

I wasn't walking anymore. My bags were bouncing against me as I dodged around people, and the corners of my eyes stung with the tears forming. You would have thought he'd been deployed to the Middle East for the past year from the way we were charging at each other.

When Jude reached me, he grabbed me up and spun me around. I held on for the ride, wondering how another person could make me feel whole again. When Jude finally set me back down, I let my purse and carry-on fall to the floor. Folding me back into his arms, he pressed into me as tightly as two people could fit together. God, it felt so good.

"Damn," he breathed into my hair. "I can't go that long again." His hand cupped the base of my neck and his other arm pressed into the small of my back.

My own arms were cinched in a death-hold around his waist. "Me, neither."

While people grabbed their luggage from baggage claim or waited in line for a cup of coffee, Jude and I stood there, frozen in time. Five minutes, ten minutes, no minutes? I didn't know. And I didn't care.

He smelled the same, all soap and man, and his skin had darkened another shade in the California sun.

"Promise me right now we'll never go that long again without seeing each other," he said, nuzzling into my neck.

His breath against my skin gave me goose bumps.

"Promise," he repeated, looking hard into my eyes.

"I will only make you a promise that I can guarantee I can keep," I said, remembering why honesty was a double-edged sword when his face fell a bit.

His thumb brushed under the collar of my shirt. "Promise me you'll marry me."

I exhaled. That was an easy one. "I promise."

His face went from dark to light in the span of two words. "Promise you'll marry me in the next six months."

Back in the danger zone.

I replied with a lift of my eyebrow.

He chuckled. "Yeah, yeah. You're so difficult, Luce," he

said, keeping me tucked under his arm as he turned toward the baggage carousel. There was only one suitcase left spinning around on it.

Grabbing my bag, Jude pretended to be overwhelmed by its size. Or weight. Or both.

"God, Luce," he said, looking from me to the bag. "If I didn't know better, I'd think you were planning on staying awhile."

Jude's continued theatrics with my bag caught the attention of a few people waiting at the next carousel over. One little boy in particular.

"Three nights is a while for a girl," I said, not able to take my eyes off the little boy gaping at Jude. No matter where we went, Jude got a lot of gaping. The little boys who stared were amusing; I only tolerated the batting-eyed females because I couldn't take out the world's female population singlehandedly. "Besides, I've got a present in there for you that took up at least half the space."

"Present?" His eyes sparkled. "A 'just because' one?"

"Aren't those the best kind?" I said, grabbing his hand and dragging him over to the airport store. I had an idea.

"I got you a present, too," he said proudly as I scanned the store.

"A 'just because' present?" I asked as I found what I was looking for. Tugging on his hand, I beelined for it.

"Aren't those the best kind?" he said.

"Yes, they are," I said, grabbing the turquoise-and-yellow football before heading to the cashier.

"Luce, I can get you one of those for free," he said, sounding confused. "An official one with the whole team's autographs if you want."

The cashier rang me up, and, before I could hand her the cash, Jude slipped a shiny black card into her hand. "I got it," he said.

It's all right. No biggie, I had to tell myself. *He's just paying for a football.*

I thanked the cashier, then sifted through my purse until I found a pen. Handing him the pen, I held the football in place. "I just want one autograph."

He did that half smile, half smirk of his that was by far the sexiest expression in the whole damn world, before signing his name just to the right of the laces.

"I feel like my number-one fan should get something better than an airport football," he said, following after me as I headed back to the baggage carousel.

"Oh, believe me," I called back, "your number-one fan will be demanding you give her something better later tonight."

He chuckled, that low-timbered one of his. "I live to serve."

Pushing the thoughts aside that were making my whole body tingle, I walked toward the little boy who was still gawking at Jude. The kid wasn't even blinking.

I knelt beside him, holding the ball out for him. "You look like a fan of Jude Ryder's," I said, grinning as the boy's eyes widened another notch when he saw the signature.

"His biggest fan," the boy said, his voice high and excited.

"You and me both, kiddo," I said, motioning at the ball when he stayed frozen.

When he finally grabbed the ball, his face lit up like only a child's could. It was amazing how a signature of the guy I loved could make a person's day. It was heavy stuff, and something I wasn't sure I was ready to process yet. Jude had been a big deal back at Syracuse, of course, but now playing for the NFL would mean a whole new level of fame.

I winked at the boy before standing up.

"Thank you," he called out as I headed back to where Jude stood a way back with my bags.

I waved at the boy as he rushed off to his parents and stuck the ball in their faces.

"I know you don't want it going public, but you're quite possibly the sweetest person out there," Jude said, his voice and eyes soft.

I grimaced with exaggeration over *sweet*.

"I think you just made that little guy's year," he said,

wrangling my duffel over one arm and grabbing my hand with his other. "A beautiful stranger picking him out in a crowd. That's one he's going to be telling his buddies ten years from now."

"That boy had eyes for nothing but you and that football," I teased as we headed for the parking garage.

"I would have come over and said hi, but the little guy looked close to hyperventilating as it was."

"Yeah, I think it's a good thing you stayed back." I laughed. "I'm certain his heart couldn't have taken it if you'd said something to him."

Fishing keys from his pocket, Jude came to an abrupt stop in front of a lifted black truck. "And I'm certain my heart can't take it if I don't kiss you," he said, resting a hand on my hip. "Right here. Right now." He stepped closer, until I could feel his body against mine. "And, Luce? I want you to kiss me until I'm weak in the knees."

That melting sensation I got whenever he looked at me the way he was now started to spread from my stomach. Lacing my fingers behind his neck, I popped up onto my tiptoes. "I live to serve," I whispered, quoting him from earlier, before pressing my lips to his.

This wasn't a soft kiss. It wasn't a sweet or shy kiss either. This was the kind of kiss you gave when you knew death was moments away. This was the kind of kiss you could feel in every part of you, and the kind of kiss that was danger-ously close to making me combust right here in the airport parking garage. Fully clothed and all.

My hands moved from his neck to the bottom hem of his shirt. Skimming my fingers inside, I played with the skin trailing along his jeans. Our tongues tangled as my thumbs skimmed lower. Moaning into my mouth, Jude dug his hands into my backside, pushing himself up against me.

Okay, yeah. If he kept pressing and moving against me like that I was about two hot seconds away from ripping both of our clothes off.

As he picked me up, I wrapped my legs around him. Pressing my back up against the truck, he bowed my neck over the hood to give him better access. His mouth moved from mine to my neck, kissing and sucking the sensitive skin until I couldn't breathe.

Somewhere in the back of my sex-crazed mind, I realized the truck's owner probably wouldn't be down with Jude and me going at it, having clothed sex on the hood, but I was long past words . . . and caring.

So when the snaps and clicks of cameras started to grow louder, I paid them no attention. All I felt was Jude's mouth and body moving over me. It was obvious that was all he cared about, too, because it wasn't until the people and cam-eras were a few cars away that either of us took notice.

"Jude! Jude!" they were shouting. "Lucy! Lucy!" More shouting and snapping, so much it shot us both out of our makeout haze.

Jude's muscles tensed over me, and, when his face lifted over mine, I saw a familiar expression I hadn't seen in a long time. Dr. Jekyll, meet Mr. Hyde.

"Jude," I begged. "Chill out," I coaxed as he set me down.

The photographers continued to yell things at us. Some comments were too vulgar to repeat. Their cameras never stopped snapping.

Angling himself in front of me, Jude stiffened further.

Shit. This would not turn out well for all the parties involved if I couldn't talk King Kong down from the Empire State Building.

"Jude," I said, grabbing his arm and trying to turn him around. He didn't budge. "It's fine. They're just pictures."

God, the muscles in his arm felt like they were going to burst through his shirt.

"They're pictures of you and me, Luce," he replied, seething as the cameras continued to go off. "Pictures of you and me doing something I don't want everyone else to see."

Why was he just standing there, letting them get more photos of him about to blow his lid?

"This is not the first time we've been under public scrutiny," I said. "And it won't be the last. And I sure as heck am not going to stop letting you kiss me like that whenever and wherever the mood strikes, so we might as well start getting used to it now." I don't know where I was finding the sense to be so reasonable.

"How's she in bed, Jude?" one of the photographers, who had no sense of self-preservation, called out.

"What did you just say, dickhead?" Jude charged a few steps forward. I didn't let go of him, so he had to drag me right along.

"Jude, stop. Think!" I yelled, realizing he'd only gotten stronger in the weeks of summer training. "Stop and think!"

My body couldn't stop him, but my words could. Coming to an abrupt stop, Jude glanced at me. It was the shortest of looks, but his whole face morphed in that silent exchange. He closed his eyes and took in a few breaths before looking back at the photographers.

Giving his shoulders an anger-defusing shake, he slid his phone from his pocket. Holding it up, Jude took a picture. "There. I've got all your faces on *my* camera now," he said, his voice controlled. Just barely. "If I see or hear about any one of those pictures being printed, I'll come after each and every one of you." Jude pointed his finger at the photographer who'd been stupid enough to ask about my skills in the sack. "Starting with you."

After they'd picked their jaws up from the ground, the

photographers started to disperse. One chanced snapping one more, but rethought that when murder flashed over Jude's face. Only when the last one was out of sight did Jude's shoulders relax. Turning around, he had the good grace to at least look sheepish.

"Sorry?" he said, rubbing the back of his neck.

I nudged him, proud of his restraint. "If I had a quarter for every time I've said—no, I've *shouted*—'Jude!' and, 'Stop!' in the same breath, I'd be a rich woman."

Picking my bags back up, he hung an arm over me. "You already are a rich woman," he said, making my stomach drop. I wasn't a rich woman. He was rich.

"And if I had a quarter for actually listening to you when you've yelled the words 'Jude!' and 'Stop!' in the same breath . . ." He grinned down at me. "I'd be middle-class."

"What do you think the owner would say if he knew what we'd just done on the hood of his new truck?" I said as Jude steered me around the side of it.

"He'd probably ask for a repeat performance."

I laughed. "Probably. Only horny pervs drive trucks like these."

Grabbing the handle, Jude swung the door open. "I'm with you on the horny part, but could we drop the perv part? I don't really want my fiancée to think of me as a pervert."

My mouth dropped open as Jude situated my bags in the

backseat. "This is yours? When did you get it? Where's your old truck?" I couldn't stop the flow of questions.

Holding out his hand for me, he helped me into the truck. I had to leap to get inside.

"This is mine. I got it a couple days ago. And my old truck is going to be scrapped as soon as possible." Shutting the door behind me, he jogged around the front and crawled into the driver's seat. Even Jude in all his gigantor size had to jump to get inside.

When he turned the key over, the engine fired to life. It was so loud, it vibrated the cab. "Now, this is a truck we could get it on in," he said, eyeing the second-row seat, where there was more than enough space for "getting it on."

"We didn't have any problem in your old truck," I muttered, clicking my seat belt into place.

Jude stopped in the middle of reversing out of the spot, eyeing the empty middle seat, then looking at where I sat at the end of the bench. "You hated that old rust bucket," he said, visibly hurt I wasn't sitting right next to him like I normally did.

Unfastening my belt, I scooted over until I was pressed against him. Jude's body running the length of mine was the only thing familiar about this truck. "It was a love/hate relationship," I said defensively. "That was more love than hate."

Clearly appeased, he hung his arm over my shoulders and continued out of the parking spot. "Well, I've still got the beater, so you can say your good-byes before he goes off to truck heaven."

"I'm not ready for him to go to truck heaven." I pouted, wondering why I was so upset. Jude was right: I wasn't his old truck's biggest fan. But now, seeing what it had been replaced with—something shiny and new—made me anxious for reasons I didn't want to admit to myself.

"I got you a little present," Jude said. "It's in the glove box."

Once he was free and clear of the garage, he gunned it. You would have thought that truck had the engine of an Indy car from the way it took off.

"My just-because present?"

"Just because I love you," he said, clearly eager for me to open it.

I was nervous, even more so after seeing the new truck, the cost of which I couldn't even begin to imagine.

When I opened the glove box, a robin's-egg-blue box with a white bow toppled out. I picked it up, already close to hyperventilating. I'd never received a gift in the blue-and-white box, but it was iconic. Every girl knew what store it came from and what was inside. It was a female rite of passage to identify this particular shade of robin's-egg blue.

I brought it to my lap and stared at it.

"Open it," he encouraged. "I've been dying to give it to you since I picked it out last week."

I smiled. It was impossible not to with that boyish look on his face. "This is a pretty fancy box, Mr. Ryder," I said, untying the bow.

"Walmart does a pretty badass gift wrap, don't they?"

I elbowed him. "Nice try." I doubted I'd ever get another Walmart present from him again. The idea made me sad.

"Open it," he said. "Nothing's too good for my girl. It's nice I can finally afford those things you deserve."

"Jude—"

Before I could say whatever I'd been planning to say next, his mouth was on mine, fast and hard. Just as quickly, it was gone. I might have thought I'd made the whole thing up if I couldn't still taste him on my lips.

"Open it," he said, his face smug.

He knew exactly what he was doing and used that to his advantage. He could have been asking me to jump off a cliff, and I was so foggy brained I would have.

I took a breath and slid the lid off.

Nestled inside was a silver cuff bracelet. Simple and elegant. Something I would have picked out for myself, if I'd allowed myself to pick out something so nice.

"Wow," I breathed, pulling it out. It was heavy and cool

to the touch.

"Do you like it?" He glanced between the road and me.

"Now, that's a bracelet," I said, not having to fake my excitement for him.

"Turn it over," he instructed. "There's something else."

Shooting him a curious look, I rotated the bracelet. There was an engraving on the inside, and the words made me weak in all the places a girl could go weak.

"'For my Luce,'" I read. *Luce* had two sparkly stones around it. My dad would love the "Lucy in the Sky with Diamonds" reference. "'Who has all my firsts that matter.'"

"Wow," I repeated. Words were failing me.

"What do you think?" he asked, looking at the bracelet proudly.

"Jude," I started. "It's . . . it's . . ." I had nothing more than one-syllable babble. Sliding the cuff onto my left wrist, I searched for the right words that would express my thanks.

Nothing.

Totally tongue-tied. I was a dancer, not a writer; my body expressed the way I was feeling a hundred times better than my words ever could.

And then it came to me.

Leaning closer, I kissed his scar. Once, twice, and then a third time before I moved to his mouth. I'd taken him by surprise. That was apparent from the way his muscles tensed.

Taking Jude Ryder by surprise was rare, and I was going to enjoy it. Sweeping gentle kisses over his entire mouth, I savored the moment. Our other kisses were so passionate and unyielding I felt like I was being consumed by them, but this one I held on to. I enjoyed the scent of salt on his skin. The way the fullness of his bottom lip felt in my mouth. The way his tongue tasted against mine.

I pressed one final kiss into the center of his mouth. "Thank you," I said. "I love my bracelet." Okay, one final, *final* kiss. "And I love you."

"Damn, woman," he said, whistling through his teeth. "Have mercy. If that's the thanks I get, I will be getting you jewelry every single day."

As I leaned my head on his shoulder, I admired the bracelet. He had a finger, and now a wrist. And he had my heart. Jude Ryder was slowly taking me over, one body part at a time.

"And you're welcome."

We sat in silence for a few minutes. I slid my fingers up and down his as he was content to draw circles on my arm. It was peaceful, and although these kinds of quiet moments had been increasing during our time together, peace wasn't a regular thing in our relationship. I hoped that one day that would change.

"Hey, I need you to put something on," he said, pulling

something out of his pocket.

My eyes narrowed at the thing dangling from his index finger.

"A blindfold?" I said. "A black satin blindfold? What was I saying about you being a horny perv?"

He shook his head. "This has nothing to do with horny . . . kinky . . . perverty," he said, sounding increasingly uneasy with each word.

I held in my laugh. "Damn," I teased. "There's a way to ruin a girl's day."

"So difficult," he said under his breath. "Just put it on. I've got another surprise for you."

Grabbing the blindfold, I slid it on. "Does this surprise have to do with any horny, kinky, perverty fun?"

"No." He chuckled.

"Double damn."

More laughter. "Luce, you are busting my balls big-time today."

"That's because I'm into that kind of thing. You know? The horny, kinky, perverty kind of thing." If I was going to be blindfolded so he could take me to some other surprise, I was going to let my snarky side run free.

It wasn't much longer before the truck came to a stop.

"We're here," he said, his voice all boyish and excited again.

"We're where?"

Grabbing my hands, he helped me out of the cab. Thankfully, he lifted me from the truck, because I didn't want to make a blindfolded jump not knowing what the hell I'd land on.

"Here," he answered, guiding me by the shoulders. We were moving over a hard surface. Concrete? Asphalt? Stone, maybe? Other than the sound of running water, fountains possibly, it was quiet. He couldn't have been taking me to a store; we weren't at the beach . . . where in the world were we?

Suddenly, he scooped me into his arms and jogged up what I assumed were stairs, before I heard a door open. Turning sideways, Jude walked inside before setting me down. My heart was already in my throat before he slid the blindfold back.

The first thing I saw was his eyes. I wanted to keep looking at them, to never look away, because I already knew what I was going to see when I did. I was scared to shift my gaze.

"I couldn't find a big enough bow to put around it," he said, turning me around. "I hope you don't mind."

Thankfully Jude had wrapped his arms around me, so when I wavered in place, he kept me upright. We were standing in a cavernous room, a space that could fit a decent-size home, and we were just in the foyer. A room a person walked through to get to others that were the size of my parents' cabin. There were two staircases going up to the second floor. One for going up? One for going down? I didn't have a clue, but it wasn't the only thing over-the-top about this place. The chandelier hanging in the center of the room was the size of a Volkswagen, the furniture was so ornate it went past the point of offensive, and the marble floors were so shiny they almost looked like an ice-skating rink.

"What *is* this?" I whispered, hoping the answer I'd arrived at was wrong.

"The soon-to-be residence of a Mr. and Mrs. Ryder," he answered, tucking his chin over my shoulder. He was grinning like a crazy man, but that changed when he saw my face.

"Luce?" he said, the excitement gone from his voice. "What's wrong?"

I closed my eyes. I couldn't keep looking around. Each new thing I saw drove me that much closer to having a full-fledged panic attack. "What is this, Jude?"

"Our home," he said slowly.

"No. Our home is back in New York."

His forehead wrinkled. "No, that place is a condemned apartment we rent. That place is a tetanus shot waiting to happen," he said, sounding defensive. "You're standing in our home. The place we're going to own outright in a year's time."

"I like our apartment," I whispered, weaving out of his embrace. Things were changing too fast. The NFL, the cross-country move, the money, the house . . . it was all moving at warp speed and I couldn't even begin to keep up. We'd been pulling change out of the seat cushions to pay our electric bill last month, and this month we were standing inside the foyer of a house that was the size of a small country.

"You hate that place." His voice was getting louder, and he was looking at me in that way again. Like he didn't recognize me.

I hated that look.

"It's a love/hate relationship that's more—"

"What the hell, Luce?" he interrupted. "What new kind of crazy have you caught?"

That trigger-touch temper of mine, like his, just shot to the surface. However, like Jude, I'd been learning to control mine. I got that in Jude's mind, he'd picked this place thinking I'd love it. I knew that at the core of every decision Jude made, my happiness was his top priority, and I loved that about him. I *knew* his heart was in the right place when he'd decided to turn us into the Joneses overnight, but I was upset about the way he'd gone about it. How could he make this huge life decision on his own without even consulting me first? We were a team. We should be making decisions as one.

Biting my tongue, I inhaled slowly before I dared to reply. "Same question right back at ya: What kind of crazy have *you* caught?" I said, nothing antagonistic in my voice, because that wasn't how I meant it. I truly was wondering what new kind of crazy Jude had caught to go out and get a place like this.

Popping his neck from side to side, Jude took his time replying. We were both working to keep our anger monkeys in their cages. "I'm renting the place right now until I get my first big check, and then the owner's agreed to sell it to me fully furnished." He stopped and took another deep breath. "You should see the lagoon and tennis court in the back. This place is hooked up."

"Lagoon? Tennis court?" My stomach was feeling more and more sick. I reminded myself once more that Jude had done this because he loved me. Not because he wanted to piss me the hell off. I bit back what I wanted to say. "Jude, we're twenty-one years old."

"We're twenty-one-year-old millionaires," he said with a shrug. "And now that I've got the means to give you anything and everything, I'm going to. I want to make you happy, Luce. That's all I give a damn about," he said, pointing at me. "You. Happy. Forever."

"Happy?" I repeated, crossing my arms. "You think this is what's going to make me happy? What did you do? Go down to the local library and check out *The Idiot's Guide to Making a Gold-digging Trophy Wife Happy*?"

I tried biting my tongue again. Man, I tried, but apparently I'd reached my quota of tongue-biting today.

"Because if I was a gold digger then I imagine this would make me very happy," I said, sweeping my arms around the room. "But I'm not. Despite your wanting me to be this girl who wants your money, I'm not that girl!"

What was I saying? What was I so mad about?

Jude's face went from shocked, to sad, to angry in two seconds flat. "No, you're not that girl, Luce. It doesn't seem like I can do anything to make you happy these days. Maybe you just don't want to be happy."

Those words were like a slap to my face. I reminded myself yet again that this house was Jude's way of showing his love for me, but my temper had taken off and I couldn't pull it back. "Here's a tip. If you're looking to make someone happy, maybe you should think about what they'd want, not what you want them to want."

Wrapping his hands behind his neck, Jude spun away from me. "And here's a tip for you. You have to be willing to let happiness in when it comes your way."

His words made me flinch.

"How is you buying a house for us in Southern California without asking me first supposed to equate with happiness? I live in New York, Jude. New. York."

"You live in New York for another year," he said, staring at the nearest wall like he wanted to bang his head against it. "Once you're done with school you can leave and move in with me."

This wasn't a slap. This was a punch. A sucker punch to the gut. "I can leave New York and move in with you here? In California? In a Playboy-size mansion?" How had there been such a disconnect between us? Where did he get off assuming he could just map my life out for me without checking with me first? "Who said I wanted to pick up and move across the country to live with you here in the land of fake tits and phony smiles?"

From the look on his face, you would have thought I'd just socked him in the stomach. "When you agreed to marry me. When you let me put that ring on your finger." His words were slow and controlled. So much so they were scary-sounding.

"So what you heard when I said yes to marrying you is that I'd willingly—no, *gladly*—give up my dreams, future plans, et cetera, et cetera, so you could live yours?" I shouted. "Because I guess I missed the fine print."

Jude closed his eyes. "What do you want, Lucy?" I cringed internally. He called me Lucy only if he was really pissed or hurt. "Because apparently I don't have a damn clue. So tell me. What. The. Hell. Do. You. Want?"

"I want to finish school. I'm going to school for dance, so I know it might seem crazy, but I'd actually like to *dance* after I graduate." I could barely look at him right now. Not because of what he was saying, but because of what I was saying to him. I didn't want to hurt him; in fact, I wanted the opposite. So when I hurt him, I hated myself.

"Okay, you want to dance." He extended his arms at his sides. "Good news, Luce. You can dance here in San Diego. Problem solved."

I snorted. "Problem not solved. If I want to dance in some crummy community theater rendition of *Swan Lake* once a year, I can dance here. I did not work my butt off dancing the past fifteen years of my life to perform half-assed dances in front of snoring seniors who paid ten dollars a ticket."

Jude's forehead lined. Well, it lined deeper. "So what are you saying? You want to stay in New York when you're done with school?"

How had we not worked this out before? Maybe because we'd been so busy living in the moment, or stumbling over our pasts, we'd forgotten to look ahead. We'd missed the future part of our relationship.

"New York, Paris, London," I said, shrugging. "Those are the cities where dancers who want to dance go."

I could see Jude's internal battle. The same WTF one I was experiencing. Why had it taken us so long to figure out that what I wanted and what he wanted might not align? "Well, shit, Luce. I didn't get drafted by the Jets. Or the Giants. Or some European league," he said, shaking his head. "I got drafted by the Chargers. I'm going to be in San Diego for a while."

I nodded. "I know."

"You know what?"

"I know you're in San Diego. I know I'm in New York."

I wanted—I *needed*—a break from this conversation. A few hours to figure out what was happening, what had been said, and where to go from here. I knew my priorities, and Jude was one notch above dance, but did Jude place me one notch below football in his mind?

I didn't think so. He'd proven I came first over and over again, but this—the house, the truck, the expectations, the assumptions—all of this was starting to worry me. I needed to sort some serious shit out, and I couldn't do it with him staring at me the way he was now. And I certainly couldn't do it inside this mansion-on-steroids.

"Where does that leave us then, Luce?" he said, his voice quiet and his face tired. He looked like he needed time to work things out as badly as I did.

Where did that leave us? San Diego? New York? Somewhere smack in the middle?

"At a crossroads," I said with a shrug.

"A crossroads?" he repeated, coming toward me. "After everything we've been through, you're telling me we're at a crossroads when I've got a ring on your finger and all our dreams are finally coming true?"

I took a deep breath before replying. "No. All *your* dreams are coming true. I'm still working on mine, so yes, we're at a crossroads."

The veins in his neck were coming to the surface. He was pissed, and I was only making it worse. "We are not at a crossroads," he hissed through his teeth.

"Oh, yes, we damn well are at a crossroads!" I yelled back.

His face went a little red. "No. We're. Not."

"Yes. We. Are!" God, were we really doing this? Fighting by repeating each other's words, like a couple of middle school kids?

"Goddammit, Lucy Larson!" he shouted. "No, we're not! And that's that, so stop talking about crossroads. In fact, just stop talking, because everything that's coming out of your mouth is plain crazy!"

I felt tears pricking to the surface and I wasn't going to

let them fall here. "You're a real ass sometimes, you know that?" I said, before running across the enormous foyer, heading toward the back of the house. I needed to get away from Jude, get some fresh air, and get my mind-set straight again. I was a mess and was only going to get messier if I stayed in the same room with him for another minute.

I heard Jude curse at the top of his lungs before his footsteps sounded behind me. "Wait, Luce," he said, but I couldn't. Not this time.

Racing down a hall, I came around a corner into another giant room. Rushing through it, I headed for the double doors that I assumed led outside.

Fresh air. A minute to think.

Shoving through the door, I found myself, presumably, in the backyard. But this was a backyard like no other. Like the house, it was spacious and elaborate. The "lagoon" I'd heard soooo much about was in front of me. There was a natural rock feature coming out of the center of it, featuring slides going into the pool. It reminded me of the pool at the hotel we'd stayed at in the Bahamas when I was ten. My brother and I couldn't be pulled away from that thing the whole week.

Behind the pool there was another building, this one more the size of a regular house. I guessed it was the pool house. I heard Jude's footsteps approaching, but I wasn't ready for him. He liked to talk things out first, think them out later. I was exactly the opposite, and I knew, given the heated topic, if we picked up where we left off before I had a couple hours to cool down, another screaming match would ensue.

I might not have matured enough to keep from yelling, but I was wise enough to try to avoid it when I could.

Striding across the back patio, I hoped whatever part of the backyard was behind the next turn would provide some temporary shelter or hiding place. The instant I turned, I knew peace and quiet wouldn't be on the agenda tonight.

Milling about a sprawling patio were a few dozen bodies. Drinks in hand, chatting with one another, they didn't notice me at first.

And then Jude came racing around the corner, still yelling my name.

Then they noticed me.

"What the—"

"F—" What I started, Jude finished.

EIGHT

"*W*ow. We suck at throwing a surprise party." A guy who looked like he could bench a semi truck came forward with a couple champagne glasses in hand.

I was still trying to determine whether I'd landed in Oz when the giant, whose shoulders and strut gave him away as a starting linebacker, handed me a glass. I took it automatically, trying to ignore everyone looking at me like I was an experiment gone wrong.

"We might have screwed up the surprise part, but we certainly won't screw up the 'party' part." The giant handed the other glass to Jude, then slid a flask out of his jacket pocket. Unscrewing the cap, he lifted it. "To the new master and mistress of this California castle. May the parties be wild and the sex even wilder." Winking back at us, he shouted, "Cheers!"

A chorus of, "Cheers!" exploded, but I was beyond words. Even one-syllable ones. I wasn't sure what twilight zone I'd found myself in, but I wanted out.

Now.

"Terrell," Jude said, coming up behind me. I could feel the heat from his body, he was that close, and I wanted to have those arms hold me right now so badly . . . so I took a couple steps away. I both was and wasn't ready for his arms around me. "What the hell is this?" Jude didn't sound angry, but he wasn't happy either.

"An attempt at a surprise party," Terrell replied. "The team wanted to christen your new crib accordingly. And what says christening better than thirty of your rowdy teammates, their hot wives, girlfriends, mistresses, dates, and everything else in between"—his eyebrows waggled in suggestion—"and booze."

Behind me, Jude sighed. He sounded as tired as I felt.

"Plus, we wanted to meet the infamous Lucy," Terrell continued, smiling at me. "I'm the guy who keeps your man from getting his ass sacked, Lucy," he said, extending his hand. It was so big, it swallowed mine whole. "Our QB here assumes it's his fancy moves, and not mine, that will keep him from going down, but I'll let you in on a little secret." Terrell leaned in. "He's wrong."

A round of laughter went through the crowd.

"Jude makes a lot of assumptions," I said, giving him a pointed look.

Terrell stared between me and Jude before grabbing the glass from Jude's hand and steering him toward a table with more bottles of alcohol than there were people in attendance. "You need something stronger than this, I'm guessing." Jude looked back at me but stayed with Terrell. The Jude I knew wouldn't have let anyone pull him away from me. Especially when I was upset and uncomfortable.

"Ladies!" Terrell hollered. "Make Lucy one of the gang."

I stood there for a few more moments, feeling like I was the last person to be picked for kickball, when one of the girls stepped away from the player she was with and approached. She wasn't dressed like the others, who adhered to the shorter-is-better policy when it came to dress selection. She was sporting an airy wrap dress and gold sandals, and, unlike the rest of the female faces staring at me like I was gum on the bottom of a shoe, she had a smile on her face. A *genuine* smile.

"So you're the Lucy Jude can't stop talking about," she said, and instead of shaking my hand, she pulled me into a hug. Like her smile, her hug was a real one.

"It's nice to meet the girl a guy can't shut up about. Reminds me of the way my husband used to be about me before we had four kids and became the laziest romantics ever." She motioned over to the group of guys Jude had been escorted to. A guy about Jude's height and weight tilted his beer our way.

"I'm Sybill, and that's my husband, Deon, over there."

"Hey, Lucy!" Deon tilted his beer at us again. "I'm the one who earns his paycheck. These other posers just like to cash 'em."

Deon received a round of shoves from the guys around him.

"That's right, baby!" Sybill said, before turning her attention back on me. "So. How are you hanging in there?"

As a policy, I didn't normally spill my guts to total strangers, but Sybill's warm smile cut right through my gut-spilling rules and restrictions. "It's a lot to take in," I began. "Weeks ago Jude was a college student, and now he's going to be playing on millions of televisions in a couple months."

"It most certainly is a lot to take in," she said. "When Deon was drafted, we were seniors in college. I packed up and moved across the country and, I kid you not, found out I was pregnant a week before his first game." She laughed, staring at her husband in a way I was familiar with. It was the way I looked at Jude. "I was so scared it would throw him off that I didn't tell him until after the game was over. We were married a month later and decided one was so much fun, we might as well have three more."

"That sounds like a hell of a lot to absorb all at once," I said, snagging a bottle of water from a table. "But look at you two now." I motioned between them, because words were useless when it came to describing their obvious connection.

"A couple who has to schedule nooky to make sure we still make time for it." She winked over at me. "But it's a good life. And I've got a good man who gave me four kids who I love so much I feel a little nutty sometimes."

Okay. I was glomming onto Sybill at these events and not letting go. Ever. We could rock our jeans and tees together while the rest of the girls flounced around in satin and sequins.

"Speaking of my four munchkins . . ." Rummaging through her purse, Sybill pulled out a phone and answered it. "What's up, Jess?"

Frowning, she motioned at her husband. "Okay, give Riley a bit of Sprite and a saltine. We'll be home in a half hour."

"Sick munchkin?" I guessed.

"Vomiting-spaghetti-and-meatballs munchkin," she said. "Hey, Deon! Riley's sick. You wanna grab the car and I'll meet you out front?"

Deon flicked her a salute and jogged inside.

"Sorry your little man's sick," I said. "I hope he feels better soon."

"Knowing Riley, he'll be up and playing Wii by the time we get home." She waved at a few of the guests before patting my forearm. "Don't let the other girls intimidate you, Lucy," she said quietly. "There's not a whole lot going on up here"—she tapped her head—"or here"—her hand moved to her heart—"but they're easily controlled. They're so shallow, all you have to do is tell them you like their new purse, or dress, or boob job, and you'll be one of the gang. Shower them in schmooze and you're in."

I looked back at where the rest of the party was, then at Sybill, who was heading inside the house. "I don't think I want in."

She threw me a smile. "Yeah, me neither. Obviously I never have been or will be an 'it' girl," she said with a shrug. "I like you, Lucy Larson. Let's be friends."

It was such a kindergarten way of putting it, but so honest. One good thing had come of this day—I had a new friend. "I like you, too. Friend."

She waved before glancing back at Jude. "Sweet pad, QB! Sorry to eat and run, but life calls."

Jude glanced between Sybill and me, not doing as good a job as I was of pretending we hadn't just had a screaming match minutes ago. "Thanks, Sybill," he replied. "I'm glad you got to finally meet Luce."

With Sybill gone, and Jude starting to make his way toward me, that group of girls to my right were a welcome distraction. I ignored the fact that their dresses were so shiny that together they created a collective disco ball. I also ignored that I would be the smallest-boobed girl in the bunch. Smallest by a landslide.

All I knew was that I wasn't ready to talk to Jude just yet, I wasn't ready to move past the nasty things we'd said to each other, and I certainly didn't want a repeat of that blowup. I'd get past it—I always did—but not yet.

As Jude drew closer, I popped over to the girls. I should have reminded myself that "popping" wasn't exactly a casual way to work your way into the group. Every flat-ironed, platinum-blond head spun toward me. How many times did I need to be on the spot in my twenty-one years of life? Really?

However, my not-so-stealthy move had worked. Jude wasn't marching my way anymore. Smart man.

Out of the pan, into the fire.

Say something, Lucy, I commanded myself as everyone waited, staring at me like I didn't belong. Then I remembered Sybill's words of wisdom. I latched on to the first thing that caught my attention.

"I love your ring," I said, nodding at the girl next to me,

her hand curled around a champagne glass.

There was another moment of silence before a chorus of "awww"s went through the group.

"That is so sweet of you to say," Ring Girl said, putting her other hand to her chest. Wow. I'd seen big boobs in my day, but these things. They could have had their own zip code. "Chad got it for me for our anniversary."

More "aww"s. The sound was like nails on a chalkboard. I didn't do "awww."

"How many years have you been married?" I asked, feeling like I had this small-talk thing down.

"Not our wedding anniversary, silly," she said, laughing like I was just too cute. "We're not married, just dating."

"Oh," I said. "How many years have you been together?"

"Two months today," she said proudly.

"You've been dating for two months, and he got you that?" Whoever this Chad was, he was a certifiable idiot. Or whoever this ring girl was, she was rather talented at what she did.

"No, she got that because she's been giving him BJs for two months," the girl to my left said under her breath before snickering. "She's obviously very good with her mouth."

The girls all joined in with her snickering, even the girl who gave the best BJs on the block, apparently.

"Wow," I said. "Good for you." I had no other reply.

Sybill was right: There was nothing going on up there.

"What about you?" a dark-haired girl across from me piped up. "Let's see your ring."

Holding out my hand, I couldn't help the smile that formed. One always did when I looked at my engagement ring. It had a special way of reminding me of Jude's and my past, as well as the promise of our future. There was powerful stuff in that ring.

"How big is that?" she asked.

Continuing to admire it, I said, "A third of a carat."

A few sharp snickers, followed by a hush. When I looked up, I found the dark-haired girl fighting a smirk. "Oh," she said, flashing her ring that was ten, if not twenty times bigger than mine. "I didn't realize they made diamonds that small."

Another round of snickers. And now I was pissed all over again. At least it wasn't at Jude. He'd worked his ass off to save enough money to buy my engagement ring, and these self-righteous bitches who had likely never worked a day in their lives were going to take a piss on his hard work?

Yeah, not on my watch.

"They come in all shapes and sizes," I said, meeting her stare with my glare. "Kind of like brains." Quirking a brow, I spun on my heel and left. I couldn't get away fast enough.

Looked like I was going to have one female friend in this

crowd this year. One true friend was worth more than fifty frenemies who laughed at my engagement ring. Bitches.

After not-so-casually slipping away from the lionesses' den, I wandered around the backyard. Since it was more like a park than a yard, it should have been easy to find a quiet spot.

I could still hear the dull roar of the party when my phone chimed in my purse. Assuming it was Jude, I was ready to hit ignore when a different but familiar phone number showed up on the screen. I wasn't really in the mood for talking, but the caller on the other end wasn't one for long conversations anyway.

"Hey, Dad," I answered, as I continued to weave my way through the landscape. I was pretty sure there was yet another god-awful, overstated fountain waiting at the end of my path, so I switched directions.

"Hello, my Lucy in the Sky," he greeted, sounding like the dad of my childhood. The dad who hadn't become an emotional and physical shut-in for the entirety of my teen years. "I'm just calling to say hi and check in."

I smiled the biggest smile I was capable of right now. Dad called every week, same day, same time. You could set a watch by Dad's calls. "Hi, yourself, and thanks for the checkup. I'm in San Diego visiting Jude."

I didn't offer anything more. If I told my dad about Jude's and my fight over the McMansion, there'd be no getting him off the phone in a few minutes.

"How's the Jude man?" he asked eagerly. I wasn't the only big fan of Jude Ryder in the Larson family. Dad was a close second in that department.

"Jude's . . ." I searched for the right word: *A shade past nuts* and *drinking the California Kool-Aid* were probably phrases I should keep to myself. "He's been really busy, Dad. I think all the sun, long hours on the field, and dollar signs are making him a little crazy."

Dad chuckled to himself.

"Crazier than normal," I clarified.

"Any updates on the nuptial front?" Dad asked, making a not-so-smooth segue.

I groaned. "Not you, too," I whined. "If it's not you, it's Mom. If it's not Mom, it's Jude. If it's not Jude, it's somebody else. What is it with everyone wanting to know every little detail about our forthcoming or not-so-forthcoming wedding?" I didn't mean to be so snappy with my dad. It was just a case of wrong question, wrong time.

"Lucy in the Sky," Dad said, sounding the picture of calm, "I don't want to just know every detail of your wedding, forthcoming or not. I want to know every detail of your whole life." I could hear that fatherly smile in his voice.

"But since you're no longer a kindergartener, how about I just settle for knowing if you're happy?"

I exhaled. Dad had a way of soothing me just with his voice alone. "That works for me."

"I mean that, sweetie. Your happiness is all I care about," he said. "If it makes you happy to stay engaged for the rest of your life, I'm fine with that." I laughed sharply. Dad might be all right with that, but I knew another man who wouldn't be too pleased. "If a shotgun wedding in Vegas makes you happy, so be it."

"Thanks, Dad," I said.

"Whatever you and Jude decide on, your mom and I are good with it," he said. "Okay?"

It was a weight off my shoulders knowing that, but the problem was, I couldn't decide what I wanted right now. I needed some time and a cup of tea to help me with my sea of indecision.

"Okay, Dad. Thanks, that means a lot to me," I said.

"Well, you mean a lot to me, Lucy in the Sky."

When I stepped out of the shower, I peeked out the bathroom window. The last party stragglers were gone. Today had been one hell of a day, and I knew that tomorrow would be, too. So tonight I wanted to forget about everything running around in my mind and get some sleep. I needed to close the door on this day and open a new one in the morning.

I'd left all the lights in the pool house off in hopes Jude would be too drunk or too tired to come looking for me. Of course, I knew that was wishful thinking. I knew he'd come. I just hoped that when he did, he would give me the space I'd tell him I needed. Jude wasn't the biggest fan of "space," given our past experience with it.

I was getting a cup from the cupboard when the knock sounded on the pool house door.

"Luce? Are you in there?" His voice was high pitched.

Before I had a chance to respond, the door opened and he stepped inside.

His face was as worried-looking as his voice had sounded. "I've been looking for you everywhere," he said, taking a few more steps inside. "What are you doing out here?"

Hiding from you. Trying to get my thoughts together. "About to go to sleep," I answered, setting the glass down. Water had sounded good until Jude had arrived. Now the only thing that sounded good was him. Especially with the way he was looking at me.

"You're hiding from me," he stated, stuffing his hands in his pockets.

"No," I said, cinching the tie of my bathrobe tighter. "I'm hiding from that place."

Jude's jaw tightened. "That place is our home, Luce. It's mine and yours."

"No, Jude. That place belongs to you and the person you want me to be. Not the person I really am."

Tapping the wall with his fist, he walked toward me. "Fine. That's not the place that you want, we'll get rid of it," he said, staring at me like I was his whole world. He knew I melted under that look. It had been days, *weeks*, and he was using my failing restraint to his advantage.

I closed my eyes and sucked in a slow breath to calm myself down. I could already feel the blood rushing to certain parts of my body at having him alone and this close. I could not, I *would* not sleep with him until I'd worked through this crap in my head.

"Tell me what you want, Luce," he said, stopping a few feet in front of me. I could smell him; I could almost taste him on my lips. I could nearly feel him. . . .

I shook my head, keeping my eyes closed. "I don't know," I admitted, sensing him stepping closer.

"Tell me what you want," he demanded, and now his body pressed into mine.

Dammit. My weakening resolve was officially about to be a lost cause.

Then his mouth moved outside my ear, and the heat of his breath broke across my neck. "What," he whispered, "do you"—his teeth sank into my earlobe "want?" His hips flexed into me, and when I felt him hard against me, that last bit of restraint I'd been clinging to slipped right through my fingers.

I opened my eyes. Now that I'd jumped, I was going to enjoy the fall.

I waited until he looked into my eyes. "I want you," I said, my fingers moving for his zipper. I was long past the point of foreplay. "Here. Now." Sliding his zipper down, I rested my mouth outside his ear. "And hard."

Jude sucked in a sharp breath, but that was all the surprise he allowed himself. His hands made quick work of untying my robe. Grabbing my hips, he hoisted me up and carried me over to the table. His mouth found mine and he kissed me like he'd never kissed me before. It was desperate, and hungry, and almost painful.

But the pain felt good. I needed to feel it right now.

After unfastening the button of his pants, I tugged them down. Grabbing him in my hand, I lay back on the table. Jude stared down at me, his face a mix of emotions. My mind, for the first time since this afternoon, was clear. And content.

As I guided him toward me, he paused. "Are you sure you're ready?" he said, his breath strained.

"Come and find out," I replied, wrapping my legs around

his waist to draw him closer.

His face creased as my hand moved up and down him, but he restrained himself.

"Jude," I whispered, "please." I lifted my hips until I could feel him right where he should be.

Moving just barely inside, he groaned. I groaned louder. The torture was insane, and if he was going to play it nice and slow, I'd just have to change his mind. Nice and slow wasn't on the agenda for tonight.

At the same time I tightened my legs around him, I flexed my hips higher, effectively taking the rest of him inside me.

"Oh, God." I sighed, feeling like I could come now that he was all the way inside me. When his hips flexed, I almost did.

"Shit, Luce," he said, breathing heavily outside my ear. "You really were ready."

Performing that hip swivel thing that drove him up the wall, I moved his hand from my hip until it was covering my breast. "Then what are you waiting for?"

His hands squeezed both my hip and my breast, and then he started moving his hips more. I'd wanted hard, and that was what I got.

Each time he thrust into me I was sure I was going to come, but I didn't. This time I was the one waiting for him. The table started wobbling beneath me as he picked up his pace. My fingers drilled into his back; all I could do was hang on and enjoy the way he was making me feel.

I heard every low growl when he slid inside, along with every tortured groan when he slid out. "Come, baby," he breathed, rocking into me faster. "I want to feel you come."

His hand slid from my hip down lower, until his thumb was circling over my clit.

I knew I was close, but my orgasm came the next instant. Jude's body touching me both inside and outside in every way sent me right over the big O edge so powerfully, I felt like I was being ripped apart from the inside. I shouted his name, feeling my muscles contract around him as he slammed into me a final time. He sighed my name so many times I lost count, before collapsing on top of me.

NINE

I could still smell Jude on my pillow, but his head wasn't sharing it with mine like it had all night. Well, all night *after* our makeup tabletop sexcapade.

But he was close. His off-key singing to the song playing on the radio was a dead giveaway. As I rolled over, a smile was already in place.

When my eyes landed on a backside, a *bare* backside, manning the coffee machine, my smile stretched wider.

"Have I mentioned lately what a fine ass you have?" I said, propping up onto my elbows, because if Jude's bare backside was on display for my ogling pleasure, I was going to enjoy the view.

He smirked at me as he poured coffee into a cup. "Only

last night, when you were grabbing it while you screamed my name."

"My. Someone woke up on the cocky side of the bed this morning." I was tempted to check my phone for the time, but that would have meant looking away. The time could wait; a naked Jude making coffee couldn't.

"I wake up on that side of the bed every morning, Luce," he said, turning around.

Like the bad girl I was, my eyes zeroed in on a certain spot. "Yes, you most certainly do." My smile could not possibly stretch further without hurting.

"Good morning," he said, holding out the cup of coffee while I continued with my staring contest.

"Yes, it is," I replied, sitting up.

"Okay, Luce, you gotta stop looking at me like that or else I'm going to be late to practice." He waited until my gaze shifted to his before he handed me the coffee. That was probably for the best. Gawking women and steaming cups of liquid don't go together well.

"If you don't want me looking at you like that, you should have put some clothes on." I raised an eyebrow at him as I took a sip. "Thanks for the coffee. Very domestic of you."

Snatching his discarded boxers from last night, he hiked

them into position before scooting next to me. "I like waiting on you hand and foot," he said, his eyes traveling down my body. "And everywhere in between."

I sighed into my cup. "Here's a pointer. If you don't want to be late to practice, you shouldn't say those kinds of things either."

His eyes cleared and returned to mine almost immediately. How he could go from dripping sex one moment to all business the next, I didn't know, but it was something that I doubted I'd ever be able to master. "You didn't exactly give me a chance to tell you last night, since you were busy ravaging me on that table that has now officially become my favorite piece of furniture"—he studied the table as a slow smile formed—"but I'm sorry for everything yesterday, Luce. I wanted the whole day to be perfect and it couldn't have gone more wrong."

No, it couldn't have. Well, at least up until the night.

I grabbed his hand and squeezed it. "I'm sorry, too," I said, so familiar with the words I could have been a certified expert by now. In the history of our relationship, "I'm sorry," "Forgive me," and "I messed up" came almost as frequently as "I love you."

"If you don't like the house, that's fine. We'll find another one," he said, draping an arm over my shoulders. "I want you to be happy, Luce, and I never would have picked this place out if I thought it was going to upset you."

I sighed in relief. Yesterday we'd battled this conversation out. Today we could talk about it calmly and constructively. Maybe this was how we needed to approach these kinds of land mines in the future: naked and in bed.

"I know that, Jude. It just took me by surprise. Everything's coming at me so fast, and sometimes I feel like I don't have a chance to catch my breath." I paused to take another drink. "You know?"

"Believe me, I know," he replied with a nod. "You don't need to explain it to me, Luce. I get it, and I'm sorry I made this whole thing harder on you. I'll call my real estate agent this afternoon and have him start looking for a different place. Okay?" He pulled me closer, tucking my head beneath his jaw.

"Will this real estate agent be looking at three-bedroom, two-bathroom houses?" I started telling myself to stay calm, so when and if this took a turn for the heated, I could better manage it.

Jude groaned, but it wasn't his full-fledged one, like he was also trying to catch himself before either of our tempers could escalate. "You realize how much money I'm making this year? Right, Luce? And how much I'll be making from now—"

"I know. I know," I said, biting my tongue so my next

comments stayed inside. "But how does that change who you are? And who I am? And what we want?" Those were, at the core of it all, the questions I needed answered.

"It doesn't change me, or you, or what we want at all, Luce," he said calmly. "All it changes is our style of life. And how many sweet rides we have in our five-car garage."

I set my coffee down on the nightstand. He wasn't getting it, or I wasn't being clear. I didn't want more cars than I had fingers. I didn't want more garages than I had hairs on my head. I wanted Jude. And a roof above us, along with a reliable car and food in the cupboards would be nice.

"I don't want to change our style of life," I said. "I thought our current style of life was pretty great."

"It is pretty great, Luce. It's pretty fucking great," he said, keeping me close. This was the way to have a tough talk, held tightly against him. "But it could be that much better. All those times I wanted to go to the jewelry store and buy you the biggest, sparkliest damn thing I could, all those times I wanted to take you to some fancy restaurant and order the most expensive thing on the menu just because I wanted you to have the best. All those winters I wanted to get you an SUV that would laugh at winter driving." He paused and leaned his head into the headboard. "I'm sick of not being able to get you the things you deserve."

What he was saying was tugging on my heart, but it

did nothing to alleviate the tension that built whenever he started talking about money. "I know you are, baby. I know you are," I said. "But the thing is, all these years you think you've been giving me second-best—"

"More like fourth-best," he muttered.

"Well, then, I must be a fourth-best kind of girl, because I've never felt cheated or that I was missing out."

We were quiet for a moment, although our thoughts were so loud it wasn't exactly silent.

"Luce? What is it about money that makes you so uncomfortable?"

Shit. He might as well have just laid me back out on that table, for how naked and vulnerable I felt with that question in the open. Jude had this uncanny ability to cut through the bullshit and see what was at the heart of what I was trying to hide. Some days I loved this gift of his. Some days I hated it.

I wasn't sure what kind of day it was yet.

I inhaled and exhaled, shoving the half-truths I was hiding behind me, trying to get to what was really bothering me. Now I was ready to say what felt like was close to the heart of it. "I come from a place where I know what it's like to have so much money in the bank you didn't even realize you could worry about something like money," I began, twisting in his arms so I could curl closer. "And I come from a place where I know what it's like to have so little in the bank you're not sure if you'll have a house to call your home the next month. I know the highs and the lows. Money can't make you happy. I don't want to pretend it can, or will."

"Luce, I know that," he interrupted. "I know it can't make you happy if you weren't already. But you and me, we've created something so damn great before all this that it can only get greater with a little cha-ching in the bank."

"No," I said abruptly. "See? That's it. I don't want my life-contentedness meter to be tied to something like money. In any way. I want them separate." I lifted one hand, extending it to the right. "Here's Lucy and the roller coaster that is my emotions." Jude was smart enough to keep from smiling his acknowledgment. "And here's money," I said, lifting my other hand and holding it off to the far left. "I don't want them to ever be connected. Ever."

"Ever? Or never, ever?" Now he was smiling. "Because there's a difference."

I elbowed him before answering. "Never, ever, *ever.*"

He contemplated that for a moment before nodding. "Okay. I think I can manage that." He sounded as sincere as he looked.

"Yeah?"

Grabbing my outstretched hands, he kissed each one. "Yeah."

Who would have guessed a round of wild tabletop sex and a night of sleep could pave the way for a productive conversation over something we'd been screaming about yesterday?

Oh, yeah. Men guessed that. From the time of the caveman, when tabletops were nothing more than flat boulders. It was time I, as a woman, figured that out and started using it to my advantage.

"Do you need anything else?" He kissed my forehead before rolling out of bed. "If I don't leave in the next thirty seconds, I'm going to be late to practice."

"I need . . . *something*," I answered, throwing the sheet to the side, "but it sounds like you've got places to be."

Jude's eyes stayed on my face, but I could tell it was killing him to do so. "You're cruel, Luce. You know that?"

"Mm-hmm," I said, rolling onto my side to give him a better view. I smiled when his gaze drifted for the shortest second.

Slapping his cheeks, he spun around and grabbed his jeans. "Why don't you go shopping or something while I'm at practice?" he said, pulling his wallet out. "There's a shitload of stores around that would be eager to cater to the soon-to-be wife of an NFL quarterback." Sliding that black shiny card free, he held it out.

I pulled the sheet back over me.

He scowled.

"Were you here for the conversation we just had?" I asked, glaring at the black card.

His scowl went another shade darker before it ironed out. "Yeah, I was." Putting the card back into his wallet, he stood there, looking helpless.

I didn't want him to feel this way. I knew Jude wanted to take care of me; that was at the forefront of his mind with everything he did. I just didn't need or want to be taken care of with a shiny black card.

"Do you think I could borrow your truck?" I asked, hoping this would ease his need-to-do-something-for-Lucy-itis. "I was thinking about going to the beach and vegging all day long."

"Of course," he said, digging into his pocket again. As predicted, he looked relieved to be able to do something for me that I was willing to go along with. "It's got a full tank, so take that baby for a spin." He held out the keys to his new truck. They were shiny, too.

Everything was so damn shiny now. I never thought I'd be so anti-shine.

"Come on, I couldn't see over the steering wheel of that thing, Jude," I said, winking to make the blow easier. "That is, if I was actually able to climb into it without your help. I'd need a step stool or a ladder."

"Do you want me to call you a driver or something?" he asked, and then his face lit up. "Or why don't you go buy yourself that new sports car I've been wanting to get you. This way you can pick out your own color."

I raised my hand and bit my tongue. "Thank you. On all offers," I said, "but I was thinking I could just take your old rust bucket."

Jude's forehead wrinkled.

"Then if I'm snoozing on the beach all day, I won't have to worry about some punk-ass kids ripping your brand-new truck off." This was partially the reason I wanted to take the old truck, but certainly not the main reason.

A flash of annoyance lined his face, but it passed. "The keys are in the ignition," he said, sliding into his jeans. "And I just changed the oil and gave it a tune-up, so you shouldn't have any problems with the old piecer."

I glared at the shirt he was reaching for. I knew clothes were the requirement, but they should have been the exception in Jude Ryder's case.

"Oil change? Tune-up?" I said as he pulled the shirt over his head. "Is this the truck you were adamant about scrapping yesterday?"

He rolled his eyes as he slid into his Cons. At least those were the same ratty old ones I was used to. "You are busting my balls, woman."

"I'm your soon-to-be wife," I said. "That's in the job description."

He froze mid–fly buttoning. "Soon-to-be?" he repeated, his eyes flashing.

Uh-oh. Not as in tomorrow or next week. "As soon-to-be as I am capable of it," I said, my heart fluttering a little from the way he was looking at me. With one look, Jude was able to melt every muscle right before they tightened in anticipation.

Jude beamed. "I'll take it," he said, and now, instead of up, his fly was going the opposite direction.

My pulse was already quickening. "What are you doing?"

Crossing the room, he leaped onto the bed. "I'm gonna be late," he said, before his mouth and body covered mine.

If there was one thing I could get used to in Southern California? The beaches and the sun. A good eight hours had ticked off when I'd done nothing more physical than turning from one side to the other. That, and unscrewing the lid from my bottle of water.

I could see myself here.

Now, if South Cali was only known as one of the premier dance places in the world, I would have been golden. The sun was starting to fall in the sky, but there was at least another good hour of UV rays to soak up, and I didn't want to miss out thanks to a severe case of hunger pangs.

To sway the leave-or-stay vote, my stomach rumbled again.

"Fine," I grumbled, making a mental note that the next time I came to the beach, I'd need to bring more than a granola bar.

Before I could start packing up my beach-day essentials, my phone chimed. I grabbed it and read the text. ALL THE GUYS WERE ASKING ME WHY I HAD THIS STUPID GRIN ON MY FACE ALL DAY. Followed by a smiley face. I BLAMED YOU.

I'LL GLADLY TAKE THE BLAME FOR THAT STUPID SMILE, I typed, wearing my own stupid grin as a few memories jumped to mind. HOPE YOU DON'T MIND WEARING ANOTHER ONE TOMORROW. Followed by a winky face.

His reply was instant. HELL, NO.

I laughed and, before I could type a response, my phone beeped again. WHERE ARE YOU? NEVER TOO EARLY TO START WORKING ON MAKING THAT STUPID SMILE AGAIN.

I'd never heard a truer statement. I typed in, STILL AT THE BEACH. AND I'M ALREADY SMILING JUST THINKING ABOUT MAKING YOU SMILE.

I sat up and tossed my sunscreen into my bag when his reply came. I'LL MEET YOU THERE AND PICK UP DINNER ON THE WAY. His message ended with a dot, dot, dot, and then my phone chimed with another message.

AND I'M SMILING ABOUT YOU SMILING THINKING ABOUT
MAKING ME SMILE.

I laughed, imagining him with the smile on his face, punching the accelerator, and adjusting his pants. ENOUGH SMILING ALREADY, I typed. HURRY UP, BECAUSE I WANT YOU TO MAKE ME MOAN.

Like I was in danger of being caught passing notes in class, I looked from side to side.

When his reply came, I almost jumped. PLANNING ON IT, LUCE.

I shifted in my seat, feeling warmth trickle into all the right places.

A few whistles sounded in front of me. I looked up as a couple of guys carrying surfboards sauntered by, gawking at a certain spot Jude wouldn't have been down with.

"Yep," I called out, giving the surfers a *really?* look, "they're boobs!"

One of them had the decency to look away. The other one just grinned bigger. That was the Jude of the two. "No, babe," the smug one called back, "those are nipples."

I glanced down. *Shit.* Yeah, those were most definitely nipples popping through for all of La Jolla beach to see. Darn Jude and all his sexting straight to high-beam hell.

I didn't have a snappy reply, but I couldn't let surfer boy have the last word. Wrapping my arm around my chest, I flipped him off with the other hand.

Tilting his chin in reply, he winked and kept walking.

Men were infuriating creatures. In all walks of life. Even while you were keeping to yourself, resting on the beach.

Needless to say, I spent the next half hour lounging on my stomach.

At least until I caught sight of a familiar form swaggering his way toward me. I hopped up and jogged over to him like I hadn't seen him in months. He had a paper sack and a sweatshirt tucked under his arm and looked freshly showered. However, the way he was looking at me was the opposite of clean.

"Where's that stupid smile you were texting me about?" I said as I approached.

"It took a vacation when I saw what you were wearing," he answered tightly. "Or what you're *not* wearing." He ran his eyes down my body, looking like he couldn't decide if he disapproved or approved.

I knew the way to make up his mind.

Winding my arms around his neck, I lifted up on my toes and planted a kiss on his mouth that started soft but didn't end up that way.

"Here," Jude said, cutting our kiss short, "put this on." He held out his old Syracuse sweatshirt and waited.

"Why?" I asked, playing dumb. On any other occasion, I

would have happily slid into Jude's ginormous 'Cuse sweat-shirt, but not when I was being ordered into it.

"Because you made me hard from a hundred yards back in that thing." He gestured at my swimsuit. "I don't like the idea of a bunch of other guys getting off looking at my girl." He shook the sweatshirt at me.

Nope. Not gonna happen.

"Who cares?" I lowered his outstretched arm and grinned up at him. "It's only your hard-on that gets to go to bed with me."

Jude snorted and crossed his arms. "Tell that to the jerk-offs who will be jerking off to you between their sheets tonight."

The overbearing act got old fast. I crossed my arms and held my ground. "I don't know what's got your boxers in a bunch. This isn't even my skimpy bikini." It wasn't. When it came to bikinis, this one was relatively tame.

He frowned as he inspected my swimsuit again. "All I'm seeing is a few tiny triangles and a whole lotta string, Luce," he said, looking tortured all over again. "And you're trying to tell me this isn't skimpy?"

I answered with a noncommittal shrug.

"Only one way to settle the skimpy debate . . ." Jude's eyes swept up and down the boardwalk, narrowing a few times along the way. "I win," he said at last. "Every single bastard within seeing distance is checking you out, Luce."

I glanced around the beach. "We'll have to agree to disagree," I said. "Because I'm positive it's not me but you they're staring at."

He made a face.

He'd arrived at a different conclusion.

"No, not for that reason," I said, giving him a gentle shove. "Do you think that maybe, just maybe, they're looking at you because you happen to be the newest Chargers quarterback?"

"It wouldn't matter if I was Peyton Manning," Jude said, pursing his lips. "With you running around in that more-string-than-swimsuit thing"—his hands gestured up and down me again—"no eyes would be turned in my direction."

I tried to hold it in, but I couldn't help the laugh that sneaked out. It was kind of cute when he was mildly upset. It wasn't as cute when he was full-blown pissed.

Jude's eyes latched onto something behind me. "Hey, jerk-off!" he hollered, narrowing his eyes. "Unless you want to be reading your monthly issue of *Playboy* in braille the rest of your life, you'd better turn your eyes now!"

I rested my hand on his side and ran my thumb in slow circles. Slow, *calming* circles. "Could you get any more territorial?" I teased.

"Ever heard of the Middle East, Luce?" he said, smirking. "Covered head to toe in layers upon layers of material." He tickled my sides. The worst was over.

"Ever heard of Europe?" I shot back in between fits of laughter. "Topless sunbathing? I thought you'd once said you were a fan of it."

"Ballbuster," he mumbled, before holding the sweatshirt back up. "Come on. Put this on?" he asked. He *asked*. He didn't order, demand, or command. He asked. Well, he almost pleaded.

"Okay," I said, because I couldn't say no. I grabbed the sweatshirt from him and slid it on. Warm, cozy, and smelled just like him. I was half considering jacking this tomorrow when I headed back to NYC.

"'Okay'?" He was looking at me like he was waiting for the punch line.

I slid the hood into position for good measure. "Okay."

"Just when I think I've got you all figured out, Lucy Larson," he said, winding his arm around my neck and pulling me close, "you go and do something totally unexpected. Like listen to me."

I slid my hand into the back pocket of his jeans as we headed toward my little slice of beachfront property. "Also in the fine print, below ballbusting," I said, hip-checking him, "soon-to-be wives are required to keep soon-to-be husbands on pins and needles at all times."

"Ahh," he said, "I really need to check out all that fine print."

"If you don't get to reading it, I'm sure I'll manage to give you a real-life demonstration of each and every point somewhere along the way," I said as we approached my beach towel. "What's for dinner? And please don't pull a can of caviar and a bottle of champagne from that bag or else I'm calling for an intervention."

He held out the paper bag for me. "Because I knew it would . . ." My brows lifted. ". . . absolutely not make you happy or unhappy, because money has no say in your happiness meter"—he popped his brows, obviously pleased with himself—"I picked up a few fish tacos from a street vendor and some cheap beer from a gas station."

He grinned like the devil and shook the bag. I grabbed it and plopped down on the towel before tearing it open. "Fish tacos from a street vendor and PBR?" I said, not sure whether to go for the beer or the tacos first. My stomach made the decision for me. "That, my love, makes me very, very happy." I pulled out a wrapped taco and tossed it into his lap once he sat down.

"Of course a dinner that cost me ten bucks would make you happy," he said, tearing the wrapper back. "Can you be any more infuriating?"

That was the million-dollar question.

Snagging a beer from the bag, I twisted the cap off and handed it to him. "Wow. You really missed the fine print if you don't know the answer to that, babe."

He bit off half the taco and rolled his eyes. "Eat your dinner," he said around a mouthful of food. "I can hear your stomach grumbling from over here."

Tearing my wrapper back from mine, I tapped his before taking a bite.

Damn. Okay, so Cali could rock the sun, the beach, and the fish tacos.

"Good?" Jude asked as I continued the love affair in my mouth.

I remembered my manners and waited until I'd swallowed my food before answering. "Good is an insult to the greatness that is this fish taco." I took another bite as Jude grabbed another beer out of the bag. After twisting the cap off, he held it out. "Finish it with a swig of this and life will be redefined as you know it, Luce."

I didn't even wait to finish chewing before I took a drink. Holy taste-bud orgasm.

"Yeah, that's the stuff," he said, clinking his bottle against mine before taking a drink.

"I. Love. You," I said, taking another bite. "So. Much. So, *so* much."

Stuffing the other half of the taco into his mouth, he stared at me in that way I'd grown accustomed to. Like I was everything he wanted and everything he ever would want. I don't know how his eyes were able to express this, but they did. Finishing his ginormous bite, he molded his hand against my cheek. "I love you. So much. So *damn* much, Luce."

Leaning into his warm hand, I clinked my bottle against his. "Cheers."

TEN

wo fish tacos, two beers, and two hours later, I was still not ready to leave. Not even close to it.

"You want the last one?" Jude asked, holding out a taco.

"It's all yours," I said. Scooting behind him, I skimmed my hands up his shirt. "You want a massage?" It wasn't so much a question as a formality. In four years, I'd never known Jude to turn down a massage.

"Hell yes," he said around a mouthful of fish taco.

Applying pressure, I worked my thumbs up the muscles of his spine. He sighed, leaning into my touch. "Does that feel good?"

"Hell yes." He dropped the taco and hung his head.

I pressed my thumbs into the exposed muscles of his neck. "How about this?" I said, never sure how much pressure

150

he'd want applied. Some days it was barely any, like he just liked the feel of my hands on him. Other days I couldn't seem to punish the muscles hard enough. "Is that still all right?" I asked, pinching the muscles running from his neck to his shoulders.

He groaned. "Hell yes."

"Sounds like it's a 'hell yes' kind of night."

He hung his neck lower, giving me better access. "Hell yes."

It'd been dark for a while, but we'd watched the sun set earlier and it was a sight I knew I'd never forget. I was starting to understand what the tens of millions of people who lived here saw in the place.

"Could you imagine doing this every night?" I said, working over a nasty knot around his shoulder blade. "Tacos and cheap beer on the beach?"

"Sounds like one hell of a life, Luce," he replied. "I'd be down with that."

"I saw a little beachfront house for rent a little way down the beach. We should rent it for a few nights during Christmas break and then we could watch the sun set every night." Having successfully worked out one knot, I moved to the next one.

"Sold," he said. "You, me, Christmas, beach, sunset. Where do I sign?"

I leaned over his shoulder as I continued to knead his back. "Right here."

His lips brushed over mine.

"I can't tell if these are all knots," I said, shifting behind him again, "or if they're insanely hard muscles, but you've definitely got something that needs working out."

He chuckled as I got back to work on a knot that was as big as my fist.

"What?"

"Luce," he said, grabbing one of my hands and winding it around his waist. "I've always got something that needs working out." My hand brushed down his jeans until he settled it over something that felt as hard as the muscles I was trying to relieve.

"A girl's job is never done," I said, gripping him.

He turned his head, his mouth searching for mine, but I had other plans. Popping up, I pulled the hoodie over my head.

"What do you think you're doing?" he asked, his eyes going dark as they skimmed my body.

Reaching for the string at the center of my back, I gave it a tug. "I'm going to work something out right here on the beach."

"Here?" His voice went an octave higher. "No. No,

you're not." His words might have been against it, but his eyes weren't. "Besides, beach sex is highly overrated."

I leveled him with my stare.

"From what I've heard," he added, giving me a tilted smile, "sand gets in all sorts of places it shouldn't."

Grabbing the tie around my neck, I tugged on it. "I'm not planning on having sex in the sand," I said, letting my top fall to the sand. Jude swallowed. "I'm more of a water girl."

Without another word, I started for the thundering waves.

"There's sharks and shit out there, Luce," he called after me.

I smiled as I continued on my merry way. How far would he let me get before he couldn't stay away? Skimming my fingers into my swimsuit bottoms, I slid them down my body.

Once they were littering the beach, I turned toward him.

He swallowed again and stood up. His Cons were already off.

"Then you'd better come save me," I called back. "From the sharks and shit." Giving a wave and a shake, I turned and bounded toward the water.

Jude cursed behind me, and a glance over my shoulder

revealed he was peeling his clothes off as quickly as clothes could be peeled. I was up to my knees before the water temperature registered. Cold barely described it. Mental note number one million and one: The ocean is more pleasurable from the beach than from the water.

"Ah! Shit! That's cold!" Jude exploded into the water, sprinting toward me. His arms wound around me after another round of curse hollering. Pressing my back to his chest, he spun me to face him.

"I guess I didn't really think this out," I shrieked, laughing. Damn, this water was really too cold to even think about getting hot and heavy in.

Jude slowed and settled me back down, but his arms didn't loosen. They tightened. He pulled me harder to him, his warmth running against my back and down lower. His hips flexed against my backside. I exhaled.

"I take that back," I said as I wound my arms behind his neck. "I totally thought this out."

I felt his smile on my neck before his tongue took its place. Jude's hands traveled up my stomach until they found my breasts.

"Nice tan lines," he breathed into my neck.

"I worked on them all day," I replied, letting my head fall back against him. As his hands and mouth moved over me, I no longer felt the chill of the water. There was nothing but warmth. A heat that ran so deep I felt it in every nerve.

One of his hands moved from my chest and trailed down my stomach. When it paused below my belly button, his finger moved against me. My breath hitched in my lungs.

"And I'm planning on working on you all night."

ELEVEN

I was so sick of saying good-bye at airports. If Jude had asked me to stay with him, I would have happily missed my flight.

I'd blinked and two days and two nights had passed. I knew the next couple of weeks before Jude was scheduled to fly out to New York would pass like each day was a year.

"Luce?" Jude popped his head back inside the truck after he'd grabbed my suitcase out of the bed. "Not that I'd mind, but if we don't hustle, you're going to miss your flight."

I held in my sigh and put on a brave face. Scooting down the seat, I patted the steering wheel. "Lots of good memories in this old rust can," I said. "Don't go and scrap it while I'm gone."

Jude shook his head as he grabbed my hand and slammed the door. "What do you see in this piece of shit?" he said, kicking the back tire as we walked through the garage.

I smiled to myself before answering. "I like things a little rough around the edges. Besides, it's what's inside that counts."

"'It's what's inside that counts,'" he repeated. "Who said that?"

"Some guy I know." I tucked my shoulder under his arm and wrapped my arm behind him.

"He sounds amazing," he said, grinning at me from the side.

I made a face and motioned my hand in a *so-so* way.

He chuckled, checking both ways before we crossed the road to the terminal. "That's not what you were saying last night," he said.

I pinched his side. "I wasn't saying much, that I recall."

"No, you weren't *saying* much. There was a shitload of moaning, though."

This earned him a few harder pinches.

"'Jude,'" he cried out, channeling me last night. "'Yes! Yes! Yes! You're amazing!'" I couldn't even pretend to be irritated with him. I was laughing so damn hard tears started to leak out of the corners of my eyes. "'*Jude . . . Amazing . . . Ryder!* Yes! Yes! *Yeeeeesss!*'"

He was causing a scene as we approached curbside check-in, but I was too hysterical to mind. My giant fiancé was bouncing, shaking, and shouting, not caring what anyone thought.

"Control yourself," I ordered amid my laughter, swatting his arm. "And if your performance is any indicator of what I act like during sex, I must look like a hippo about to give birth."

Dropping the Lucy Larson Orgasming Show, he laughed with me. "Nah." He laughed one more note before his expression changed. "It's the damn sexiest thing I've ever experienced, Luce."

Thankfully his words were no louder than a whisper, but as we approached the ticket counter, I was sure the heat rushing into my face, paired with Jude's crooked smile, gave away the gist of what he'd just whispered into my ear.

From the sly smile on the employee's face, he caught more than just the gist.

While I waited for my ticket, Jude handed my suitcase off and gave the guy a hefty tip. It was only a month ago when that tip would have paid for a movie-and-dinner date.

The ticket counter employee handed me my ticket, but he had eyes for no one but Jude. I knew that look, but it was weird sharing it with middle-aged males.

"You're Jude Ryder," the employee said, looking, sounding, and acting starstruck. "Aren't you?"

Shoving his hands in his pockets, Jude winked over at

me. "Jude *Amazing* Ryder," he managed with a straight face. I couldn't perform the same feat.

Coming up behind me, Jude wrapped his arms around me. "What's so funny?" he teased.

Thrusting a pen and a newspaper at us, the poor guy looked like he was about to burst a blood vessel. It was so odd the way people treated Jude now, like they idolized him. "Could I have your autograph?" His voice was shaky.

"You bet," Jude answered, uncapping the pen as the employee unfolded the front page of the local newspaper. On it was a huge photograph of a man and a woman at night. In the ocean. Bare-ass naked.

"Shit," I murmured, twisting in Jude's arms, hoping he hadn't seen it yet.

Nothing good would come of Jude seeing this.

His eyes were locked on the picture, like he wasn't sure what he was seeing. The confusion shifted toward red-faced anger in the time it took me to plant my hands on either side of his face.

"Jude," I said, trying to sound calm. Trying to *be* calm for him, when I felt anything but. Calm was impossible when a full-frontal naked shot of me was plastered on who knew how many thousands of papers. "It's all right. Calm down," I continued, trying to get his eyes to focus on mine. But they would not look away from the picture below the headline,

"Ryder Has Game Both On and Off the Field." The photographer must have snapped the picture right when he'd joined me in the water and spun me around. Other than his face and arms, that was all of Jude the stupid pap had caught. But with me, they'd had to make use of the photo-blur tool in a couple of places.

Jude snatched the paper from the man's hand and glowered at him. "What the hell is this?" Rolling it up, Jude stuffed the paper into the back of his pants and waited.

Once the employee realized Jude wasn't going to move until he got an answer, he shrugged. "A newspaper." He had the decency to look ashamed.

"That's not a newspaper," Jude said, seething. The muscles of his jaw rolled beneath my hands. "That's a naked picture of my fiancée."

Dammit. His face had just gone from red to purple. Soon we'd be past the point where anything I could do would talk him down.

"You got any more of those back there?" Rushing behind the counter, Jude inspected the area. I followed him.

"Jude," I said, "stop."

"No, no," the employee said, raising his hands. I could tell he hadn't meant any disrespect when he'd asked Jude to sign a naked photo of him and me, but I also knew the man would never, ever try something like this again.

"Who else has one of these?" Jude demanded after he was satisfied no more newspapers were stuffed behind the counter.

The man looked from Jude to me with his brows knitted together, his expression reading, *Seriously?* "Whoever subscribes to or picked up a Sunday paper today?" he suggested, slinking away from Jude.

Smart move.

Just then, Jude's gaze drifted inside the terminal, where a man in a suit was depositing quarters into a . . .

Shit.

Jude turned and sprinted away before I could offer an apologetic smile to the ticketing employee.

"Jude!" I shouted as I entered the terminal. In addition to good-byes, I was also sick of making scenes.

He didn't glance back—he didn't even slow down—he just kept barreling at the man who was just lifting the vending machine door to grab his morning paper. Before he'd had a chance to unfold it, Jude was on him.

Shit, shit.

I was running now, too, but was still a hundred feet away.

Snatching the paper out of the man's hands, Jude towered over him, glowering like he was the one responsible for my teeth, tits, and toes winding up on the front page.

"Jude!" I yelled louder this time, trying to get his attention.

It worked. His glare shifted toward me for the shortest moment, but it was enough. Jude's shoulders were lowering and the rage on his face had dimmed as I got to him.

Panting from my two-hundred-meter dash, I laced my hands around his forearm. "Deep breath in," I instructed. "Deep breath out. Think." I took my own breath, watching his chest rise and fall. *"Think."*

When I was certain Jude wasn't going to hammer the guy into the ground, I loosened my grip on his arm. "Sorry about that," I said, addressing the man, who was gawking at Jude like he was a tiger who had escaped the zoo. However, he didn't look scared, just intrigued. This guy had no survival instincts whatsoever.

"Might I suggest tempering that anger of yours with some yoga and meditation, young man," the guy said, in an incredibly unflustered voice. Like he hadn't just been charged by two hundred and fifty pounds of muscle and fury.

Quirking a brow, he inspected Jude one more moment before turning and heading on his merry, no-survival-instinct way.

"Dammit, Jude," I hissed, snatching the paper out of his

hands. "Could you act any more unbalanced?"

He didn't need to answer me. We both already knew the answer to that.

Watching the man in the suit meander away, Jude inhaled. "Can you believe this?"

"What? Yoga and meditation?" I said, hoping to lighten the mood. "Sounds like it might work wonders for that temper of yours."

When Jude turned to me, his eyes narrowing even more, I realized lightening the mood wasn't on the agenda for the day. "Not the yoga shit," he said, flashing the stolen newspaper in front of my face. "This shit."

I winced when I looked at the picture again. That photographer could not have been in a better position. If my hair was two shades lighter and my boobs three sizes bigger, I could have been a Playmate.

"Oh," I said, hoping my parents never saw this spread. I mean . . . *photo.* "That shit. Yeah, that sucks."

"'That sucks'?" Jude couldn't have looked more flabbergasted by my blasé attitude. Truth be told, of course I was pissed as pissed could be, but what could I do? It was out there, on lord only knew how many thousands of doorsteps and briefcases. My losing my cool wouldn't help Jude hold whatever he had left of his. I needed to control myself for him, because it was apparent he couldn't do it for himself.

"'That sucks'?" he repeated, slapping the photo with his hand. "You're naked for the whole goddamned world to see, Luce. My fiancée is going to be the fantasy of every jerk-off in the county tonight. And you have nothing more to say than 'That sucks'?"

I counted to five before answering, because the reply that wanted to roll right off my tongue wasn't going to help calm him down. It would have done the opposite. *Calm, calm, calm*, I reminded myself before replying.

"Is there another word you'd like me to use to describe it?" I asked, working to keep my voice flat. "Is there a certain way you'd like me to be acting right now?" *Good job, Lucy. Keep the temper in its cage.* "So if 'that sucks' doesn't work for you, how would you describe it?"

"This is fucking war," he said, his eyes onyx.

Shit. He was a rare shade of pissed.

Pulling his phone from his pocket, he punched in a number at the same time he charged toward the newspaper vending machine. He could have been about to beat the crap out of it, just as much as he could have been about to light it on fire. When Jude was in the rage zone, I never knew what he might do. The only thing I knew was that the end result was never a good one.

However, what he did next wasn't even on my top-ten list. Jamming a few quarters into the machine, he dropped the door and, instead of tearing the machine to pieces, he grabbed the entire stack of newspapers in his arms.

Okay, he was in the rage zone that leaned more toward crazy than angry.

That was just as bad, if not worse.

"Jude," I hissed, glaring at a few people who'd stopped to watch the show, "what in the hell are you doing?"

"I'm taking every goddamn newspaper in this machine," he answered, depositing his armload into the closest garbage can, "and then I'm going to go find every other newspaper machine in the airport and do the same. And then I'm going to every damn newspaper machine in the city and destroy every last one of these motherfuckers until the only copy left is the one I own."

My mouth was open. It had dropped at some point during his little speech, but I wasn't sure when.

"Hammon," Jude seethed into the phone. I felt sorry for whoever was on the other end. "You checked out the morning paper—"

Jude's face darkened. "If you don't go shred that front page right the hell now you will not be my agent by lunchtime."

He was quiet for a few seconds while Hammon was saying or doing who knew what. I didn't doubt he was actually shredding the paper now. Given Jude's annual salary and multiyear contract, Hammon could retire a happy man in five years' time if he played his cards right and didn't piss Jude Ryder off.

"Done?" Jude said, crossing his arms.

Damn, he'd really been waiting while Hammon shredded my porn-o-rific photo.

"As soon as I'm off the phone with you, I want you to call the newspaper and I want you to find out the name, address, and phone number of the editor, the owner, the asshole writer who wrote this thing, and the photographer who's about to be a dead man."

Just when I thought he'd worked past the extreme temper, I was reminded how Jude's anger ran deep. It was like a volcano: dormant most of the time, but when it exploded . . . it *really* exploded. Jude's past made anger a part of his present and future; that was the fact. However, he had a choice about whether he let that anger rule his life. Up until now, he'd done a hell of a job keeping it contained. Well, controlled, at least. But now he was really losing his shit in a scary way.

"Why?" Jude said, cracking his neck. "Is that a question you're sure you want to ask me?"

It took Hammon all of a second to reply.

"Thatta boy," Jude said. "Time to earn your commission." Hanging up, he pocketed his phone and glared at the floor.

His anger was unrestrained. He'd lost all control and was running on nothing but impulse. What could I possibly say or do to talk him down? I knew nothing short of a miracle would work at this stage.

So what, in the entire world of words and responses, did I lead with?

Perhaps the worst.

"Gibbons."

Jude couldn't have looked more startled than if I'd just stripped out of my clothes and started streaking down the terminal.

"Gibbons," I repeated, because now that I was heading down this insane track, I might as well keep chugging along. Plus, his eyes had already lightened into a steely gray.

"Luce?" Jude came closer and pressed the back of his hand against my forehead.

He ran his hands over me like I was one notch below a padded room. It would have been irritating if he wasn't so visibly concerned.

"I'm fine," I assured him. "Really."

Pulling me to him, he continued to study me. "Then what are you rambling on about?"

I rolled my eyes. "Gibbons."

Another flash of worry in his eyes. "Gibbons?" he said slowly.

I nodded.

"Luce, what the hell's a gibbon?"

So far, as certifiable as it was, my plan to trick Jude's monster back into its cage was working.

"It's like a monkey," I said, wrapping my arms around him. His every muscle was standing on alert. "I used to see them at the zoo when I was a little girl."

He held up his hand. "You know I love to know every little thing you're willing to share with me, Luce, but what the hell does a gibbon have to do with your tits being on the front page of the paper?"

I pretended I wasn't talking to a man one thread away from snapping for good. "If you'd be quiet for one minute so I could get out more than three words at a time, then you'd learn what a gibbon and my tits have in common." I paused and plastered on a smile for him.

He stayed quiet. Jude had learned a lot in the years we'd been together.

"I remember learning that gibbons are mostly monogamous. They choose one mate and spend the rest of their lives with that mate. They take care of their mate, protect it, clean it, feed it—you name it and these gibbons do it. Both the male and the female. There isn't a distinction between sex." Jude's eyebrows pulled together. "These gibbons live in their own little world. They don't let anything, or any other gibbons, get in the way of the bond they've formed. They live in their bubble from the rest of the world, and don't let what's going on outside their bubble come inside it."

What the hell was I saying? I really was about to have a total and irreversible break.

And then every single wrinkle on Jude's face flattened. Looking into my eyes, I watched his eyes go from steel to silver gray. When his hand brushed my cheek, I knew my lunacy had appealed to his and had somehow managed to cancel it out. "Luce," he said, one corner of his mouth turning up, "are you saying we're gibbons?"

My smile formed. I had my Jude back. "Well, *you* might be one. You're the hairy one."

A few laughs later, his mouth dropped to mine. "Come here, my beautiful, smart, sexy gibbon."

"And calm," I added, around his kisses. "I'm a calm gibbon." I couldn't get anything else out, because his mouth made words impossible.

As he kissed me, I felt the tension leave him. Each time our tongues touched, every slide of our lips, every touch dimmed his anger.

"At least the new and improved calm Lucy Larson can still kiss the hell out of me," he said, after pressing a final kiss to my forehead. "Mind telling me how you were able to keep from blowing a gasket?"

I grinned at a man over Jude's shoulder who'd been hoping to grab a morning paper. Not today, not this stand.

"Yoga and meditation," I replied, shifting my smile Jude's way.

His eyes rolled. "Well, whatever's responsible for your being the calm to my crazy, I'm proud of you, Luce," he said, before his eyes wandered down my body. His forehead wrinkled. "My being proud of you aside, I don't understand how you can be so damn cool about all of this, Luce."

There was a lot of "all of this" going on right now. More than normal. "All what?"

"A naked picture of you plastered on the front page," he said, keeping his voice controlled, even though the sinews of his neck were surfacing. "Your boobs on display for the entire world. I mean, shit, those are my boobs. Not the entire world's to enjoy."

The anger had morphed into hurt, and, in Jude's case, that meant nothing around us was in danger of being destroyed. I let myself exhale. It felt like I'd been holding that breath for ten minutes straight.

Speaking of time . . . if we didn't wrap this up soon I was going to miss my flight.

"No, baby," I said, glancing down at them, "these are *my* boobs. I just give you an all-access pass to them." He half scowled, half smirked at me as I continued. "And the only reason I'm able to stay cool is because I know there's going to be no end to this kind of stuff, Jude. You're in the public eye in a big way now. There's going to be no shortage of scandals, or photos, or rumors, or whatever else comes with being a hotshot quarterback." Dropping my hand to his, I weaved my fingers with his. "Even before the NFL, there was no shortage of this kind of shit in our lives."

I paused and let him work those words out. Our path had never been smooth, and though I often found myself wishing for it, our future probably wouldn't be, either. I'd figured this out freshman year, chosen to accept it, and gotten on with my life . . . with Jude.

There were worse things than bumps in the road.

Plus, I had a man like Jude, who loved me like there was no tomorrow. Bumps in the road were a small sacrifice to make for that kind of love.

"Okay. Two things," Jude said, rubbing the back of his neck as he liked to do when he was working things out. "One—I do believe when you agreed to be my wife, that whole 'what's mine is yours' clause applies, so your boobs are, in fact, mine." I crossed my arms while he continued walking on thin ice. "Just the way my body belongs to you, Luce," he added with a wink. "And two—are you saying you want to—that you're *okay* with—living in our own little gibbon bubble?"

The words *gibbon* and *bubble* coming from Jude Ryder's mouth were all kinds of funny. But he meant what he said. Seriously.

"If I get to live in that bubble with a certain guy I love"—I ran my thumb down the scar on his cheek—"then yeah, I want to live in a bubble." It was the only option, really. Unless I wanted to be downing some hard-core over-the-counter narcotics before I turned twenty-two, Jude and I would have to figure out a way to separate ourselves from the public eye and the scrutiny that was sure to follow. "How about you? How does bubble living sound from your size twelves?"

"With you, Luce," he said, grabbing my hand as it left his face. Holding it to his mouth, he kissed my palm softly. That kiss, pressed to that patch of skin on my palm, had a direct line to every nerve ending in my body. "I'll take any kind of living, so long as I get to do it with you at my side."

"At your side. On your side. Side by side . . ."

He lifted his hand. "Are you saying you're with me, Luce, no matter what comes?"

"I'm saying I've always been with you, Ryder"—I kissed one corner of his mouth, and then the other—"and I always will be."

His grin was so wide, his scar disappeared into his cheek. This was my favorite smile of his. Not because it made his scar disappear, but because it eased it for a few moments.

His cocky smile-smirk was a close second favorite.

"You." He pointed at me before turning his finger on himself. "Me. Bubble." His finger now circled around us before making a flicking motion. "The world."

"Sounds perfect," I replied, my eyes shifting toward the security checkpoint. I was going to miss my flight if I didn't leave now. When I looked back at him and saw that familiar glimmering of longing and want in those gray eyes of his, my stomach bottomed out.

Okay, thirty seconds.

"Three weeks," he said, followed by a groan.

I groaned my reply.

Grabbing me close, he dropped his mouth to my ear. "Better make it a good one then."

I made it the best damn one yet.

TWELVE

That next Monday, I found myself in a predicament.

Not only because the past day and a half since I'd last seen Jude had gone by so agonizingly slowly that it didn't seem fair, and I still had nineteen days to go, but because I was unprepared for the dress code at my new job.

I had a half hour before eight, and I knew the only thing worse than showing up for the first day under- or overdressed was being late. I shot a quick text off to India, praying she'd have some idea whether my position at Xavier Industries warranted a skirt and a blouse or was more of a pants-and-shirt kind of place.

As I waited for her reply, I hoped it would be more the cotton-and-wrinkle-free kind of workplace.

As I was hooking my bra into place, my phone chimed.

I frowned when I read her reply. ANTON'S AN OLD-SCHOOL, *MAD MEN* STYLE CHUMP. AS YOUR FRIEND, I HAVE TO ADVISE YOU TO DRESS UP. BUT AS HIS SISTER, I REALLY WANT YOU TO SHOW UP IN CUTOFFS AND SANDALS JUST TO PISS HIM OFF.

I sighed and pulled my black pencil skirt from the hanger. As I was stepping into it, my phone chimed with another message from India. GOOD LUCK. GIVE 'EM HELL.

I typed DITTO and hit send before pulling my white button-down blouse out of the closet, along with my black heels. Once I was changed, I hurried out of the apartment. Although, thanks to the tightness of the skirt, "hurrying" anywhere was a joke. The fastest I could go was a shuffle.

Once I was in my Mazda, it took me only ten minutes to get to the office. As I passed a familiar building, I realized my new job had yet another perk—my dance studio was close by. Time would be in short supply this summer, and if I wanted to keep dance a priority, I'd have to come up with some creative scheduling. Maybe I could squeeze in some mornings before work, or during a lunch break, or whenever I could carve out an hour or two after work. Thankfully, my summer class was an independent study, so as long as I clocked four hours of studio time every week, I'd pass the course.

After double-checking the address on the outside of the building with the address and suite number I had in my phone, I found a parking spot and headed to my first day on the job.

I was always nervous on a first day of anything, but this morning I was all butterflies. I would have thought I'd be more chill, since I kind of knew Anton, but that seemed to create the opposite effect. Maybe because he was India's brother, and I didn't want to put either of them in an awkward position if things didn't work out, or maybe I was nervous because administrative assistant sounded like a pretty professional job for a college student.

As I was heading through the revolving door, my phone chimed. I slid it out of my purse. I stopped in the middle of the foyer so I could admire the picture. Jude was in his gym gear inside the locker room, extending a handful of roses. *Red* roses. The text read, SORRY I COULDN'T BE THERE TO HAND THESE TO YOU IN PERSON.

Just like that, the nerves were gone. One picture and a handful of words from Jude and I was calm as calm could be. Before heading toward the elevator, I texted back, I'M ONE LUCKY BITCH.

I was lucky for so many reasons. All of those reasons starting and ending with Jude.

Once inside the elevator, I couldn't resist checking out the picture again. When I looked away, a few of the people around me were staring at me like they couldn't possibly imagine why I was beaming on a Monday morning.

If only they knew.

The doors whooshed open on the fifth floor and I headed down the hall, still running on grins and giddiness. When I came to the door that read, XAVIER INDUSTRIES, I ran my hands down my skirt, rolled my shoulders back, and only once I was sure I looked what I felt like an admin assistant should did I open the door.

The office wasn't huge, nor was it exceptionally welcoming, but it was how I envisioned a cubicle city–type office would appear. It smelled like copy machine, and there was even a rubber tree plant stuffed in the back corner where the watercooler stood. It looked like I was the first one here, because I didn't see a single top of a head over the maze of cubicle walls, or any computers humming to life.

The lights were on, though, and someone had to have unlocked the door, so I couldn't be the lone ranger at Xavier Industries. Taking a few more steps inside, I saw what I guessed would be my desk, situated outside a large enclosed office.

I didn't know this because of the nameplate in front that read, LUCY LARSON; nor did it have anything to do with the nameplate on the door behind the desk that read, ANTON XAVIER. I knew it was my space because there were a dozen vases dotting the desk, brimming over with red roses.

That beam that was starting to hurt my smile muscles burst again as I reached for the white envelope on one of the arrangements. *So maybe I could kind of be there in person.* The note was signed with an, *XXXO, Mr. Amazing.*

Talk about a great way to start a first day at a new job.

Plus Mom and Dad had left a voice mail for me on the drive over, wishing me good luck and a great first day.

"I wish I could say I'd come up with the idea," a voice sounded behind me.

I spun around, my mouth dropping. I could have been looking at a male India, only a couple inches taller, maybe a shade darker. I would have mistaken Anton and India for twins if I didn't know Anton was a few years older.

"What idea?" I said, figuring that if he wasn't going to start off with a common greeting, I didn't need to either.

"The flowers," Anton replied, gesturing at my desk. "It's your first day and your boss didn't think to order flowers to welcome you. Good thing someone else did."

I decided not to mention that if Anton had thought to order flowers for me and Jude ever found out, Anton would be speaking an octave higher for the rest of his life.

"I wasn't sure what the dress code was, so I hope I did all right," I said, looking down at my outfit. In contrast, Anton had on a stylish navy suit and a maroon pencil tie. I was definitely underdressed if this was the standard.

"You couldn't be more all right if I'd dressed you myself," he replied with a smile.

"Oh," I said, diverting my attention from him. He was staring at me in that unblinking way, not sexually, but in a searching way that made me uncomfortable. I didn't want to be inspected. I wanted to clock in, make my money, and clock out. "That's good."

Anton came toward me and extended his hand. "Nice to finally meet you in person, Lucy Larson," he said, his smile so white and perfect it didn't seem real. "And if I had known you were even prettier in person than in a picture, I never would have hired you."

I rolled my eyes. He was a flirt. Like brother, like sister.

"Why's that," I shot back, realizing my smart-ass self was going to fit in fine here, "because you'd no longer be in the office running for best-looking?"

Anton's head tipped back as he laughed. His laugh, like his voice, was clear and almost musical. "India warned me you were a firecracker. For once, I'm glad she was right about something," he said, his shoulders still shaking. "But no, that's not the reason. At least, not the main reason. My dad keeps one rule, and one rule only, in business. He says all the rest you can bend along the way if need be, save for one." He paused, studying me again. I watched his pupils, and never once did they wander south of my face.

"What's that?" I said, since he was obviously not going to say any more until I inquired.

"The fifty/fifty rule when hiring an admin," he said, with a shrug like it was common knowledge.

"This ought to be good."

Anton slid a hand into his pants pocket. "Make sure she's over fifty and fifty pounds overweight."

"I didn't realize I was coming to work for a chauvinist," I said, followed by an exaggerated sigh. "Why's this the number one rule?"

He mimicked my sigh. We'd spoken a few sentences, but I had a feeling I had met my match. "So there's no temptation," he said.

Flashing my left hand in front of him, I waited for him to take note of the ring on a certain important finger. "In case India forgot to mention it, I'm engaged. So there'll be no temptation whatsoever."

Anton studied the ring for another moment before he smiled broadly. "Forbidden fruit. Wanting what a man can't have. I don't think that worked out so well for Adam and the whole fall-of-man thing." His smile pulled higher as he waited for me to reply. He was enjoying this banter.

Since it was my first day on the job, I decided to bite back what I wanted to say to him.

"Anytime you're ready to tell me what I'm here to actually do . . ." I said, gesturing at my desk and computer. "I didn't get all dressed up for nothing."

"No." Anton chuckled, coming around the side of my desk. "You certainly didn't." Continuing past the desk, he opened the door to his office and sauntered in. When he got to his desk, he glanced back at me where I hovered at the door. "Anytime you're ready for me to tell you what you're actually here to do . . ." He gestured at the chair in front of his desk and waited.

"I didn't realize we were playing tag," I muttered, just loud enough for him to hear.

He smiled and fired up his laptop.

Anton's office was posh—if you were into the modern twist on 1960s cool. Like India had said, it was a scene pulled from *Mad Men*, right down to the fancy crystal bottles of liquor displayed on a shelf behind his desk. Like his little sister, Anton had expensive taste.

I took a seat in the chair across from him and waited.

"Do you know much about what we do here in this office?" he asked, his eyes fixed on his laptop, all business. He could flip the on and off mood switch as fast as I could.

Should I have done research? It was too late now.

"Nope." Super. Real intelligent-sounding, Lucy.

"I love an honest woman," he said, his eyes flicking to me. "And one who isn't ashamed about it."

From business to banter in two seconds' time. Anton was going to keep me guessing. "And I love a man who gets to the point," I said, "sometime today."

Getting back to his laptop, he started typing. "Here's the quick rundown on Xavier Industries' White Plains branch," he said, typing furiously. His fingers were almost a blur over that keyboard. "We're a customer-support call center here. We have twenty employees and triage close to eight hundred calls a day."

"A call center?" I was confused. "Xavier Industries is a board game development company, right?" I could have sworn that was what Indie said.

"That's right, but developing, distributing, and selling the board games is only half the battle. The other half is keeping those retailers and customers happy." His war with the keyboard came to an end. Punching one final key, he leaned back in his high-backed leather chair.

Thank the heavens I wasn't majoring in business, because this made no sense to me. "Happy? Isn't that the reason they're buying one of the games? So they'll be . . . *happy?*"

"Yes, happiness is definitely a desired side effect. However, humans as a species have this need to report or review or vent or share their opinion to someone who cares." He waved his hands before folding them over his desk. "That's what we're here for."

"To care?"

Anton looked at me like my confusion was cute. "To *pretend* to care."

"Oh-kay," I said, shifting in my seat. I understood why so many politicians came from business backgrounds. They'd been bullshitting their way to the top for decades. "And my job is to pretend to care?"

"No, you won't be taking any of the customer calls. You're working for me." He leaned forward. "So your job is to enthusiastically care."

The more he said, the farther down the rabbit hole I fell.

"Can you define 'care' in basic job duties?" I asked. "Like sharpening pencils, making copies, that sort of thing?"

Sliding a drawer of his desk open, Anton dropped a thick folder in front of me. "For starters, I'd like you to go through these call sheets and make note of how long each call lasted, along with how many minutes the caller had to wait on hold before reaching an associate."

I gawked at the folder—it was larger than any college textbook I'd ever seen. "Is this supposed to take me all summer?"

That slow smile of Anton's slid back into place. "I'll give you until lunch."

I was earning my pay here at XI.

I'd been sure I'd been on the receiving end of a good deal, but I realized by lunchtime that it was Anton who'd been on the better receiving end.

I didn't know how I did it, or who'd slowed time down in order for me to get it done, but I was on my last sheet of that dictionary-size folder when Anton's door whooshed open.

"Lunchtime," he announced, sliding into his jacket that had just enough sheen to it for me to know it had cost a small fortune.

Glancing at the time on my computer, I felt my eyes bulge. It was almost one o'clock. "Oh, man. I'm sorry, Anton. I got so caught up in this project that I didn't even realize what time it was," I said, spinning in my chair to face him. "What do you normally get for lunch? I'll run out and grab it right now."

His eyebrows knitted together like he was insulted. "If India found out I'd reduced you, in any way, shape, or form, to a glorified coffee runner, she'd skin me and leave me in the woods for the bears."

I capped my pen and dropped it back into the holder. "And if you ever give me another project like that and expect me to finish it before the year is up, I might just do the same to you." I smiled sweetly.

"Have you talked to all your bosses like this?" he asked, leaning into my desk.

I raised an eyebrow. "Only the ones who deserved it."

Shaking his head, Anton motioned for the door. "Come on. Time for lunch."

"Huh?" Another brilliant gem from the mouth of Lucy Larson.

"Food. Sustenance. You. Me." He motioned to the door again. "Now."

Two things stopped me short from accepting Anton's invitation right then. The first being Jude. And the second being Jude. He was about as territorial as I was, and I knew I wouldn't have been okay with another woman taking him to lunch on a whim.

"I think I'll stay and finish this up," I lied. "I brought a snack with me."

"Enough with the protesting already. You've put up a good fight, but it's useless, because I always get what I want." Anton's eyes gleamed, while I felt my temper switch begging to be flipped. "Plus, it's a company tradition passed down from my dad. Rule number two in the business world: You always take an employee out to lunch on their first day. That's just good business."

There'd been a lot of times in my life when I'd felt like an idiot. This being one of those times. Hoping Anton didn't think I was acting like too much of a nut, I slid back into my heels and stood up.

"Far be it from me to stand in the way of time-honored traditions and good business," I said, grabbing my purse before coming around the desk.

Anton had the door open and was waiting. Almost everyone in cubicle city was back from lunch, and just like this morning, whenever I'd looked up from my heap of paperwork, they were watching me.

Staring was perhaps the better word.

"I'll have my cell if anyone needs to get hold of me," Anton announced before closing the door behind us. "Don't worry. They'll get used to you in a few days."

I followed him toward the elevator. "What will they get used to?" I hadn't been aware I was something or someone who required getting used to.

"They're a bit starstruck. It's not every day you get to work in a call center with a girl who's with one of the most talked-about NFL quarterbacks, and one who was just photographed nak—"

He paused as my eyes bulged before narrowing on him. Shit, shit, shit, shit, shit.

Shit on a stick.

The whole office had seen that picture? Anton had seen that picture?

A few of those male stares made a bit more sense today. They'd been staring at me like they were seeing me naked because they had, in fact, seen me naked.

Shit.

"You saw it?" It wasn't really a question, but I needed it confirmed.

Anton had the decency to look a little sheepish.

Just then the elevator doors opened.

Saved by the elevator.

"You want to talk about it?" he asked, trying, but failing, not to smirk.

"No," I hissed, crossing my arms. I guess I hadn't thought that picture would span the whole country. I should have known better.

"Don't worry. I didn't look," he said, his voice soft. "I couldn't stop the others from seeing it, but I didn't. I'm sorry that happened." His expression bled sincerity. The first I'd seen from Anton.

The anger rolled right off me. "Yeah. I'm sorry, too," I said as the doors opened on the first floor.

Sensing I didn't want to talk about it more, or finished talking about it himself, Anton waved at someone in passing. "There's this great place right around the corner. Makes everything from scratch every morning. Soups, breads, sandwiches, that kind of thing." He waited for me to go through the revolving door first. "Sound good?" he asked when he joined me out on the sidewalk.

"Sounds good."

It turned out the café was no more than half a block from the office. Even though it was past the height of lunch hour, the place was still bustling. The scent of fresh bread and basil hit me full-on as soon as we made our way inside.

Anton weaved a path to the only open table, waving at a few of the waitresses behind the counter, who blushed almost immediately. As suspected, Anton was a flirt. A certified ladies' man.

We'd barely taken our seats when one of the starry-eyed waitresses was dropping glasses of water in front of us. "Hey, Anton," she said, brushing her hair behind her ear.

I waved my hand in greeting, but I was invisible.

"Hey, angel," he replied. When he looked at her, you would have thought she'd just died and gone to heaven from the dreamy look on her face.

Just as quickly as she'd arrived, she left in the same fashion. Anton obviously rendered most girls speechless. Good things I wasn't most girls.

"Angel?" I said, giving him an unimpressed look. "That's the best you've got?"

He took a sip of his water, the amused expression of his settling on his face. "Are you questioning my game?" he said. "Because I've got more game than I know what to do with."

"Says you and every other male in history," I tossed back. "But for a man who claims to have mad game, that was weak. I think my sixth-grade boyfriend won me over with 'Hey, angel.'"

"Well, Miss Know-it-all"—Anton leaned forward— "Angel happens to be her name." An eyebrow peaked and he waited.

I had nothing. I didn't know anything either. Obviously.

"So . . ." I said, taking a sip of water, "how 'bout this weather?"

Anton laughed, clearly more amused than insulted at my latest bout of know-it-all-itis.

"Why have you, India, and me not gotten together and verbally sparred the night away before?" he said. "We'll have to remedy that."

"It seems we already are," I said, smiling my apology.

"Hey, Anton." Same greeting and moon eyes, different waitress.

"Hi, honey," he greeted, giving me a sideways glance. "As in your name, Honey. Would you mind taking our order?"

Honey didn't go as stupefied as Angel had when Anton leveled her with those baby browns. "At your service," she replied, biting her lip in a suggestive, anything-but-innocent way.

"Lucy"—Anton motioned at me—"you know what you want?"

"I'll have the Caprese salad, please," I said. Honey didn't once look at me or from Anton as she scratched down my order. The restaurant staff had obviously been drinking the Anton water and was thirsty for more.

"Anton," Honey said, her eyes lidding, "what would you like?"

I grabbed my glass and took another sip of water. This chick meant business. I doubt she would have objected if Anton told her to meet him in the men's bathroom in five.

"What's your soup of the day?" he asked, returning those flirty eyes.

"Tomato bisque."

I never knew bisque could sound so lewd.

"Ooh, I'll have that," he said. "I'm living on the edge today."

"Wild man," I said, handing Honey my menu. "Watch out."

"So, Lucy," he said, "since my sister never shuts up about you, I feel like I already know you."

I could only imagine what India had told him. In fact, I didn't want to imagine.

"Okay, I'm going to take off the 'boss' hat and put on the 'friend' hat and ask you about something I probably shouldn't . . ." He cleared his throat and leaned forward. "Tell me about your boyfriend—"

"Fiancé," I clarified. "And India's told you everything about me and nothing about Jude?" The girl loved Jude. Well, all the girls loved Jude, but India loved him in a platonic sort of way, not the make-me-moan kind of way.

"Here's what I know of Jude from India. And these are her words, not mine," he said, shifting in his seat. "He's fine, has a nice ass, and can make you blush after four years together."

"India." I sighed. "All of those things happen to be true, but there's a lot more to Jude than that."

Anton nodded. "I would hope so," he said. "What made you fall in love with him?"

This was not the conversation I was expecting to have with my boss on my first day, but expectations, in my opinion, were a wasted effort. Disappointment was at the end of every expectation.

"It wasn't so much what made me fall in love with him," I began, staring out the window. "It was more that I couldn't not fall in love with him."

"That whole, 'the stars aligned and fate predestined it' kind of thing?" he guessed, his smile telling me he thought he'd gotten it right. But he was wrong.

"No. More like we made the stars realign and fate had nothing to do with it."

Before he could respond, my phone rang.

"Sorry," I said, about to hit ignore when Anton gave me a nod.

"Take it," he said. "You're off the clock, and I've still got my 'friend' hat on."

"Okay," I said. "I'll be quick."

Anton nodded and waved me on.

"Hello," I answered, twisting in my seat. "Is this Mr. Amazing?"

Jude's low chuckle came through the phone. "You better believe it, Luce," he said. "How's your first day?"

"It's going about ten times better now, thanks to this guy who sent me about a million roses."

"A million *red* roses," he said.

"Thank you. You really are pretty amazing, both in and out of the"—I substituted a throat clearing for the word I was going for—"room."

"I'm so damn proud of you, Luce," he said, over some yelling and grunting in the background. He must be taking a phone break during practice. "That's one badass job you got yourself."

"Wait. You're proud now?" I said, thanking Angel with a nod when she dropped my salad in front of me. Anton thanked her with a wink, which sent her over the flustered edge. "When did this happen?"

"When I decided to stop being a selfish jackass," Jude answered. "Would I prefer you to be here with me so I can crawl into bed with you every night? Hell, yeah. But if this is what you need to do, I don't need to understand it to support you along the way."

I went a little soft in the knees right then. Good thing I was sitting.

"Aren't we turning into the mature one?" I replied, glancing over at Anton. He hadn't taken a bite of his soup and was obviously waiting for me before digging in.

I encouraged him with a wave. Very gentlemanly of him, but there was no sense in his soup getting cold while I wrapped up my call with Jude.

"So what are you up to now?" Jude said. "You're not going to get in trouble if the boss catches you on your phone, are you?"

"The boss already did catch me on the phone," I answered, smiling at Anton. "But I think he's all right with it, since he's sitting across the table from me at lunch."

Jude was silent on the other end—for so long, I had to check to make sure I hadn't lost the call. "Jude?"

"You're at lunch with him?" His voice was low, controlled.

Not good. "Yeah?"

"Alone?" His voice was still low, but quavered a little.

Not good at all. "Yeah?"

Jude exhaled sharply. "Does he know you're engaged?"

His voice was making me squirm in my seat. Like I'd done something wrong.

"Yeah."

He took a few long breaths before replying. "Let me talk to him."

"Why?" I asked, knowing that was a bad idea from a mile off.

"Because maybe he needs a reminder that you are engaged to *me*," he said. "And therefore off-limits to *him*."

I glanced at Anton. He was still waiting patiently, oblivious to the guy on the other end of the phone who would gladly reach through the speaker and strangle him if it was possible. I scooted my chair back and lowered my voice, hoping Anton would take a clue and excuse himself for a bathroom break or something. "Jude," I whispered, "even if he does or doesn't know, accept, or care that I'm engaged. I. Know," I said firmly. "I know I'm engaged, and that's all you need to concern yourself with." I shot Anton another look. It was obvious he was pretending to not be intrigued by my conversation.

"You know you're engaged?" Jude said, snorting. "Then what are you doing agreeing to go on private lunch dates with your boss?"

He was getting fired up. So was I. The difference was that I chose to keep my fire to a smolder.

I never thought I'd be classified as one of the cool, calm, and collected people out there, but I was starting to surprise myself.

I unclenched my fists before replying. "Because I was hungry. Because he asked. Because it's a company tradition to take new employees out to lunch. Because there's nothing remotely intimate between us. Because I was sure you trusted and *supported* me enough to make my own wise choices. And"—surely there were about a hundred more reasons—"and because I was hungry."

Anton cleared his throat. "Lucy," he said, sliding out of his seat, "should I go?"

I shook my head.

"Yes," Jude snapped, overhearing him. "Yes, he damn well should."

"Jude," I warned.

"Put him on the phone, Luce," he said. "I need to talk to him."

Anton stood up to go and I shook my head again, and pointed at his seat. I wasn't going to let this argument between Jude and me be resolved by default. He needed to trust my discretion, my choices, and my decisions. He needed to trust *me*.

Anton sat back down hesitantly, looking as uncomfortable as a person could be.

"No."

"Luce," he replied.

"Jude," I threw back. "No."

He kind of sighed, kind of groaned, and was quiet again. I was familiar enough with his frustration to know he was rubbing the back of his neck now, while every inch of his face was creased. "I'm across the country, Luce. Completely helpless while you're at lunch with your boss who's probably some pretty guy in a suit who thinks that because all the girls before you have caved to his charms, you will, too." I was glad he wasn't here to see me, because a small smile parted my mouth. Jude had nailed it; Anton was a pretty guy in a suit. "What do you expect me to do, Luce?"

This was an easy answer. And next to impossible to deliver. "Trust me."

Something short and quiet came from Jude's end, but I didn't catch it. Another few moments of nothing. I swear, half of this call had been in silence while one of us processed what the other was thinking. I suppose you could say we'd finally graduated from the Think Before You Speak Academy.

"Damn," he said under his breath.

I totally got that response. "See why it was so hard for me?"

"Yeah. I'm starting to get why you turned into a crazy person back in the day," he said, understating just what I'd become "back in the day." Psychotic, rabid, shot-flames-from-my-nose lunatic would have been a more accurate description. "Okay, I'll trust you. I will not trust him, or any other man who thinks it's okay to take out an engaged woman alone on a lunch date. Not cool in my book."

My smile wasn't small any longer. I had Jude's trust, even in a situation where he really didn't want to extend it. "Is that some man rule I missed?"

"Man rule number two," he said solemnly. "You don't mess with another man's woman. Ever."

"And what's rule number one?"

"Don't mess with me." From his tone alone, I knew that cocky half smile of his was in full bloom.

"Words to live by," I said. "Although I think I've messed with you plenty." In more ways than one.

"You, and only you, are the one exception to that rule, Luce."

"Well, there's an exception to every rule," I said, realizing I was long past being rude, having been on the phone so long. "It's been nice chatting, but I've got to get back to my—"

"Date."

"Lunch," I clarified. "I love you. Thank you for the call, the flowers, and the trust. I'll give you a ring later tonight once Holly and little Jude are settled in."

"Give Hol a hug for me. You've got the football for little Jude, right?"

"I will, and yes," I answered.

"One more thing," he said.

"Anything."

"Put him on the phone," he said, only partly teasing.

I groaned. "You can talk with him in person when you fly out, so I can monitor what you're saying."

"Ballbuster," he muttered.

"Love you."

"Love you, Luce."

Ending the call, I gave Anton an embarrassed smile. "I'm sorry about that."

He lifted his hand, waving like it was no big deal.

"No, really. I'm sorry." My first day at work, and I'd just sparred with my fiancé on the phone for almost ten minutes at lunch. Not something that would guarantee me an employee-of-the-month plaque anytime in the near future.

"It was entertaining," he said. "I don't think I've seen that much drama since India forced me to watch the season finale of *The Real World* back when I was in middle school."

I wasn't sure if he'd intended this as a jab or as a joke, but it stung. It was none of Anton's business, but I had to set the record straight. "Jude's dramatic. I'm dramatic. Together we make a pretty big production." Cutting into my Caprese salad, I took a bite. Food at last.

Anton finally dropped his spoon into his soup. A gentleman. Not exactly what I'd expected from a brother of India's. "That sounds unhealthy."

My brows came together. I wasn't going to let a guy who thought ordering tomato bisque was living on the wild side tell me what was and wasn't unhealthy.

"Maybe for you, but not for me."

There. That was a way to roll up about an afternoon's worth of explanations into one sentence.

"Forgive me for speaking my mind, but I am a Xavier,"

he said. "How is controlling healthy for anyone?"

"Jude isn't controlling," I said, taking a breath. "He's protective."

"There's a difference?" he asked, having a spoonful of soup. It was probably cold by now.

"Yeah, there's a huge difference. Controlling is completely different from protective." I was tempted to whip out my phone and go all Webster's on his ass. "Jude's protective of me because he knows exactly what kind of nasty crap is out there in the world and he doesn't want me to ever experience it. And if I did, he's both willing and capable of protecting me." I tried to keep from sounding defensive. I liked Anton, but his questions were starting to bug me. "However, even though I know he wishes I'd let him do it, he lets me make my own decisions. The only person who controls me is *me*."

Anton pursed his lips. "Controlling, protective, possessive. I'd lump all those into the same category," he said, watching me. "Unhealthy."

This guy didn't know when to back off. Neither did I.

"What did you major in, in college?" I asked, hoping that if I tried a different path of explanation I could win the conversational battle.

"I doubled in political science and economics," he said, seeming unfazed by my abrupt turn in conversation.

"Okay, so in political science terms . . ." I mused, rolling my fingers over the table. Lightbulb alert.

"Jude isn't a tyrant. He doesn't rule over me or expect that I obey his every word. He's more like an adviser," I explained. "An adviser who not only offers good advice but who knows how to kick ass if required to."

Anton took a couple more sips of soup, stalling. "So you've got drama, he's"—he purposely cleared his throat—"*protective,* and you can't tell me exactly why you love him, just that you couldn't not love him. Lucy, don't slap me too hard, but that sounds like you're smitten. Or infatuated. Not in love."

Boy, I wasn't catching a break this afternoon. From Jude to Anton, these guys were going to make me lose it. I inhaled and counted to five. It didn't matter what Anton thought, nor did it matter what anyone else thought. I wasn't going to let doubt back into my mind. I loved Jude. He loved me. He'd proven himself again and again, over the course of four years. I was through with doubt.

"We'll have to agree to disagree," I said, setting my fork down, because I was finished with lunch and this conversation. "We should probably get back."

"Lucy," he said, "I didn't mean to offend you. I speak my mind, when most of the time I shouldn't."

"Because you're India's brother, my boss, and a pretty

cool guy, I think we should make a pact to not speak about my relationship again." I stared at him straight on. "Because I will not, for another second, let you try to put down what Jude and I have. You don't understand us. That's fine. You wouldn't be the first and you sure as hell won't be the last. But I can't be your friend if you keep saying these things."

"You can't hear anything you don't want to hear?"

"No, that's not it. With Jude and me, we've been through more in four years than most couples would go through in four lifetimes together. I get that the odds are not in our favor. I also don't care." Wow, I was on a roll. Time to get off my soapbox before I slipped off and broke my neck. "I'm sick of hearing people tell us how not right we are for each other. Just because you don't see it doesn't mean we're not true."

Anton lifted his hands in surrender. Good call. "Fair enough. I think I can manage that."

"We'll see," I said. I had my doubts about how Anton was going to "manage."

THIRTEEN

My apartment sounded like a herd of rhinos had been set loose on it.

The little man was doing his namesake proud, hollering and grunting like a caveman. I'd had a long day at work, my feet were killing me, and I was exhausted, but I couldn't get to my apartment fast enough.

It felt like forever since I'd had someone to look forward to seeing when I got home. So long since voices other than mine or the ones coming from the TV had filled my apartment.

Stopping in front of the door, I knocked. It felt a little strange knocking on my own front door, until I heard the *clop, clop, clop*ping of little caveman feet thundering toward the door.

"Aunt Luce is here! Aunt Luce is here!" Although Luce sounded more like *Woose*.

The door opened so hard it bounced against the wall. "Aunt Luce!"

I propped a hand on my hip. "Have you seen a little boy, sir? His name's Jude, and he's about this tall." I held my hand out at his shoulder level. "His uncle Jude and I got him a present."

"Aunt Luce, it's me!"

"What? No way. You are way too big to be little Jude."

He rolled his eyes. Not even four years old and the kid could manage a solid eye roll. No doubt he'd perfected that move from his mama. However, he was the spitting image of Sawyer, his father. So much so that when his face lit up with his smile, I forgot where I was and who was standing in front of me. "Mom says I'm growing like a weed, and I'm not little Jude anymore. I'm LJ," he declared, standing a little taller.

"LJ, eh?" I said. "Says who?"

"Says Thomas," he said, pointing back into the apartment.

A loud crash, followed by Holly firing off a string of, "Fudge, fudge, fudgity, fudge." Sounded like I was needed.

"Is LJ too big to give those really good hugs of his?"

LJ gave this a moment's thought before shaking that mop of golden brown hair. "Nah."

I opened my arms and he dived right in. "Good. Because I've been dying for a good hug." Planting a kiss on his cheek, I headed inside. "Are you already demolition-derbying my apartment?" I shouted over at Holly, who was furiously picking up Jude's old football trophies that had toppled off their shelf.

"I've got a little boy who believes he's a T. rex half of the time," she replied, setting the last trophy back into place. "The question isn't if this place will be demolished; it's when." Holly crossed the room, looking more frazzled than I'd ever seen her. I suppose traveling across the country with a little one would do that to a girl. "Are you sure you don't want to rethink this, Lucy? It's not too late, you know. I haven't finished unpacking all our junk."

"If you even think about leaving, I will literally tie you up and hold you prisoner," I said, hugging LJ tighter.

Giving me a hug from the side, Holly mussed LJ's hair. "Well, it's your security deposit and sanity."

Apparently two momlike girls fussing over him was his limit. Making a face, LJ squirmed out of my arms. "How was the flight?"

"It was a whole heck of a lot better than it could have been, thanks to my friend children's Benadryl," Holly said, watching LJ beeline for the kitchen. "Hey, give Thomas two minutes to himself."

"Hey, Thomas! Didn't have anything better to do tonight?" I called into the kitchen. I hadn't noticed he'd stuck around after picking Holly and Jude up from the airport when I walked in, but Holly and LJ had a way of taking up a person's attention.

Waving a spoon in the air, Thomas grinned. "I told Holly I'd hang around for a while and chill with LJ while she got settled in," he said, right before LJ tackled his legs.

"Jude Michael Reed!" Holly shouted. Damn, she had the mom tone down so well I flinched. "If you don't calm down and start acting like the sweet, good little boy I know you can be, poor Thomas will never come back to see us."

Thomas's eyes shifted to Holly, and even though they were dark brown, I would have sworn they went a little soft. Holly had already left an impression on him. He waved his spoon again. "I've got three little brothers, so I guarantee you there's nothing he can do to me that hasn't already been done."

Turning off a burner, Thomas grabbed LJ and tossed him over his shoulder before galloping around the room in circles. The poor neighbors below us.

"So that's your dance partner?" Holly said, watching the two of them charging and squealing around the room.

"That's him."

"I can see why Jude went ape shit when he found him

undressing you," she said, heading back toward her suitcase.

"That's not exactly a revelation, Holly. Jude does, would, and will go ape shit on anything that remotely resembles a man who tries to help me undress." I followed her and plopped down on the sofa.

"Yeah, but Thomas is cute," she said, stealing a glance at him.

My brows came together. Thomas was good-looking in a beautiful kind of way. Dark, long hair, eyes almost as dark, and flawless alabaster skin. He was easy on the eyes and had caught the attention of more than the majority of female dancers at Marymount Manhattan, but their cute and Holly's cute didn't seem like they would have aligned. Holly was more on the same page as me: she liked the rough, rugged, raw, handsome, all-male type.

"You think Thomas is cute?" I asked.

"Don't you?"

I shrugged, watching Thomas and LJ where they now wrestled on the ground. "Yeah. But—"

"Yeah, yeah, I know," Holly interrupted. "He plays for the other team. That's obvious. Look how thoughtful he is, how well he dresses, and how his eyes never wander below my neck."

I was about to clarify Thomas's sexual orientation when LJ went off like a fire alarm. I made a mental note to pick up some Excedrin next time I was at the store.

"Aunt Luce, is this for me?" he asked. Well, he yelled.

"LJ. Were you going through Aunt Lucy's things?" Holly said as he sprinted toward us with a present in hand. Jude had even had it wrapped in yellow-and-teal paper.

"It was in her bedroom," he said, turning the present over in his hands.

"What were you doing in her bedroom? I told you Lucy's bedroom is off-limits."

"I forgot to tell you," I said, grabbing LJ and tossing him into my lap. "You guys are going to take my room and I'm going to be out here."

"What?" Holly said, like she'd heard me wrong. "No. No way, Lucy Larson. We came on the understanding we'd inconvenience you, not straight-up displace you."

Thomas crashed down beside me. His hair looked like it had been whirled around in a blender a few times.

"Will you listen to me for once, you stubborn brat? You and LJ are taking my room. He needs a quiet spot where he can sleep, and there are two of you. I already ordered a twin mattress and a couple room dividers to set up out here for me, so it's done." I arched a brow and waited. Holly liked to argue with me almost as much as Jude did.

What she did next, though, I wasn't expecting. I'd been braced and ready for another five rounds of back-and-forth.

Instead she threw herself down beside me and pulled me into a hug that was so tight it almost cut my airway off.

"I don't know what I'd do without you and Jude." She sniffed into my hair. I'd never seen her cry. In fact, I'd come to the conclusion she couldn't cry.

"You'd be fine, Holly," I assured her, just like either Jude or I did when she tried to give us more credit than we were due. Holly had crossed the proverbial Nile all on her own. Jude and I had just been there to provide a little help along the way. Patting her back a few times, I winked at LJ. "Well. Are you going to keep staring at that thing all night or are you going to tear into it?"

His face lit up right before a hurricane of wrapping paper flew into the air.

"A football!" he said, jumping up and down. "A real football. Not a baby one." Arching his arm back, he launched it straight into Thomas's stomach.

Thomas grunted, fumbling with the ball like he didn't know whether to throw it or pirouette with it.

"Holy snickies," Holly said, examining the ball in Thomas's hands. "Are those signatures on that thing?"

"Snickies, yeah," I replied, realizing I'd have to really watch my mouth now that an innocent set of ears was around. That, more than anything else, seemed like it would be the hardest part of this situation.

"As in the signatures of a certain Jude Ryder and the rest of his teammates?" Holly was gaping at the ball now.

I shot her a smirk. "No. Jude Ryder and the rest of the members of the Bad Boys Club."

"In that case," she said with a slow smile, "where are the phone numbers?"

Thomas handed the ball back to LJ before popping up from the couch. Zeroing in on the door, he shifted. "I'd better get back," he said. "I've got an hour's drive ahead of me."

Holly and I exchanged a look. Thomas had seemed ready to spend the night on the couch, and now he couldn't get out of here fast enough.

Hopping up, I followed after him. "Thanks again, Thomas," I said, opening the door for him. "I owe you a solid."

He paused in the doorway and looked back to where LJ was tossing his ball to Holly. "No, you don't. I haven't had this much fun since karaoke night, when you sang a drunken version of 'Hey Jude' before falling off the stage."

I scowled at him. That was a night I didn't like to remember. Jude had been in town that weekend, and the bartender had been a bit heavy-handed with my drinks that night. The result wasn't pretty.

Thomas still couldn't take his eyes off Holly, so I began to hatch a plan. "How about you let me make you dinner

Friday night, then? As a way to express my undying thanks."

I waited while he worked out something in his head.

"Come on. You can stay the night here, so you won't have to worry about driving late at night."

His eyes widened at that. "Are you sure?"

"Hol," I called over my shoulder, "are we sure we want Thomas over for dinner Friday night?"

After launching the ball into LJ's arms, she glanced over at us. I swore I heard an uptick in Thomas's heart. "Seven o'clock," she said. "Don't be late."

I grinned victoriously at Thomas and waited.

"It's a date," he said at last, before his face reddened. "I mean, it's a dinner. A dinner date . . ." Another shade redder. "I mean Friday's the date, and dinner's the event." Wincing, he turned around. "I'm going to go die now."

"Thanks for everything!" Holly shouted as he headed into the hall. "It was nice meeting you, Thomas."

He stuck his head back into the apartment. "It was nice meeting *you*, Holly."

She shot him a smile that made the poor guy go another shade darker. Giving me a wave, Thomas hurried down the hall. He didn't make it two doors down before he tripped over . . . his own two feet.

"You all right down there, Grace?" I called out as he caught himself before he bit it.

"I'm not exactly feeling like myself tonight," he replied, glaring at his feet like they'd betrayed him.

"I wonder why." I gave him a wry smile.

His shook his head. "Good night, Lucy."

"Good night, Grace."

He gave me a thumbs-up before making it down the rest of the hall in one piece. I'd never seen Thomas trip like that, not once in our three years of performing together.

"What did you do to that boy?" I asked as soon as I closed the door.

"Made him think twice about having kids," Holly said, getting back to work on unpacking her suitcase.

"No, he has the Holly bug so bad—"

"*Jude!*" Holly shouted, rushing over to where LJ stood in front of my potted fern. His pants were around his ankles. "Please, please, please don't tell me you just peed on Aunt Lucy's plant."

LJ pulled up his pants and shrugged. "It looked thirsty."

I burst out in laughter, but was silenced almost as quickly when Holly turned her power glare on me.

Giving me a look that said, *Just laugh one more time, I dare ya,* she marched over to LJ. "Where are you supposed to go potty?"

"The bathroom," LJ said, like it was obvious.

"Specifically."

"The toilet." He sighed.

"So why did you just pee in Aunt Lucy's plant?"

"I told you. It was thirsty."

Auntie intervention in order. Grabbing the watering can from the counter, I headed over to where Holly towered over LJ. "You're right; it was thirsty. But I know for a fact my little fern is allergic to little-boy pee"—I elbowed Holly before she elbowed me right back—"so next time it's thirsty, you can use this to give it some *water*." I handed the can to LJ. "This will be your job here. To keep the plant happy and healthy. Think you can handle that?"

LJ inspected the can, turning it over a few times before nodding. "Yeah. I'll take care of the plant, Aunt Luce," he said, sounding as solemn as an almost four-year-old boy could. Then his eyes shifted to the TV in front of the sofa and they lit up. "Mom? Can I watch *Yo Gabba Gabba*?"

Holly checked the clock on the kitchen wall. "Go for it."

After carefully placing the watering can beside the plant, LJ skipped over to the TV and grabbed the remote.

"Does he need help with that?" I asked.

"Are you kidding? He's known what time and what channel *Yo Gabba Gabba!* is on since he was two," she said, looking from the plant to me. "Sorry about that. Like I said, a little caveman."

"Don't worry," I said, "and if it makes you feel any better,

I'm pretty sure that wasn't the first time it was peed on. I'm almost certain Jude had that honor after we burned through a couple bottles of champagne New Year's Eve and the bathroom was just too far to go when he had to *go*."

"Men," Holly said, curling her nose at the plant. "They look for any excuse they can to whip that thing out. Age isn't a factor. Obviously." Her eyes landed on LJ, who was enraptured by a show that looked like it was conceived during an acid trip.

"Come on. Let's get your stuff moved into the bedroom so you guys can get some sleep," I said, grabbing another suitcase of theirs. "I'm sure you're beat."

"Like a punching bag," she said, grabbing another suitcase and following me. "Aunt Lucy and I are going to finish unpacking. Let me know if you need anything, LJ."

"Are the brownies done yet?" LJ asked, his eyes glued to the TV.

Holly glanced at the timer on the microwave. "Another twenty minutes."

"Okay," he said, sounding like twenty minutes was an eternity. "I love you, Mom."

All the stress lines on Holly's face ironed out. "I love you, Jude."

"It's LJ," he said, looking away just long enough to meet Holly's gaze.

"Sorry, I forgot," she said. "I love you, *LJ*."

Damn. The kid could pee on any and every surface in the apartment if he kept saying stuff like that. The apartment felt full again. I felt full again.

Mostly.

I knew no matter how many bodies I packed into the place, it would never be enough to fill the void Jude had left behind. No one could fill that empty place except for him.

Heaving the suitcase on top of the bed, I unzipped it and got to work. I'd already put on fresh sheets and emptied out the closet and drawers to make room for Holly and LJ.

"Lucy, I still don't feel right taking your room," Holly said, tossing her bag onto the bed as well. "I mean, it's your place. You should get the bedroom."

"Would you stop already?" I said, opening the top dresser drawer before layering LJ's pants into it. "It's done. My decision's final. End of subject."

"I love it when you talk bitch to me," Holly said, snagging a few hangers from the closet. "It gets me all excited."

I laughed and tossed her LJ's coat to hang up. "How's the job search going? Any luck so far?"

I loved that I was friends with a woman who believed in creating her own destiny.

"I start tomorrow night," she said proudly, sliding a teeny-weeny dress onto a hanger.

"Amazing. You can find a job in this town from across the country in a weekend's time. It took me weeks, and even then, I had to have a friend's older brother throw me a job bone."

Holly shrugged. "I had to have a friend's help, too." She smiled at me before situating a few hangers back into the closet.

"What salon did you get on with?"

"Les Cheveux Chic," she said. "And it's only, like, a half mile away, so I can walk to work."

"Wow. That's one of the best salons in town, Holly," I said, impressed. "Way to go."

"Yeah, well, I guess they were desperate for someone, with all the new business they've been getting, so when the owner heard I'd been clipping and dyeing my share of heads for five years, she pretty much hired me right then over the phone." Holly scooped an armload of bras and panties from her suitcase. I think every color of the rainbow was represented, as well as every pattern and fabric. Not a bad collection for a girl who claimed to go sans underwear half the time. "However, my schedule sucks balls. I'm working nights and weekends and have a grand total of one day off." Sliding open a dresser drawer in the closet that had been Jude's, she dropped her racy unmentionables inside.

"What hours at night?"

"Six to ten Monday through Thursday," she answered. "Apparently the salon's trying to be friendlier to working women."

"And here I'd been under the impression working women worked nights," I teased, pulling out the next drawer.

"Who's been telling on me?" Holly threw back, slingshotting a bright yellow thong at my face.

I dodged it before it landed on me. "I bet working those night shifts when you have all those professionals coming in, you'll make a ton in tips."

"Probably," she said with a shrug, "but I'm having a hell of a time finding child care for Jude. It seems every day care in this town closes by six o'clock, and if I can't find day care, then I can't take the job."

I smiled. It was nice to be able to help out. "I happen to know of a certain auntie's child care that's got an opening and is available twenty-four-seven."

Holly froze, right before her face wrinkled. "No way, Lucy. No, no, no way," she said. "You've done about ten times too much already. There's no way I could let you babysit my little man four nights a week plus the entire weekend. No. Way."

I rolled my eyes. Holly didn't understand that I wasn't doing this strictly out of the goodness of my heart. I wanted someone to fill my time so I wouldn't mope around pining for Jude. I couldn't imagine anyone who was more up to the task of distracting me than LJ.

"Yes way," I replied, sliding the drawer closed.

"Don't you even think about arguing with me on this, Lucy Larson," Holly warned, wagging a finger at me. "Because I will win."

I wasn't planning on arguing. I was planning on being victorious.

"Holly, you and LJ are like family. I love you both. Let me do this."

My pleas were working. A little.

"Come on. This solves both of our problems. You need someone to watch LJ and I need someone to keep me company." Holding up a little shirt of his that read, LADIES' MAN, I continued. "It's a win-win."

Holly's mouth had fallen open about midway through my last spiel. Shaking her head, she looked at me like I was certifiable. "Are you serious, Lucy?" she asked. "You do realize what you just witnessed isn't just a sugar high, right? That's the way he is all day, every day. It's nonstop, on-the-top-of-your-game supervision."

I crossed my arms. "Are you done yet?" I asked.

"Are you done yet?" she mimicked.

"No, I'm not. I can go all night long, baby," I said. "I'm not giving up until I get my way, so why don't you save us the time and effort and just cave already."

A few moments passed in silence. Nothing but the sound of that trippy-ass music filling the apartment, before her eyes went a little watery. "Come here, you stubborn, sweet woman," she said, flapping her arms.

I let Holly hug me until I felt like I was going to pass out again.

A couple hours later, the apartment was dark and, other than LJ's little man-snoring, quiet. In two hours' time, we'd managed to get them unpacked, worked out a weekly schedule that detailed when I'd be watching LJ as well as a chore and shopping list, bathed LJ (which was more like what I imagined it would be like to wrestle with a slippery sea lion), and cleaned up not one, but two cups of spilled milk.

Neither LJ nor I cried over it, but Holly was close when spill number two wound up on my coat. I'd sent her to bed, promising I'd send LJ in right after he'd had his third try at a cup of milk.

I added *spill-proof cup* to the shopping list before tucking him in next to Holly, who was already so deep in sleep she didn't even shift when LJ crawled in beside her.

Until my bed got here, I was camping out on the couch, which was pretty comfortable when you paired it with a couple of cozy blankets and pillows. Almost as soon as my head hit the pillow, I felt myself drifting off to sleep. The day had been exhausting for me, too.

That was when my phone rang.

I snapped awake. I couldn't believe I'd almost forgotten Jude's and my nightly call. Blinking to clear my sleepy eyes, I accepted the Face Time request.

"Hey, handsome," I said, sounding as tired as I felt.

"Shit. Did I wake you, Luce?" His forehead creased, but his mouth stayed formed in a smile.

"If you'd waited another thirty seconds you would have," I said, shifting onto my elbows. "It was one hell of a day."

"Good or bad hell of a day?"

"Pretty great really. Just busy. And exhausting," I said. "Even better now that I get to end it with you." I took him in, letting myself soak up as much of Jude as I could through the phone. This was all I got for another twenty-four hours. He was back in his hotel after finally coming to his senses that we didn't need a ten-thousand-square-foot home for our first one. Jude was sitting up in bed, and he was shirtless.

Had I really been tired less than a minute ago? It didn't seem possible with the way my blood was pumping through my veins right now.

"So . . ." he began, his smile twisting, "you look pretty tired, but I wanted to see if you felt like having some sweet dreams tonight."

My inner thighs tightened. "I'm not exactly alone any-more," I whispered, glancing back at the bedroom. "I can't have regular phone sex with you when a three-year-old's under the roof."

"Just be quiet," he suggested.

I laughed out loud before catching myself. "When was the last time I was able to be quiet during . . . *that*?"

An eyebrow arched. "Never. But there's a first time for everything, Luce." He was so damn confident, I almost wanted to tell him no just out of principle. But I knew I wouldn't. My body had already started the spiral to the top from his words alone.

"You do know if I have to attempt this whole quiet thing, I'm not going to be able to talk dirty to you. Right?" I said, skimming my fingers down my stomach. My skin was extrasensitive from anticipation.

Jude shifted in bed before holding his boxers in front of the camera. "That's a sacrifice I'm happy to make." And then he threw them to the side, giving me a full-monty view.

I swallowed, and then slid my hand under my leggings.

"Aunt Luce?"

I jolted, dropping the phone in the process. "LJ?! What are you doing up?" My voice was two octaves too high.

"I heard voices and wanted to make sure you were okay,"

he said, coming around the side of the couch sporting his Avengers pj's.

The phone had slipped behind the sofa cushions, but I could hear Jude's low laugh coming through it.

"I'm okay," I said as I pulled the phone free. "I was just saying good night to Uncle Jude." Checking the screen to make sure the view had changed, I flashed it in front of LJ.

"Uncle Jude!" His face lit up like Jude was cooler than bubble gum.

"Hey, little man. How's it going?"

"Good, but don't talk too loud, okay?" he asked, lifting his finger to his mouth. "Mom doesn't know I snuck out of bed."

"You got up to check on Aunt Luce?"

LJ nodded.

"Good job," Jude said. "You're the man of the house now, so I'm trusting you to take care of your mom and Aunt Luce."

"Jude, he's three," I said, turning the screen toward me. He'd shrugged into a shirt faster than he could get mine off.

"I'm almost four," LJ said proudly.

"Yeah, Luce. He's almost four."

"All right, man of the house," I said, turning the screen back toward LJ. "Say good night. It's way past your bedtime."

"One more minute?" LJ begged.

"Yeah, one more minute?" Jude's voice joined in.

I sighed. "Fine."

LJ did a little dance.

"Phone five," Jude said, as LJ high-fived the screen.

"Thanks for the football, Uncle Jude. Will you teach me to throw it one thousand yards?" It was dark, but LJ's eyes were twinkling.

"I'll teach you to throw it ten thousand yards."

"Wow," LJ replied, dumbfounded.

"I'll take you to the park when I come visit in a couple weeks. In the meantime, practice snapping your arm back and following through on your throw."

LJ's eyes squinted while he stored these instructions away.

"You'll be throwing like a pro before you know it."

"And . . . time," I interrupted, realizing that if I was going to be watching this kid six days a week, I'd have to get used to being a responsible adult.

LJ groaned and hung his shoulders.

"Listen to your aunt Luce, little man," Jude said. "From one guy to another, here's a word of advice: You're going to have to figure out what battles are worth fighting. And this isn't one you'll win."

LJ contemplated that pearl of wisdom for all of a second

before nodding his head. "Okay. Good night, Uncle Jude. Good night, Aunt Luce." He waved and started for the bedroom. "I love you."

I turned the phone so Jude could watch him go. "Love you, little man."

When I heard the bedroom door click shut, I spun the phone around. "That was a major crisis averted," I teased, as his smile grew when he saw me.

"That, Luce, was a major crisis delayed," he implied, letting those words settle.

Jude Ryder . . . hopeless optimist.

"No, Jude," I said, propping the phone up against a stack of coasters on the coffee table. "That was a major crisis called on account of weather."

"Luce, no way." He groaned. "You got me all excited and now you're giving me the airtime cock block?"

I turned onto my side, trying not to laugh. "No. I'm going to sleep," I replied, blowing him a kiss. "Good night. Love you, Jude."

A good minute after I'd closed my eyes, he sighed. I never knew so many emotions could reside in one sigh. "Good night. Love you, Luce."

That night, my dreams picked up where Jude and I had let off. Ecstasy.

FOURTEEN

I'd fallen asleep on Monday night and it was Friday when I woke up.

It was amazing how time could move so fast when your life was filled with a nine-to-five office job, mac 'n' cheese dinners, *Yo Gabba Gabba!* dates, precious hours squeezed in at the dance studio, and nightly calls from the love of my life.

So far, Holly loved her job, and I actually looked forward to getting home so I could hang with a three-almost-four-year-old every night. It was impossible to experience any degree of self-pity when you were in the presence of a kiddo who was as happy and energetic as LJ. Plus, after chasing him around for four hours, I was able to fall asleep as soon as my head hit the pillow.

Much to Jude's dismay.

I was smiling to myself as I played through the many puppy-dog faces and pleas that Jude had come up with this week, when Anton burst out of his office.

"Checked tie or striped tie?" he asked, bobbing two ties in front of me.

Apparently personal wardrobe consultant was now one of the many hats I wore here at Xavier Industries. Work had been going well. I was learning the ropes, and I was so busy the days flew by. I'd done so much typing and created so many spreadsheets, I was sure I could complete my job with my eyes closed.

"What's the occasion?" I asked, powering down my computer. It was a few minutes after five on a Friday night.

"Dinner with a blind date," he said, inspecting the ties critically. "Some girl my friend went to school with. She's a graphic designer, likes glam rock, and runs marathons. That's all I know about her, which is why I'm coming up empty in the tie selection endeavor."

If Anton thought selecting the right tie was the be-all-end-all when it came to getting a second date, I understood why he was still single.

"The checked one," I said, tapping it with the end of my pen.

The skin between his brows lined. "So confident. So

certain," he said, holding the checked tie up. "How did you decide?"

I used the Pythagorean theorem and square-rooted the null set. I was an insufferable smart-ass.

"It's the one I like," I said, shrugging.

Anton's face relaxed. Nodding, he appraised the tie with new eyes. "The checked one it is," he said, heading back for his office. "Thanks, Lucy. Have a nice weekend."

"Do you need anything else?" I asked, already shouldering my purse. I had our first ever Friday-night dinner to prepare for five tonight, and, while Anton had been true to his word and not brought my relationship up again this week, I felt uncomfortable being alone with him.

And it made me mad. Other than some harmless flirting, Anton had been a true gentleman, going so far as to walk me to my car every night to make sure I got to it safely. I shouldn't feel uneasy to be alone with another man, and the fact that I did made me even more uneasy.

"No, it's quitting time," he said from his office. "I'm out of here, too, so I'll walk you out." Reappearing with the checked tie in place and a tweed vest instead of his suit jacket, he held open the office door and waited for me.

I turned off the lights and went through the door as fast as I could. He'd put on some cologne that was spicy and sweet-smelling, and the fact that I noticed set me on edge.

We walked in silence to the elevator, and our silence dragged on while we waited for it.

"Do I make you uncomfortable?" Anton asked.

"When you ask those kinds of questions, yeah, you do," I said, almost bolting inside the elevator as soon as the doors opened.

Anton took one giant step inside and stopped in front of me. "Why?"

I found it hard to believe that he needed to ask me why. "Because of the way you're looking at me right now. And because of the things you say." I took a couple steps back until I was up against the elevator wall. "You're my boss. You're my friend's brother. You can't look at me like that, or say those kinds of things to me."

"Why?" he asked, tilting his head.

His calm, one-word replies were starting to piss me off.

"Because," the genius inside me answered.

"I've been in relationships with women who have worked with me, Lucy," he said, looking at me too intently. "And I've been in relationships with my sister's friends. Believe me, that's not what's stopping me from pursuing you."

Shit. That look on his face, combined with the tone of his voice, made me wish I could put another five feet of space between us. Thankfully, the elevator jostled to a stop and the doors opened. I was out of those doors faster than I thought I could move.

"So, yeah, there it is," Anton said, rushing up beside me. I'll take "Get a Clue" for a thousand, Alex. "I'm attracted to you, Lucy. I want to pursue you, and I want you to want to be pursued by me."

If I didn't reply, could I wake up tomorrow and pretend none of this had happened? I shoved through the revolving door and powered toward the Mazda.

"But I won't act on my attraction out of respect for—"

I spun on him. This was too much, too late in the day. "Out of respect for a guy who would kill you where you stood if he ever found out what you just said?"

He shook his head. "No. Out of respect for you."

I laughed harshly. "You've got one hell of a way of showing respect for me," I said, fumbling with my keys.

"I respect you enough to tell you the truth," he said, stepping to the side when I swung the door open. "I want you to know you've got options."

I bit my cheek to keep from nailing him with words I'd regret later. "I don't want options."

"Sure you do," he said. "Every girl does." And those words, paired with his expression, which was way too condescending for my liking, brought the words I'd been trying to keep under wraps right to the surface.

"Go fuck yourself, Anton," I fired off before slamming the door and peeling out of the parking lot, never once checking the rearview mirror.

I was quivering. Shaking from the emotions that were spilling out of me. It felt like every emotion possible was present and accounted for, although the loudest ones were anger and confusion. Anger for the obvious reasons. Anton had no right to say those things to me, an engaged woman. Not to mention, an engaged woman who was also his employee. No right at all.

Confusion because I didn't understand why Anton had said them in the first place. He was intelligent and purposeful to a fault. He didn't do things on a whim, so I could assume he'd planned this whole spilling-of-the-guts elevator ride. And that confused and pissed me off more.

My life was complicated enough already. I didn't need some guy I'd just met in person five days ago professing his attraction to me. Anton either had a screw loose or was over-confident. Neither was a recipe for an acceptable "option," like he'd said.

Not that I wanted options in the first place.

Dammit. Now I was thinking about options, thanks to my lovely boss screwing with my Friday night.

I wanted to call Jude. I wanted to tell him everything that happened and everything I was feeling about it. I wanted to talk to my best friend about all of it. Unfortunately in this case, my best friend also happened to be the guy I loved, and the guy I loved would fly off the handle—and across the country in a heartbeat—if he knew any other man, Anton especially, had said those kinds of things to me.

So I didn't call him. Instead I glowered at the road and threw a few punches into the steering wheel. By the time I got home, I felt better. And worse. Better because I reminded myself that no matter what any guy said or did, I'd never love anyone but Jude. It felt good to be reminded of this. And worse because I was going to be jobless again come Monday morning. I couldn't . . . no, I *wouldn't* work for a man who confessed to having a thing for me. That was a whole heap of drama I didn't need in my life right now. Not to mention I'd just told my boss to fuck himself. I might not have a ton of job experience, but I knew I was on my way to getting myself fired on the spot.

As I headed up to my apartment, I forced myself to shelve the Anton issue and forget about it until Sunday night, when I had to call him and tell him to put an ad in the paper for a new admin. I was going to enjoy tonight. It wasn't often I was able to have some of my best friends in the same place, and I wasn't going to ruin it by moping.

So Anton was attracted to me. Big deal. It was a free country and he could be attracted to whomever he wanted.

As of right now, his attraction was out of my mind.

Heading down the hall, I could already smell dinner and hear laughter streaming from the apartment. I was grinning by the time I opened the door.

"Aunt Luce!" LJ greeted me as soon as I came through the door, like he was standing guard.

"LJ!" I greeted him back, sniffing the air. Chicken enchiladas, one of my faves.

"Right this way," he said in a dignified voice, before grabbing my hand and pulling me into the bathroom.

"What are you up to, crazy man?" I laughed as he towed me along. He was strong for an almost-four-year-old.

"I picked out some jammies and slippers for you," he said, pointing at them balanced on the sink ledge. "Once you're comfy, we can have some dinner and I'll even bring you your plate." His face was so lit up with excitement, it rubbed off on me.

"Thank you, kind sir," I said, bowing formally. "But to what do I owe the honor of all this special treatment?"

"Mom says you've been working hard all week and you're our angel and you deserve some DLC," he recited, backing out of the bathroom.

"You mean TLC?"

He rolled his eyes at me. "Nope. DLC."

I covered my mouth to keep from laughing. "Well, I'm looking forward to my DLC tonight."

He beamed before shutting the door. The next sound I heard was his footsteps pounding into the kitchen as he shouted, "She's getting comfy! She's getting comfy! I want to pour her cup of apple juice now!"

I couldn't get out of my skirt and blouse fast enough. I'd worn the same black skirt twice this week, thanks to my lack of business attire, and I had been hoping to remedy that sometime this weekend. Maybe now instead of getting new outfits, I could get LJ a new pair of swimming trunks so we could swim at the public pool.

LJ had clearly handpicked my jammies for the night without any help from Holly. The top he'd gotten right. I always wore some variety of a camisole to bed. However, he'd matched it with a pair of Jude's boxers that had four-leaf clovers on them that read, GET LUCKY, and then, to top it off, LJ had loaned me his slide-on slippers featuring the most terrifying of the *Yo Gabba Gabba!* characters: the red, warty dude with one eye.

Once I'd slid into my tank and hiked Jude's boxers into place, I squeezed on the slippers. Only because I couldn't resist, I took a good look in the mirror and burst out laughing. This outfit was too rad not to share. Snapping a picture with my phone, I typed a quick message: BET YOU WISH YOU WERE HERE TO ENJOY ALL THIS SEXINESS, before sending it to Jude.

Opening the door, I rolled my shoulders back and turned that hallway into a runway.

India was the first to catch sight of me working it, and the beer she'd been sipping shot straight out of her nose.

Sputtering and laughing at the same time, she nudged Holly, who was chopping up a head of lettuce. "You go, girl!" India said, snapping her fingers. "You get on with your bad self!"

Holly, followed by Thomas, burst into laughter next, tossing in a few whistles and catcalls for good measure.

I came to a stop at the kitchen and struck a pose. More laughter. India even let a snort pop out, which, of course, only made everyone laugh harder.

While I was busy holding my pose, a little hand grabbed mine. "You look beautiful, Aunt Luce," LJ said, his voice and face full of awe.

"All thanks to you," I said, clicking my slippers together like Dorothy before heading over to the sink. "What do you guys need help with?"

"Just stay out of the way," Thomas whispered, nudging me as he upended a bag of chips into a bowl. "India was ready to cut a bitch when I dropped the cilantro on the floor."

"I heard that, Tinker Bell," India said, shooting a glare Thomas's way.

"Sure, go for the easy insult. Yes, yes, I am a male dancer who's majoring in ballet," he said, flinging a chip India's way. "You're just jeals because my butt looks better in a pair of jeans than yours does."

"Enough already, you two," Holly ordered, bringing a bowl of guacamole our way. "I've been playing referee all afternoon and I'm done."

"He insulted my butt," India said, hiking a hand onto her hip.

"I didn't insult it," Thomas responded. "I just stated that mine, in fact, is nicer to look at."

When I realized I'd been washing my hands the whole time India and Thomas had been snapping back and forth, I shut off the water.

Groaning, Holly slammed the bowl down on the counter. "Fine. India, turn around," she demanded, twirling her finger in the air. India didn't argue; she even popped her hip to the side to sway the ass vote her way. "Nice. I give it a nine out of ten."

Only India would be insulted that her ass had just been ranked a nine out of ten.

"Okay, Thomas. Your turn," Holly said, waiting, but Thomas wasn't moving. He was frozen in place.

Familiar with that deer-in-the-headlights look, I helped him out. Grabbing his shoulders, I spun him around. I even tucked in his tee and highlighted his derriere with my hands, Vanna White style.

Inspecting Thomas, Holly tilted her head to one side, then the other, before her eyes went a little dreamy. Coming up behind him, Holly slapped both hands into Thomas's cheeks and squeezed.

He jolted with surprise, but didn't put up any argument.

"Thomas wins," Holly announced, giving his butt a little love pat before retrieving her bowl of guacamole.

"Whatever." India sulked, carrying a tray of enchiladas to the table. "What I got back here's a perfect ten, baby."

"Taste this," Holly said, sticking a finger topped by a dollop of guac in front of my mouth.

"Eww, no way. I don't like avocados." I wrinkled my nose and sidestepped her before she shoved her finger into my mouth.

"Thomas, you try then." Lifting her finger to Thomas's mouth, she paused. Maybe because of the way Thomas was looking at her, or maybe because of the way she was looking at him, but it was clear they were both *very* conscious of each other.

Her other hand dropped to the bend of his elbow right before he opened his mouth. Holly slipped her finger inside and, just as Thomas's lips closed around it, LJ came running into the room.

"I didn't spill even a little bit," he announced proudly as he set the pitcher on the counter.

This shook them both out of their stupor. Clearing her throat, Holly pulled her finger back. "What do you think? Too spicy?"

Thomas looked like he'd need a two-by-four to the head to clear his mind. I was about to go searching for one when he shook his head. "No."

I supposed a lame one-word reply was better than no reply.

"Maybe not enough salt?" Holly suggested, looking everywhere but at Thomas. Her eyes had suddenly become allergic to him. "There's definitely something missing."

Thomas's face got all deliberate. "From where I'm standing," he said, "it's pretty darn perfect."

I was beginning to feel like a third wheel, so I started making my way to the table when a knock sounded at the door.

"Yay! He's here," India said, clapping as she rushed to the door. "Someone who will be on my side."

I didn't know India was going to invite her latest boy toy over for the night, not that she would have cared if I knew or approved or not. I was contemplating dodging behind my room dividers so I could change when she threw the door open.

"Anton!" she said, tossing her arms around his neck.

Anton. My exact same response, minus the enthusiasm. Actually, with the complete opposite of enthusiasm.

He was still in his checked tie and vest when India dragged him inside. He had the decency to make an apologetic face when he looked my way. That was, until he really saw me. Or saw what I was wearing. He was grinning by the time he got to the slippers, but that grin died as soon as he noticed the look I was leveling on him.

"What are *you* doing here?" I asked, sounding as impolite as a person could. "I thought you had some sort of hot blind date tonight."

"The bitch canceled on him last-minute," India answered for him, "and when my big brother texted me that for the first time ever, he'd been stood up, I couldn't not invite him over to our first Friday-night dinner to lick his wounds. Besides, we've got Corona on ice, and Mama made some Jell-O shooters for the after-little-man-goes-to-bed party," she said, nodding over at LJ, who was too busy tossing his football up in the air to pay us any attention.

"You don't mind, do you, Lucy?" India asked, finally taking a second to *look* at me.

Instead of smacking Anton square across the face like I

wanted to, I plastered on a fake smile. "No, why would I mind?" I said, going to the kitchen to grab another place setting. "Why wouldn't I want my boss and my friend's brother to join us for dinner?"

I was laying it on thick. That was obvious from the way Holly and Thomas were studying me, like I'd tripped a wire in my brain or something.

"I'm sensing the sarcasm," India said, when I marched back to the table and slapped a plate down.

"You mean I wasn't subtle?"

"Not exactly," she said, as I took out a little frustration on the napkin I was folding. "Bad day at work?" she guessed.

"Understatement," I muttered before I looked up and caught Anton staring at my cleavage. So much for Saint Anton who was impervious to what was south of a woman's neck.

"I'm going to go," Anton said, lifting his hands and retreating toward the door.

"Best idea you've had all day," I said, crossing my arms.

"Hold up, you two," India said, grabbing her brother's arm and pulling him back. "What in the H-E-L-L is going on here?"

Thomas and Holly had drifted up to the table and were watching the whole thing like it was one big ol' train wreck they couldn't look away from.

"I can answer that with four words," I said, crossing my arms tighter. "Anton is an A-S-S." I glanced over at LJ, who was oblivious. Nothing but him and his football. I mourned that kind of simplicity.

India's face scrunched up while Anton's dropped. "You're right. I was an"—he glanced over at LJ—"A-S-S. A huge, insensitive one. And I'm sorry." He took a few steps my direction but stopped once I stiffened. "Will you forgive me?"

"Will you promise to stop acting like a huge, insensitive A-S-S?"

"I can't guarantee that," he said. "But I can promise that I'll try." A couple steps closer, until I could smell that damned cologne of his. "So? Forgiven?"

"Forgiven? I don't know," I answered truthfully. "But you can stay." Wanting to put some space between us, I headed back into the kitchen. I was tempted to hack up the other half head of lettuce just to get some of my frustration out, but held myself back.

Instead, I cracked my neck, popped my knuckles, and grabbed a Corona. I didn't bother with the lime.

"Lucy, my girl, I don't know how you managed to get the first apology I've ever heard from my brother, but that ought to make you eligible for your own national holiday," India said, taking a seat at the table. "Lucy Larson Puts Jack-A-S-S-E-S in Their Place Day."

"Indie, that's an everyday holiday in my life," I said, selecting the seat as far away from Anton as I could.

Holly lifted her beer and clanked it against mine. "Amen, sister."

"Can I sit next to you, Aunt Luce?" LJ asked, squirming up beside me.

"It's all right with me if it's all right with your mom."

"Mom? Is it all right?"

"Knock yourself out," she said, cutting LJ's enchilada into bite-size pieces.

Thomas dished everyone an enchilada before taking his seat across from Anton. "So what's your story, Anton?" he asked. "Other than being an A-S-S?"

Anton chuckled. "I'll save you the details, since it's a pretty boring one."

"I doubt that," Thomas said around a bite of enchilada. "I mean, how can a guy named Anton, who is next in line to run a multimillion-dollar company, not to mention a guy who can seriously tick Lucy Larson off, have a boring story? It's impossible."

I dived into my dinner, hoping that if I had a mouthful of food I wouldn't fire off anything that was better kept to myself.

"Trust me, it's about as exciting as French vanilla ice cream."

I choked on my food. Seriously choked.

LJ stood up in his chair and gave my back a few whacks while I sipped some apple juice. When I looked up from my choking incident, everyone was staring at me.

"What?" I said, expressing my thanks to LJ with a smile. "I've always found French vanilla to be rather exciting. That's all."

"Do you think the psych unit is closed for the night?" India mumbled.

I scowled at her as I contemplated if eating my dinner was going to be more dangerous than not eating it.

"Since my big brother's having this rare moment of modesty, I'll give you the four-one-one on Anton Shaft Xavier."

"Wait." Thomas waved his fork. "Your middle name is Shaft?"

Anton shrugged. "Our parents are huge *Shaft* fans."

Thomas clapped his hands, clearly in awe. "There is no conceivable way your life story is boring with a middle name like Shaft."

"The only person whose life story is more exciting is mine," India said, taking a swig of her beer. "Okay. So ASX in a nutshell . . . which is strangely ironic, since it's very close to A-S-S." She grinned like this was a revelation. "He was the captain of his lacrosse team back in high school. Was student body president his senior year. Dated every cheerleader on the squad by the time he turned eighteen." Anton sighed, and grabbed India's beer before she could stop him. He took a long swig. "He got a scholarship to Dartmouth, graduated summa cum laude, went to the Olympic trials for the lacrosse team; he summited K2 three years ago, sailed across the Atlantic on his own two years ago, and one year ago he lost his fiancée."

Anton choked on his beer. A lot of choking going on tonight. "Shit, India," he said, before Holly leveled a look at him. "I mean, S-H-I-T, India."

"What do you mean, he lost his fiancée?" Thomas asked, leaning forward. "Like, one day he woke up and couldn't find her?"

Anton lifted his hand. "Let's just drop—"

"No, like 'one day he woke up and got the call she'd been killed in a car accident' lost her," India explained.

"S-H-I-T." Anton sighed, shaking his head at India.

I felt a little sick. Sick to my stomach and sick in the head. Anton had been engaged and she'd died. Recently. I never would have guessed Mr. Too-smooth-for-his-own-good had such a tragic past. Anton seemed more like the friends-with-benefits kind of guy, not the put-a-ring-on-it kind of guy.

"Why didn't you say anything?" I asked India. She'd shared about every other personal detail of her life with me.

I didn't understand how she'd forget to mention this one.

"Anton didn't want me telling the whole world about it," she said.

"Which obviously worked out fantastically," he said, keeping his glare aimed her way.

"What?" she said. "It's been a year, Anton. I know it's not something you forget, but I'd like to think it's something you'll eventually move on from."

"As fun as this conversation is," he said, smiling tightly, "think we could drop it and move on to topics that don't involve death and fiancées?"

India huffed, apparently not ready to *drop* it just yet. Whether it was sympathy or empathy or some combination of the two, I spoke up.

"Anyone seen any good movies lately?" I asked, trying to sound casual. "I haven't seen one in forever and I have no clue what's playing. I'm thinking of taking Jude to one when he's in town."

"So much for not talking about fiancés . . ."

"So help me God, India," I seethed. "I will put you in time-out and leave you there all night if you don't take it down a notch. Or three."

"I'll let you borrow my spot if you want," LJ piped up, pointing to the stool in the corner he'd spent some hard time sitting in.

"Give me some love," India said, extending her fist at LJ. "You're like my brother in crime."

LJ bumped her fist with one of his own, and then India went back to her dinner, looking like she was planning on staying silent for a while.

Figured. I should have known to put India next to the three-year-old if I wanted her to behave.

"I've been hearing great things about this new spy movie set in the forties," Thomas said, clearing the air. I went to the fridge to grab him a fresh beer as thanks.

"Ooh, yeah," Holly said, pointing her fork at Thomas. "The previews for that movie looked killer."

"You guys should go next Friday after dinner," I said, handing the beer off to Thomas. "I could tuck LJ in and you two could go get a drink first and catch the late show."

Holly was looking at me like I had three heads. Thomas, however, tilted his beer at me. "That sounds great. What do you think, Holly? You up for it?"

Holly's curious stare shifted to Thomas. "Sure, but do you really want to make the drive again next week?" she said finally. "Are you sure you want to go with me? Isn't there someone else you'd rather—"

"I'm sure," Thomas interrupted.

Hello, Mr. Obvious.

"Okay, then," Holly said. "It's a date."

Thomas swallowed. "It's . . . yeah."

I smiled into my lap. These two were both so hot for each other, I was dying for one of them to cave and just admit it already. I wasn't sure who would be the first to do it, but I hoped it would be soon.

After that, dinner was fine. No more awkward moments, followed by even more awkward silences. An hour later, nothing was left of dinner other than a few chip pieces. India and Holly had called mercy and unbuttoned their jeans a half hour earlier, but I—the one in elastic-band box-ers—was good to go.

Anton took dish duty while Thomas cleared the table. LJ and the girls piled a stack of blankets and pillows on the liv-ing room floor before making the world's coolest fort with every last sheet I had in the place.

"I've got to take a picture of this," Anton said, rolling his sleeves back down as he wandered from the kitchen.

"No pictures!" LJ said, crawling out from beneath it. "This is top-secret."

"Good point," Anton replied, pocketing his phone. "This gets out to the public, every little boy's going to have one of these."

Fiddling with the controls, I managed to get the DVD player to cooperate.

"What are we watching?" Thomas asked, crawling inside

and throwing himself down close to Holly.

Coincidence? I think not.

"*Ice Age!*" LJ replied, plopping down right in between Holly and Thomas.

India had already claimed her spot and was two Jell-O shots deep when I crawled in beside her.

When Anton stuck his head inside, I got all self-conscious again. Of course his eyes landed right on me, and a smile crept into position when he saw I was also looking at him.

"Room for one more?"

I was about to say no when LJ hushed him.

"The movie's starting," he said. "No talking unless you want to wind up in the time-out corner."

"India," I whispered, shaking her. She was almost asleep. "Indie. Trade spots."

No response.

India was sandwiched between me and Thomas, who had LJ and Holly on his other side, which left the space beside me empty.

Although it didn't stay empty for long.

"This spot taken?" Anton whispered, crawling beside me.

"Would you believe me if I said yes?"

"Okay. Now you're just hurting my feelings," he said, punching a couple of pillows into position.

"I didn't think you had any."

He chuckled. "Would you let me know once you're ready to move past this afternoon? You know, just so I'm not holding my breath."

My mood was lightening up, and I wasn't sure how I felt about that. "You start holding your breath now, and I'll say 'when' once I'm ready to forgive you."

"If I did that, I'm afraid I'd be dead before you'd even considered it," he whispered.

Apparently, even whispering wasn't allowed. LJ sat up and shushed us. "Aunt Luce," he said in that warning voice I'd used with him a half dozen times a day.

I mouthed, "Sorry," before zipping my mouth closed and throwing away the key. That seemed to satisfy LJ.

"Whose phone is that?" Holly said, looking down the row of bodies.

"Mom," LJ whined before hopping up and pushing pause on the DVD player. As he scampered toward the bathroom, I checked my pockets for mine. Hold up, I didn't have pockets. In fact, I hadn't seen my phone in a couple hours, since I'd changed in the bathroom. It was late, so that meant it was a certain someone making his nightly call.

A Face Time call . . .

I muttered a curse right before LJ rounded the corner, phone in hand.

"Hey, Uncle Jude," he greeted with a wave.

I cursed again, when what I should have been doing was leaping up and getting as far away from Anton as the apartment would allow.

I didn't hear what Jude said, but I could guess from LJ's reply. "Yeah. She's right here." Flipping the phone around, LJ came toward me and handed it off.

Jude's face went from light to dark in the time it took his eyes to move from me to the space next to me.

"Luce," he said, the muscles of his jaw working. "Who the hell is that?"

"Jude," I said, feeling my temper fire to life. "Nice to see you, too."

Holly jumped up and stopped LJ from unpausing the movie. "Let's get your pajamas on, LJ," she said, steering him down the hall. One thing Holly had learned about Jude over the years: When he was pissed, he wouldn't take the time to spell out select words that weren't meant for little ears. Thomas rushed after them.

"It would be nice to see you, too, if you weren't horizontal next to another guy." Jude's glare didn't leave Anton once, like he was hoping he'd combust if he stared long enough.

"Let me guess who this chump is . . ." he said. "The man whose gravestone is about to read, 'Anton Xavier.'"

I knew I should be embarrassed that my fiancé was acting like this. I knew I should be mortified. But I was too angry for that.

"And you must be the very noncontrolling Jude Ryder," Anton replied, sitting up on his elbows.

If there was a silver lining to this testosterone showdown, it was that the jabs wouldn't leave bruises.

"Anton," Jude said, sitting up straighter. "You're shorter than I pictured you."

Kill me. Kill me right now. Why wasn't I hitting that end button? Why hadn't I hit it the instant LJ handed that sucker over to me?

Because I was an idiot, that's why.

I hopped up and headed for the kitchen, hoping Anton would stay where he was so I could start with the damage control. Of course Anton shot up and was only two steps behind me when I stopped in the kitchen.

"Jude," Anton said, moving in front of the screen. "Your head's smaller than I thought it would be."

"Cute. Real cute." The veins in Jude's neck looked ready to burst. "I hope you're gutsy enough to say something like that to me in person."

"I'm gutsy enough."

Jude grinned a tad manically for my liking. "Something to look forward to."

I was starting to wonder if their next display of manhood would include whipping their dicks out and comparing size. I elbowed Anton, hoping he'd take a clue. Not happening.

"You planning on being at Friday-night dinner two weeks from now?" Jude asked.

"If I'm invited."

"You're not," I said instantly.

"Yes, he is," Jude said, that joker smile turning up a notch. "That is, if you're gutsy enough."

"I'll be here." Anton did what I guessed to be a Face Time stare-down with Jude.

"No, you won't. You're not invited," I said.

"I invited him, Luce."

I moved the phone closer, until my face took up the entire screen. "And I just uninvited him."

"Sorry, Luce. But that apartment's just as much mine as it is yours. And I invited him."

I was losing my grip. My fiancé and my boss were fighting over me like I was some shiny trophy. This was the last straw.

"Fine. You want to invite Anton? Invite Anton," I seethed, as my hands began trembling. "You boys have fun, because I sure as shit won't be here." Jude's forehead lined as his eyes finally softened when they took me in. "Now, if you boys are done cockfighting, you're going to leave right now," I ordered, pointing Anton in the direction of the door. "And I'm hanging up on you," I said, narrowing my eyes at Jude.

"Luce," he began, but I was true to my word. Before Jude could get another word out, I did what I should have done three minutes ago.

I punched end.

"Lucy, I'm sorry," Anton said.

"Get out," I said, pointing toward the door. "Just get out. I've had enough for one day."

Anton looked like he wanted to say more, but for once he kept quiet. After letting out a long sigh, he headed for the door and didn't look back.

FIFTEEN

*J*ude's calls started coming in thirty seconds later. I didn't answer them. I wasn't ready.

India had snoozed through the whole Face Time call from hell, and Holly, Thomas, and LJ had stayed hidden in the bedroom until the coast was clear. When it was, Thomas came back into the living room, wrapped me up in his arms, and didn't let go until I'd almost fallen asleep.

He carried me to my bed and tucked me in before crawling back into the ginormous fort and falling asleep himself.

It was a little past midnight, and I was stuck in that place between sleep and awake, when I finally answered Jude's call. It wasn't an exaggeration to guess he'd called at least fifty times.

"Hey, Mr. Persistent," I said in a sleepy voice.

"Luce." He sighed. I could feel his relief in that one word.

"You were out of line tonight, Ryder," I said, reminding myself to stay calm.

"I know," he replied, his voice all low and rough, like he hadn't said a word in days. "But so were you, Luce."

"Huh?" I sat up in bed. "I wasn't the one verbally threatening to kill a man."

"No. No, you weren't. But you were the one cuddled up to him and practically sharing a pillow."

"Yeah, Anton was next to me. So was India. And Thomas. And Holly. And LJ, too. We were all camped out on the floor watching *Ice Age* in a kick-ass fort." With all the FaceTime calls Jude and I had been doing, it felt strange just talking to him. I couldn't read the expressions on his face; I could only guess how he felt from his voice.

"That man is into you, Luce. I know you don't believe me, and I know you want to believe he's just a friend, but friendship is the farthest thing from his mind when it comes to you." His voice was so controlled, so restrained. I was proud of him . . . still irritated, but proud.

"We weren't even close enough to touch elbows, Jude."

"But that doesn't change the fact that he wanted to touch you and easily could have, since you were lying right next to him."

With everything that had happened tonight, I'd pushed aside the bomb Anton dropped after work. I'd planned on telling Jude, because that wasn't something I thought I should keep from him, but now, after Jude was already pissed to the moon and back, he'd surely charter a plane and fly across the country tonight just so he could kick Anton's ass in person. Was it a lie if I omitted it for maybe a week?

From the guilt that trickled into my veins, I guessed it was.

"Now, Luce. I'm sorry for the way I lost it tonight. That's on me," he said, interrupting my thoughts. "But I need you to keep your distance from Anton. I know you want to believe the best in everyone, but not everyone has the best intentions, Luce."

"How do you expect me to keep my distance? He's my boss. I file his paperwork and submit his expense reports and make PowerPoint presentations for him Monday through Friday." After taking a few hours to cool off, I realized I'd been a tad rash in wanting to quit. I had a job, a good, paying one, and I didn't want to pack up my cardboard box all because my boss had admitted he was attracted to me. Anton certainly wouldn't have been the first boss to hit on his secretary.

"Remind me again why you're so insistent on having your own job?"

I sighed my answer.

"Okay, okay. So you can't physically keep your distance

from him, but keep your emotional distance from him. That's all I'm saying, Luce," he said, sounding more tired than anything else. That was the same way I felt. "And no more lying next to him with a bunch of blankets and shit, dressed in nothing but a tiny tank top and my underwear. Okay?"

"Are you asking or telling?"

"Do you really need to ask, Luce?"

"After the whole *thing* tonight . . ." I said, trying not to replay it in my head. "Yeah, I need to ask."

"Asking. I'm always asking, Luce," he said. "Sometimes I just ask with a little extra enthusiasm."

I heard an almost-smile in his voice and could feel my own starting to bloom. "Sometimes? More like all the time."

He gave his low laugh. "Yeah, you're right. But the only reason I'm asking with enthusiasm is because I care about you, Luce. I care about you more than I've ever cared about anything else. I'd do anything, sacrifice anything, and say anything to protect you."

"I wouldn't put Anton Xavier high on the list of what I need protecting from," I replied.

"I would," he answered instantly. "And if you're having a tough time understanding where I'm coming from, just put yourself in my shoes. What would you do if you found out I was working for some rich, fine chick who would do anything to get me into bed, and then you called one night to say good night and found me cozied up next to her?" He paused, probably more to drive the point home than to catch his breath. "Would your reaction be so different from mine?"

I wanted to snap back with, *Of course it would*, or, *Hell yes*, but I didn't. Because I knew he was right. Jude had made me understand his point of view, and that was a feat worthy of the Nobel Peace Prize.

"No, it wouldn't," I admitted reluctantly. "I'd claw that bitch's eyes out through the phone if I needed to."

Jude was laughing in earnest now. Hearing him laugh made me chuckle, too. "So we understand each other, Luce."

"Always," I said, yawning around my laughter. "Sometimes it just takes us a while to get there."

"Sometimes?" he said. "How about all the time?"

I lay back down and burrowed into my pillow. "Thanks for calling fifty times and apologizing."

"Thanks for answering on the fiftieth call and accepting."

The moment after we hung up, I was free of the rest/ awake limbo land. I didn't wake up once until my little-man alarm clock was bouncing on my bed, bearing pancakes in the shape of footballs.

It was Friday night again. Our weekly dinners with our thrown-together family already felt like a time-honored tradition. Last week we'd made manicotti and garlic bread, and this week we were making our special guest's favorite meal: cheeseburgers and fries.

Jude had flown in earlier this afternoon, and even though I fought tooth and nail to get the day off so I could pick him up at the airport, Anton had had a big day full of meetings and conference calls, and said that if ever he needed an admin, today was the day. So I'd been stuck at the office when Jude had landed. I knew he was probably already at our apartment, just waiting.

This afternoon had been a torturous practice in patience.

I was watching my computer screen like a hawk, so when it changed over to five p.m., I was out of my seat and halfway to the door before anyone else had powered down their computers over in cubicle city. Anton had gone to an off-site meeting an hour ago, so I didn't have to check with him to see if he had any last-minute tasks for me before I left.

Once I was inside the Mazda, I fought every instinct to NASCAR my way back to the apartment. I forced myself to follow the speed limit, and I even made myself pull over at the mall to make a quick purchase.

My watching LJ evenings and weekends was working out better than any of us could have imagined. He listened to me as much as a minicaveman could, he helped me with chores around the apartment, and I could even take him out in public without having to worry about leaving behind a trail of chaos.

However, the store I was heading to now wasn't one I wanted to take a little boy into. It didn't take me long to pick out what I thought Jude would like best, since he wasn't hard to please when it came to lingerie. I paid for it, and was back to the Mazda in less than ten minutes.

Once I was in my parking spot, I checked the mirror. Applying a coat of lipstick and adding a touch of bronzer, I was good as good could be right now. I'd worn my new cobalt skirt and a sleeveless wrap blouse, paired with a patent-leather pair of red heels that were sure to drive Jude a little wild. These were his favorite shoes of mine, although he preferred it when I wore them with nothing.

I was hoping that was exactly what he had planned for tonight. Logistics-wise, we were going to have to get creative, but you know what they say: Necessity is the mother of invention.

I jogged up the stairs as fast as I dared in these four-inchers, and continued the trek down the hall. As had become the norm, I could hear laughter as I approached the apartment, but for the first time in weeks, my Jude's was thrown into the mix. My heart hurt hearing him without the filter of a phone. His voice, his *laugh*, was meant to be experienced filter-free.

I threw the door open and burst inside. The room went silent following my dramatic entrance. I didn't notice anyone else; I couldn't have even told you who was there and where they were standing. All I saw was him.

And all he saw was me.

I barely had time to drop my bags before he made it across the room. His arms wound around me and he pulled me hard against him.

I was home.

"Luce," he breathed, weaving his fingers into my hair.

I wrapped my arms around his neck and dropped my face into the curve of his neck. I inhaled his scent. I inhaled him. "I missed you, too."

"I missed you more."

"Oh, yeah?"

His mouth dropped to my ear. "Yeah."

"Prove it," I said, pressing my lips into his neck.

Leaning back, he cupped my face in his hand, holding it steady while his mouth lowered over mine. He kissed me gently, almost tenderly. It was sweet and soft, and the kind of kiss that could have melted me into a pile of mush if he hadn't been holding me so strongly.

His lips moved mine apart before his tongue entered my mouth. When it touched mine, gliding and exploring with the excitement of a first touch and the familiarity of a last touch, a slow moan escaped out of me. My hands left his neck, roaming the rest of his body like they couldn't get to the next place fast enough. His hands followed my lead, up, down, around and around. Gliding, squeezing, digging. It was enough to make my head spin.

When my teeth grazed the tip of his tongue, the breath caught in his lungs, before he shoved me back up against the wall. His body pressed against the front of me was as hard as the wall against my back. He was hard in all the right places. All the places that made heat surge into the center of my body.

"Okay, this is family dinner and movie night." Holly's voice entered the world Jude and I created whenever we were together. "Not swingers night at the seedy theater that has a back entrance."

I groaned in protest when Jude's mouth left mine, but his hands didn't. They stayed on the curve of my hips in such a way that I could still feel that desire between my legs growing.

"How was that for proving it?" he said, his chest rising and falling hard.

"I'll let you know later tonight," I said. "After everyone is tucked in my bedroom and you tuck me in." I arched a brow in suggestion.

His Adam's apple bobbed. "Do you think it would be

rude if we told everyone it was time to get lost?"

I laughed and grabbed his hand in mine. "Maybe just a little." Towing him behind me, I made the rounds.

Holly was standing behind LJ with her hands covering his eyes. "Are you two done?" she said with a wink.

"No promises," Jude answered.

"Yes," I said, elbowing him. "For now, at least."

"Flippin' rabbits," she muttered with an eye roll before uncovering LJ's eyes.

LJ had on a Chargers jersey that was a couple sizes too big, and his tongue was blue from licking the lollipop in his hand that was as big as his face. If he was hoping this little guy would be tucked in and asleep before midnight, Uncle Jude shouldn't have loaded him up with a thousand grams of sugar a couple of hours before bedtime.

"Why are Aunt Luce and Uncle Jude flippin' rabbits?"

My eyes bulged as Jude tried to muffle his laugher behind me. It wasn't working out so well.

Holly froze on her way into the kitchen. "Because they like to be . . . petted." Holly shook her head. Seeing her like this, tongue-tied, was a rarer occurrence than a solar eclipse. "Because they like to . . . hu—"

"Because they're cute and fluffy," Thomas interrupted.

LJ's eyebrows came together for one second before he got to work on his lollipop. "Oh, okay." Running over to his toy box, he started rummaging through it. Crisis averted.

Holly thanked Thomas with a smile.

"Good save, Thomas," I said, grabbing a beer from the fridge for Jude. Angling it against the counter, I drove my palm down on it. The cap popped off, tinkling when it hit the floor.

"Damn," Jude said, when I handed him the beer. "You know how turned on I get when you do that."

"Oh, God, you two. Really?" Holly groaned, sounding more jealous than irritated. Grabbing something off the floor, she marched toward Jude and me. Holding up LJ's Spider-Man bouncy ball, she stared us both down. "You know how back in the day they used to put balloons between boys and girls at school dances to make sure they kept their distance?"

I gave her a *really?* look. "You're not ramming that thing against my boobs."

"You're right, I'm not." She gave me a sweet smile before jamming the ball in between Jude and me. South of our belly buttons. "There, now the rest of us can actually eat tonight, since you won't be able to grind up on each other every two seconds."

Jude looked down at the ball between us and burst into laughter. "Man, Luce. You been telling on me again?" he said, flexing his hips against the ball, successfully shoving me against the fridge. "You know I like it kinky, but even for me, this might be a stretch."

I sighed. "I'm sure it wouldn't stop you."

"No," he said, tilting his beer at me. "No, it wouldn't."

"Mom?!" LJ shouted from the toy box. "What's kinky?"

Jude's face froze in surprise. Holly gave him a shove before clearing her throat.

"It's when a chain gets tangled up," Thomas said, all matter-of-fact.

"Oh," LJ replied, before going back to unloading the entire contents of the toy box.

"Nice save, my man," Jude said, lifting his chin at Thomas.

Thomas shook his head as he continued to stack cheeseburgers onto a serving tray. "So today I'm 'your man,' but not too long ago I was Peter Pan. What earned me the upgrade?"

"First off, I called you Peter Pan because I'm a jealous dick who'd just found you undressing my girl," Jude explained. "And you're 'my man' because you've been looking after the three most important people in my life."

Thomas fought his smile. "What do you know? The dumb jock is deep."

"Yeah, yeah," Jude said, taking a drink of his beer. "I've heard enough dumb-jock jokes to last an eternity."

"And I've heard enough Peter Pan jokes to last two," Thomas tossed back, before heading to the table with a tray holding more cheeseburgers than we could eat in a week.

Jude took another drink before examining the bottle. "PBR?" he said, looking impressed. "Luce, you know how to treat me right."

I wrapped an arm around him because, after three weeks of being apart, I didn't want to be apart anymore. "Nothing but the best for my man."

"Come on. Let's eat," he said, ringing an arm around my neck. "I'm starving."

"Me, too," I said, lowering my voice, since young ears and sexual innuendos shouldn't go together. "But not for food."

Jude stopped in place. His mouth lowered just outside my ear. "You keep up that kind of talk and I will throw you down and do you on this table, too."

Goose bumps were already rising, but when his teeth grazed my earlobe, those goose bumps exploded to the surface even quicker.

Fine. Two could play at this foreplay game. I had to rise up on my tiptoes to settle my mouth at his ear. "I'm so ready for you my panties would be wet . . ." I said, going one step further and sucking the tip of his earlobe between my teeth, "if I was wearing any."

His breath hitched between his teeth.

Flashing him an innocent smile, I continued to the table. Just as I was sitting down, he came up behind me. "Thanks to you and that filthy mouth, I've got to take a little time-out in the bathroom."

"What?" I said, spinning in my seat. "We're just about to eat dinner. A cold shower can wait."

I chalked up a point for Lucy Larson. She'd won this round of verbal foreplay.

"My dick's so hard a cold shower wouldn't even touch it. And I'm not going to sit through dinner with a hard-on tenting my jeans," he said into my ear. "I'm going to go rub one out. I'll be right back."

Speaking of wet panties . . .

"I'll help," I said, jumping out of my chair.

He grabbed my hand and pulled me along. "Good. Your hands are softer than mine."

We'd just about made it to the bathroom, so close I was already reaching for the top button of Jude's jeans, when a solo knock sounded outside the front door.

A solo knock followed by three fast ones.

I wanted to cry from the letdown. If we'd been two seconds faster, we already would have been behind that closed door and my hand would have been sliding up and down—

"Lookie here. We've got a welcoming committee," India

said after swinging the door open.

With Anton at her side.

"Shit."

Did that just slip out of my mouth?

"'Hello. Nice to see you. Good of you to make it,'" India said, stepping inside. "These are a few commonly accepted greetings when welcoming someone to your place." Smirking at me, she gave Jude a quick hug. "It sure is nice to have my arms around your sexy-ass body again. Any idea why we had to shove through a mini army of paparazzi camped out on the sidewalk?"

"Hey, Indie," Jude said, his eyes locked on Anton. "I hope you kicked each one of those bloodsuckers in the junk on your way up."

I sighed. I must have been too absorbed and focused on getting up to the apartment to notice that the small crowd of people outside our apartment had cameras around their necks. It seemed wherever Jude Ryder went, so did the photographers. Looked like we wouldn't be leaving the apartment all weekend, which, actually . . . wasn't such a bad deal.

"I hope you are hooking up my girl tonight, because she needs some sweet, sweet lovin'," India said, patting his cheek before heading down the hall. "It's been a while since I've seen Lucy's cute little freshly F-U-C-K-E-D face."

"Don't worry," Jude answered her, continuing his stare-down with Anton, who didn't look the least bit threatened. "I plan on taking care of my girl. All. Night. Long."

I flushed so hard I could feel it bleeding into my neck. "Hi, Anton. Nice to see you," I said, wrapping both hands around Jude's arm. "Even for you, this is one hell of a ballsy move."

"Lucy," he replied with an amused smile.

I shot him a tight smile before tugging on Jude's arm. Yeah, that wasn't happening. "Now, if you're done talking about our sex life with my boss . . ." I pulled again, harder this time. Nope. One of the downsides to being with a man who could bench a school bus was feeling like the biggest wimp in the world. "I've got a half dozen cheeseburgers with your name on them."

Jude squared himself in front of Anton, not taking the cheeseburger bait. "You must be Anton."

How could he make a few harmless words sound like a death threat?

Anton looked pointedly at Jude's arm draped over me. "And you must be Jude."

"In the flesh," he said. "No more phones keeping us apart if you try to cuddle up to my girl again."

"Jude," I warned for quite possibly the millionth time in my life.

"Okay. How do we do this?" Anton said, sliding his hands into his slacks. "I haven't been in a fight over a girl since fifth grade. Do we take it outside? Throw down right here in the doorway? Schedule an appointment? I'm in uncharted territory here."

I would have laughed had the whole situation been so not funny. Where was everyone else when I needed them to help me separate these two? A peek over my shoulder revealed my answer.

"Oblivious" was the name of the game back in the kitchen.

"Let's get one thing straight right now. We are not fighting for a girl. Luce is *my* girl. She will *always* be my girl." The veins were starting to bulge in Jude's neck. We were two stages away from fists flying. "What we're fighting over is the way you look at my girl. The way I know you think about her. The way I know you want to have her. That's what we're fighting over." Jude straightened his back to stand a little taller. He had a way of making his three-inch advantage seem like he was towering over Anton. "But let's be honest. Since you and I both know you don't stand a chance in a fight against me, why don't we just pretend I've just kicked your ass into next year and you stop trying to weasel your way into Luce's better judgment, heart, or pants. Got it?"

"I've never been one to take the easy road," Anton replied, as calm as if he were conducting a business meeting. "And I don't like being told what to do, so I'm afraid that's a no-go, big guy."

"Anton," I hissed, wondering if he had a death wish. From what he was saying, I would guess he did.

"So how are we going to do this?" Anton repeated, taking a step forward. I'd underestimated Anton. I'd figured him for more the pacifist, antiwar kind of guy. I couldn't have been more wrong. He wouldn't back down from a fight any sooner than Jude would. Anton just wore a suit to the battle.

"I'm gonna kick your ass," Jude replied, taking his own step forward.

Yep. They were going to do this. Right here in the doorway.

"Dinner's ready!" Holly shouted. "If you don't want me tossing yours out the window you'd better have your butts in your seats in three."

When the end of time was upon us, Holly Reed was here to save us.

"Later, then," Anton said, shouldering past Jude.

"Looking forward to it," Jude said, glaring holes into Anton's back.

"Real mature," I said, nudging him.

"I thought you said that guy didn't have a thing for you, Luce."

I still hadn't told Jude what Anton had said to me that afternoon a few weeks ago in the office. No time seemed to be right for unloading that dirty little secret. Least of all now.

"What's your point?"

"That douche has a serious thing for you. A *serious* thing."

I rubbed his arm, trying to soothe him. "How do you know that?" I asked, pretending I wasn't sure if he was right.

"Because when he looks at you, it reminds me of the way I looked at you when we first met."

"And how was that?"

Jude grabbed my hand in his and led me to the table. He sighed. "Like it was all over. Like the girl I was looking at was the one I was going to spend my life with."

"And you don't look at me that way anymore?" I teased.

"I still do, but there's a confidence behind that look now. A confidence because I know you're mine." Jude pulled my chair out for me and moved his mouth closer to my ear. "That guy looks at you with the uncertainty I did at first. When I wasn't sure I could ever have you," he said quietly. "That guy wants you, all right, but I'm going to make damn sure he knows that he will never have you."

"Hey, Tarzan," I said as he took his seat next to me.

"Tone it down a notch or ten."

He slid me a smile. "You know that's not my style, Luce."

"Then why don't you take a cheeseburger and stuff it in your mouth before you start throwing around any more ass-kicking threats at my boss." I motioned at the tray of burgers Holly was holding out for Jude.

"So, Lucy," Anton said from the other end of the table—positioned so he and Jude could pick up right where they'd left off in their staring contest. "I haven't had a chance to talk with you about this yet, but I was wondering if you'd be able to stay on in the fall once school starts."

Oh, boy.

"Lucy's going to be busy—"

I raised my hand, cutting Jude off. "I can answer for myself, thank you very much."

Jude raised his hand in surrender, clearly amused.

"I'm going to be busy"—I shot Jude a look—"with school. I really piled on the coursework my senior year, and then I'll be going back and forth to San Diego to see Jude a bunch, too."

Jude's hand fell on my knee. "Not as much as I'll be coming back and forth here to see you."

"I could work around your schedule," Anton said as everyone else chewed their dinner in silence. Even LJ knew something was going on. "In just three weeks' time, you've proven to be quite the asset at Xavier Industries. I can't just let you go."

Jude squeezed my knee, more out of irritation than in reassurance.

"I'll double your salary," Anton announced before taking a big bite of his cheeseburger.

Jude opened his mouth, but I wasn't going to let this go any farther without adding my two cents.

"It's not about the money," I said.

Anton arched an eyebrow.

"Well, it's not totally about the money. I just won't have the time. I want to commit to the things in my life that are more important than money," I said, grabbing the ketchup bottle and squirting a glob onto my plate. "Besides, Jude's making boatloads of money. I'm sure he can lend me a few bucks if I need it."

I peered over at Jude. This was a source of discomfort for me, a matter of pride, and admitting to a table of my closest friends that I'd be willing to lean on Jude for financial support made me feel very . . . vulnerable. In the I'm-naked-where's-the-nearest-palm-leaf kind of way.

But taking one glance at Jude's face eased the way I was feeling. He didn't just look happy; he looked relieved. Like

I'd just removed a heavy weight from his shoulders. I didn't understand it, but I didn't need to in order to be glad I made him feel that way.

"I thought you liked making your own money. Being independent. Multimillion-dollar fiancé or not." Okay, Anton didn't just have a death wish courtesy of Jude. He had a death wish compliments of Lucy Larson.

This time it was my hand that moved to Jude's leg, giving it a squeeze.

"That's right. I do like making my own money," I said, wanting to dunk one of my fries in ketchup and sail it across the table at Anton's face. "But if Jude ever needed any of it, that money would be all his. And I think he feels the same way about the money he makes."

"Damn straight I do, Luce."

I loved the way he was looking at me right now, like he'd never been prouder of me. I wanted nothing more than to straddle him in that chair and kiss him until we were both blue in the face.

But I had someone else who needed to be put in his place.

"Anything else?" I said, challenging Anton with my eyes.

"I've got a whole lot of 'anything else's," he said, dropping his hamburger onto the plate. "I've got so many more 'anything else's I could go on all night. But how about I start with one word that pretty much sums it up." Anton wagged his finger between Jude and me. "Un. Healthy."

Jude bolted up from his seat. I didn't know what route he would take to get to Anton, but I wasn't ruling out his flying straight across the table.

"That's enough!" Holly scrambled out of her seat, too. "My three-year-old behaves better than all of you." She looked down at LJ, who was trying to stuff a fry up his nostril. "And that's not saying a whole lot."

She looked at Anton. "Behave." Then turned those crazy eyes on Jude. "Behave." And then me. "Behave." Taking a seat, she pulled the fry from LJ's nose. "What's Mom always telling you about using kind words, baby?"

LJ sat up in his seat, quite pleased to be included in this conversation. "If you can't say anything nice, don't say anything at all."

Holly mussed the top of his head. "Any questions?" she asked the table.

Nada.

Other than a few more death glares aimed at each other, Jude and Anton didn't say another word to each other over dinner, although it wasn't exactly a quiet dining experience. Between LJ and India and Holly trying to talk over each other while Thomas tried and failed to add in his two cents, my ears were ringing by the time Jude started on his third cheeseburger.

"Where are you putting all of that?" I asked, done in at half of one of those burgers.

He shrugged as he chewed off a tennis ball–size bite. "I have a feeling I'm going to need my energy for tonight."

Ah. There was that flirty foreplay I'd missed. "Good feeling."

He grinned at me as he continued to chew. I still hadn't adjusted to it: Jude being über-rich. He had close to no table manners, lived in Levi's and a white Hanes undershirt, and thought the Hamptons was a seventies rock band. You never could have known by looking at him that he was a millionaire.

And I loved that about him.

I hoped he'd still be sporting Hanes and Levi's in ten years.

"So how was that movie you guys went to last Friday?" India asked, waving a fry at Thomas and Holly.

"It was all right," Thomas said.

Holly couldn't have looked more offended.

"But the company was phenomenal," he clarified, giving her a wink.

"That's what I thought," she said.

"Did you guys make out or do anything freaky after?"

Holly choked on her burger. Thomas went red, a rare shade of scarlet, thanks to his fair skin.

"India," I said, "could you be any more awkward?"

"Is that a rhetorical question?" she asked, while Jude thumped Holly's back.

"Yeah. I suppose it is."

India blew me a kiss before returning to the grand inquisition. "Well? Spill," she said, looking between Holly and Thomas. "You two have so much pent-up S-E-X-U-A-L tension for one another I've almost passed out from lack of oxygen."

"God, India," I said, tossing a fry at her. She dodged it, so it flew into Anton's chest.

I smiled. Even better.

"No," Holly said, covering LJ's ears. "We didn't kiss or do anything else of a freaky or kinky nature, since you just have to know."

Jude covered his mouth, but it wasn't keeping his laughter contained.

"And just for future reference, we won't ever be kissing," she added.

Thomas's head whipped to the side. "What?" he said to Holly. "Why not?" So much for playing the cool guy.

The skin between Holly's brows creased. "Because I'm a girl," she said slowly, like she was confused, "and you like boys."

Thomas's and my mouth fell open at the same moment.

Maybe I should have been more direct with Holly about Thomas's attraction to her, but I thought it'd been obvious. I hadn't realized she still thought he was gay after the first night we all had dinner.

Judging from the hurt look on Thomas's face, I didn't think he'd ever be the same after this blow.

"You think I'm . . . I'm . . . *gay*?" Damn. He couldn't have sounded more insulted either.

Holly's shoulders slumped as her hands fell away from LJ's ears. "Aren't you?"

"I've got the little man," Jude said, standing and grabbing LJ. He tossed him over his shoulder, much to LJ's delight. "You want me to teach you how to throw a football ten thousand yards now?"

"Yay!" LJ replied, giggling as Jude walked him down the hall before disappearing into the bedroom.

That man was getting laid so good tonight.

"So wait." Holly shook her head. "You're not gay? You like women?" This was clearly rocking her worldview.

"What? No!" Thomas twisted in his seat.

"No, you're not gay, or no, you don't like women?" Holly asked.

"No, I'm not gay!" This was the first time I'd heard Thomas raise his voice. I suppose if there ever was a time for a guy to lose his cool, it was when the girl he had it bad for thought he was gay the entire time.

"Whoa." Holly gave her head another shake. "This revelation is . . . profound."

"Unbelievable. My whole life people have assumed I was gay because I was a dancer. People judged me because I slipped into a different kind of spandex than the other guys in the locker room." Thomas shoved his seat back, stood up, and headed for the door. "I didn't think you were one of those people, too, Holly."

"Thomas," Holly called after him. "Wait."

"I don't think so," he said, continuing to storm for the door. "I'm going to find some boys to kiss." When he slammed the door, it shook the walls.

"He's not gay?" she said, more to herself than anything else. "Did you know?"

"He's been my dance partner for three years," I replied, staring at the door. "Of course I knew he wasn't."

"Why didn't you tell me?"

"Because I thought you figured it out after the first night you met him," I said, hating the way Holly was looking at me—like I'd betrayed her.

"I did think that, until we went on our date last Friday," she said. "Until he kept bringing up this guy Samuel. He was talking about him making breakfast that morning, and how he always leaves his wet towels on the floor, and . . ."

Holly's face blanched. "Oh, my God, Samuel is Thomas's roommate, isn't he?"

I clucked my tongue. "Bingo."

"Shit," she said, slamming her fist down on the table.

"Do you like him, Hol?" I asked, feeling like I already knew the answer.

She bit her lip and nodded.

"A lot?"

Another nod.

"Then what are you still doing here?" I said. "Go after him."

"Please, Lucy. Even if he did like me before I called him gay, he's never going to say another word to me."

"There's only one way to find out," India piped up. I was surprised it had taken her this long to give her two cents. She usually wanted in right away. Beside her, Anton was staying quiet for once in his life.

"You think I've got a chance in hell that he's still going to like me after what I just said?" Holly's arms were flailing about—a sure sign she was about to lose it.

India propped her chin on her fist and gave Holly a once-over. "Girl. I think that man would still like you if you told him to go get bent every time you saw him. He's got it bad for you. Bad squared."

"Lucy?" Holly said, her eyes shifting from me to the door.

"He definitely likes you. And I think you definitely like him, too," I said. "So why don't you go after him and definitely like each other."

The corners of Holly's mouth twitched. "Anyone have some lip gloss handy?"

India slid a tube out from her back pocket. "Always handy," she said, tossing it to Holly, who managed to catch it despite being in the middle of that hair-flipping/hair-teasing thing she loved to do. Slicking on a coat of gloss, Holly headed for the door like a woman on a mission.

"Good luck," I called after her.

After the door slammed closed for a grand total of twice in the past two minutes, Jude and LJ reemerged from the bedroom, football in hand.

"Uncle Jude taught me how to hold the football like he does," he announced, skipping to the table.

"Everything all right?" Jude asked, coming up behind me and rubbing my shoulders.

"I hope so," I said, feeling like my eyes were about to roll into the back of my head from the magic his fingers were working on my muscles.

"Movie time!" LJ said, rummaging through the DVD

collection. "Can I be in between you and Aunt Luce in the fort?"

Jude's eyes locked on Anton, and they narrowed. "You are the only man I'll let come between Aunt Luce and me."

So much for the drama being behind us.

SIXTEEN

*H*olly and LJ were in their bedroom—presumably asleep, since I hadn't heard a peep from there in the last ten minutes. India was racked out on the couch, hopefully in a drunken stupor where the trumpets of the second coming could have blasted and she wouldn't have stirred. Poor Thomas had the floor, but I'd layered a few blankets for padding so he wouldn't wake up with *too* much of a stiff back.

After reappearing thirty minutes later, Holly's hand in his, both of their faces flushed and their lips swollen, Thomas and Holly cuddled up beside each other inside the fort and hadn't spoken another word. Whatever was said or done had been effective.

Thankfully, Anton had taken the hint that he wasn't welcome for our Friday-night sleepover and had gracefully bowed out, saying he had an early morning racquetball match scheduled.

You can imagine the fun Jude had with that little tidbit of information.

The apartment was, at last, quiet.

Locking myself inside the bathroom with my purchase from earlier, I brushed my teeth. Twice. I rubbed in a little satsuma lotion and ran a brush through my hair. I inspected myself in the mirror. Pretty damn hot. After three weeks of celibacy, Jude was going to bust something when he saw me in my little number. Hell, after three weeks of celibacy I was about to bust something just thinking about what was waiting for me behind a pair of room dividers.

I took another look in the full-length mirror on the back of the bathroom door. Something was missing, but I couldn't figure out what. My bra was a sheer pale pink material. So sheer you could see my nipples through the fabric. My panties were the same color, but made of lace, and even had garters that were fitted to a pair of sheer black nylons that had seams running up the back. Black patent-leather heels finished the outfit. If you could call this an "outfit."

Everything from the neck down was spot-on; it was from the neck up that I needed something. Something that was as sweet-meets-sexy as the rest of my getup was.

The lightbulb went off.

Pulling out the drawer that was overflowing with Holly's toiletries and hair goodies, I rummaged around until I found what I was looking for. Just as I was pulling it out, a soft knock sounded on the other side of the door.

"Luce?" Jude whispered. My body tightened in anticipation just from his voice. "You take any longer in there and I'm going to bust down the door and do you on the bathroom sink."

That image was appealing on so many levels. "It wouldn't be the first time," I whispered back. "Just go chill. I'll be out in thirty seconds."

"That's thirty seconds too long," he said back, before I heard his footsteps padding down the hall.

In even more of a hurry, I wound the wide black satin scarf around my head, tying it in the perfect bow that I slid to the side.

Innocent schoolgirl meets not-so-innocent seductress.

Smiling at myself in the mirror, I grabbed my bathrobe and put it on before cracking the door open. It was dark and quiet. Jude was a mere twenty feet away.

I didn't want to make a noise, which actually took quite a bit of focus when I had a pair of stripper heels on my feet, so that twenty feet might as well have been twenty miles. Tiptoeing the last few steps, I slithered in between the room dividers.

Jude was lounging on the mattress, stripped down to his boxers. His skin was even tanner, and against every physical law known to man, his muscles had grown. His eyes were closed, but they snapped open the moment I slipped inside the "room."

"Sorry I kept you waiting," I whispered.

"Me too," he said, tucking his arms behind his head. "My balls are so damn blue by now, they are solely responsible for creating a new shade in the blue spectrum."

I started to laugh, but caught myself. The last thing I wanted was to wake one of the four sleeping bodies in this apartment, because I could not handle a serving of delayed gratification tonight. If I had balls, I could guarantee mine would have been bluer than his.

"Let me make it up to you," I said, shrugging out of my robe. Before it had dropped to the floor, Jude's eyes had widened beyond their capacity.

"Consider yourself made up," he said, his eyes running over me.

I tried to ignore what was rising in his boxers, but I couldn't. I needed that inside me. I wanted it now.

I crawled across the mattress to him, holding myself above him to purposely drive him a little crazy. When my face was directly above his, I stopped. I smiled down at him, reveling in the power I so obviously had over him. "How's it going down there?" I said, lowering my mouth so it was just above his. So close I could taste his breath coming from his lips.

His hands grabbed my hips as his hips flexed up to meet mine. "It's going to be a lot better down there when I'm buried deep inside you."

I wasn't sure if the moan that escaped me was due to his words or the continued pressing of his hips against mine, but I'd place an equal bet on both.

Fresh out of willpower, I lowered myself onto him, letting all my weight curve against him. I felt his erection running from the bottom of my panties to the top of my belly button. I moved up and down against his body. His mouth was no longer gliding against mine; it was sucking and nipping.

When I slid up him a third time, I almost came right then. I was so ready it was dampening his boxers, but I didn't want to before he was inside me. I lifted my hips to remove the temptation of friction, and tried to catch my breath.

Tried and failed.

"That's a nice bra, Luce," Jude said, sounding about as breathless as I felt. One hand left my hip and traveled up my stomach before cupping my breast. His thumb and finger caught my nipple and gave it a gentle tug. "I wonder what your nipples taste like through it."

In one seamless move, Jude's mouth took the place of his fingers. His tongue played with my nipple before he took it into his mouth. He started out gentle, but that changed. The harder he sucked, the closer I got to coming.

Leaning back, I freed myself from his mouth. I wasn't going to come until he was moving inside me, and since it was obvious I couldn't hold off much longer, I grabbed the waistband of his boxers and pulled them down.

"What?" Jude whispered, grinning at me. "All done with the foreplay?"

How could he not be? I felt like I was ready to explode if I had to wait another minute, and here he was, casually relaxed and reclining, seemingly happy to grind and suck the night away.

"I need you inside me, Jude," I said, grabbing hold of him. That got a reaction from him. "Please."

I was just lowering my hand down him when he lifted his hips, successfully rolling me off him. I was on my back and he was hovering over me before I knew how I'd gotten there.

"Say that again," he whispered, before running his mouth down my neck.

"What?" I breathed.

"Beg me," he said, right before his teeth sank into my neck. I flinched, but more from pleasure than from pain.

"Please," I said, pressing my pelvic area against him. "Please, Jude."

His mouth stayed on my neck, gently sucking at it. His hands skimmed down my waist, continuing on past my hips and gliding around the front of my panties. That thumb of his stopped over my clit and circled it.

"Yes." I sighed, flexing against his touch. "Please, baby. Do me."

His thumb came to a stop, right before he tore the lace away. "With pleasure," he said, right before he thrust into me.

I practically screamed in relief before Jude's hand covered my mouth.

"Shhh," he whispered, his voice gravelly as he moved deeper inside me. "I'm going to make you come hard, Luce, but I need you to be quiet so we don't wake the whole house."

He slid out, and I wanted to cry.

"Can you be quiet?" he asked, waiting.

"When was the last time I was able to be quiet?" I said, trying to get him back inside. But he wasn't having it. He wasn't going to enter me again until I agreed.

"I'll be quiet," I said, as quickly as I'd ever said three words.

"Good," he said, just barely entering me, "but just in case . . ." Grabbing the satin scarf I had tied in my hair, he slid it down over my face until it was covering my mouth.

That, with the smallest amount of him inside me, almost caused me to come yet again.

His mouth found my other nipple this time, and right as he took it deep inside, his hips flexed and he thrust even deeper inside me. I almost screamed out again, but my promise fresh on my mind, along with the scarf covering my mouth, served to keep it contained. His pace picked up until he was breathing as heavily as I was. I was proud of myself that I'd managed to hold my orgasm off, but when his mouth moved from my breast to just outside my ear and he started whispering words, I started to spiral out of control.

"That's right, baby. That's right," he breathed, not only moving faster, but harder now. "I want to feel you come, Luce."

My body lost all control, and I was powerless to hold it back any longer. I felt all my muscles tighten around him as he sank inside me one last time, finding his own release. My moans started seeping around the scarf, growing so loud Jude had to cover my mouth with his hand.

Jude's body trembled over mine, while mine was shaking more violently. A sheen of sweat covered his face when he lifted it above mine. Even though he was breathing rapidly, he was still able to smile. He untied the scarf covering my mouth right before his lips took its place. The way he kissed me, with such patience and tenderness, didn't help calm my shaking body.

"Marry me," he said in the space between our mouths.

Thanks to the ecstasy I was still swimming in, this question didn't put me on edge like it normally did. "Soon," I answered him.

He ran his fingers through my hair and gave me one last kiss. "I'll take that," he said, gathering me in his arms as he got comfortable. "That's an improvement over 'someday.'"

I didn't know if *soon* meant tomorrow, or next month, or next year, but . . .

"Damn, you two. That was freakin' hot."

Jude and I tensed at the same time.

"How's a girl supposed to get to sleep after that?" India continued.

I would have been embarrassed if I wasn't still in my postsex stupor.

"Sweet dreams once you do," I replied.

Jude chuckled into the back of my neck, and, with his arms around me, I was asleep before I even knew I was falling.

SEVENTEEN

I'd blinked my eyes and when I'd next opened them, summer had passed me by.

It was the first day of class my senior year. Between working forty-plus hours a week, watching LJ another forty hours a week, taking a couple more flights to visit Jude, hosting Friday-night dinner and movie nights, and trying to squeeze in a couple precious hours of dance every morning, I felt like I had a severe case of mono.

After that Friday night featuring fireworks by Jude and Anton, Anton showed up only when Jude was in San Diego. It was a smart move. Overall, Anton was a good guy, and when he followed my rule and didn't bring Jude up, we managed to get along most days. Thanks to the job he'd given me, I'd been able to build a decent rainy-day fund, and we'd even figured out a way for me to sneak in a few hours during the school year. Jude wasn't thrilled with the idea, but he knew better than to push me on the issue. Anton was my boss, my good friend's brother, a friendly acquaintance. Nothing more.

After some creative schedule juggling, I was still able to help Holly out with LJ, and Thomas was able to fill in on Wednesdays, when I had a night class. Thomas and Holly had been an item, a *hot* item, since that night they figured out Thomas was indeed straight, and were ready to admit they were attached to each other. Thomas had become a permanent fixture at the apartment. I was about to invite him to move in, but was worried about the problems that would arise from sharing one bathroom among four people who each liked to take long showers.

My last class of the day had finished early, and since I had some time before I had to be back to watch LJ, I headed to the dance studio in White Plains. I hadn't gotten in near as much dance time as I'd wanted to this summer. What with the circus my life had become, it seemed that somewhere along the way, my priorities had started to shift. Not necessarily change, but realign. I was starting to get a better grasp on the concept that the world doesn't revolve around Lucy Larson.

A concept I was still trying to work out in my mind.

The studio was empty, and I took a moment to enjoy it.

Moments of quiet and alone time were so rare now, I savored them. It was ironic how a few months back, all I'd felt was lonely, and now I craved a few minutes of lonely.

I tied on my pointes and took my time stretching. I was in the middle of a quad stretch when my stomach turned. Followed by a clench and a rumble.

I grabbed my stomach, hoping it would pass.

When the whole turn, clench, and rumble repeated itself, I hurried off the stage and headed for the backstage bath-room. I hadn't thrown up in years, but I don't think a person ever forgets the queasy way she feels before she throws up. That was an unpleasant series of events that was forever branded into my mind.

I could taste the bile crawling up my throat as I raced inside the bathroom. There wasn't a second to spare before my stomach tightened one last time as I heaved into the toilet. I coughed and hovered there, just in case. After a minute had passed and I was fairly certain there wouldn't be any after-shocks, I flushed before heading to the sink to turn the faucet on. I rinsed my mouth and doused my face with cold water.

I was already feeling better by the time I dried my face, but I wasn't going to chance it. If I was catching something I wanted to nip it in the bud before it got worse. I exchanged my pointes for my flats, slipped my sweater over my cami, and headed back to the Mazda. I was going to be watching

LJ all night, and was hoping to take a quick nap before I started going sixty miles per hour until bedtime.

As I climbed the stairs to the apartment, that stomach-churning feeling was returning. By the time I was unlocking the door, it had returned with a vengeance. After another sprint to the bathroom, I barely made it in time to throw up for the second time in an hour. Thankfully I'd skipped lunch, or else this would have been an even more unpleasant ordeal.

"Lucy?" Holly knocked on the door, sounding concerned. "You okay in there?"

I groaned as my stomach churned again. This time it had mercy on me.

"I'm okay if you consider dying okay," I said, wondering why the sink felt so far away.

The door opened and Holly slipped inside.

"Where's LJ?" I asked, not wanting the little man to witness this. The kid would never be the same.

"Passed out under the table," she said, looking concerned. "You got sick?"

"What gave that away?" I said, glad I'd just cleaned the toilet yesterday, since my cheek was resting on the seat.

She glanced at the toilet, her nose wrinkled.

"Oh, shoot. Sorry," I said, flushing.

Holly grabbed a washcloth and ran some water over it.

She knelt beside me and wrapped it around my neck. It was cool and made me feel better right away.

"I must have eaten something bad," I guessed. My stomach was seriously pissed at me and revolting.

"You had Kashi cereal for dinner last night and your standard apple for breakfast," she said, pulling my hair back and braiding it. "I don't think it's anything you ate."

"Then it must be some kind of flu bug," I said, starting to feel better. For how long, I wasn't sure.

"It's early September, Lucy. This isn't flu season." She wrapped a tie around the end of my hair before sliding the braid under my sweater.

"Then I must be one of the fortunate few who catches that rare summertime bug," I said, not wanting to talk about why I was sick, but rather how I could get better. Fast.

Holly sighed and scooted around until she was looking at me. "When was the last time you had your period?"

I was startled at first by her question, which was as abrupt as it was random. Two seconds later I understood what she was getting at.

"You think I could be pregnant?" Now, in addition to feeling sick to my stomach, I felt a little faint, too.

"Well, it's not like you're exactly abstinent, Lucy," she said.

"I'm on the pill," I replied, feeling like I was trying to

convince her as much as I was myself. I'd missed a pill here and there, but was usually so careful.

"Yeah, but did you miss the part where it says the pill is only ninety-nine percent effective in preventing pregnancy?" Her voice was as soft as Holly's had ever been. She wasn't saying this to upset me, but upset was just the way I felt.

"But sometimes we use a condom, too." Though not often.

"So that means sometimes you don't," she said, grabbing my hand. "I'm not a doctor, but I'm pretty sure 'sometimes' isn't a guarantee that you won't get knocked up."

I was starting to panic now. I was breaking out in a clammy sweat, and my hands were trembling, because I knew what Holly was saying could be a possibility. I was on the pill, and we used a condom during the times I was supposed to be at my most prime for getting pregnant, but she was right: I wasn't abstinent, so I couldn't rule pregnancy out 100 percent, given the way I was feeling today. As much as I wanted to.

"When was your last period?" she asked again.

I couldn't think. I could barely breathe, so it took me a while to answer her. "Um . . . a couple of months ago. I think." This wasn't happening. It couldn't be. "But I don't get my period every month. It's irregular." It was a common thing for dancers to have sporadic periods, or even for them to stop completely. The lifestyle, paired with the low body fat, really messed with our cycles.

"Yeah, but you still get your period, so you could be pregnant." Holly scooted toward the sink and pulled out one of the drawers. Shuffling inside it, she pulled out a pink-and-white cardboard box. "There's only one way to know for sure."

This whole thing got even more surreal as Holly waved the pregnancy kit in front of me.

I shook my head. "I don't think I can do it." One part of me already knew Holly was probably right, and I wasn't ready for that to be confirmed. I wasn't ready to think of how my life would change in a total and forever kind of way.

She opened the box and pulled out a white stick. "I'll help you."

I don't know how long I stared at that white stick, but Holly had to help me up, because I wasn't capable of moving. After telling me what to do, she waited with me while I peed on the test. A test that felt like it was holding my whole life in the balance. Like all my dreams, and hopes, and my future rested on the outcome of one or two pink lines.

After capping it, Holly set it down on the sink. "We have to wait two minutes."

Two minutes might as well have been two decades. I wanted to sneak a peek just as much as I didn't. Holly hugged me the whole time, rubbing the back of my neck and patting my back. It was moments like these when you were most thankful for your friends, because there was no way I could have made it through this without her.

"Okay, I think it's time," she said, giving my braid one gentle tug.

"Just tell me," I said, closing my eyes. "I can't look."

"All right, Lucy," she said. I heard her pick the stick up from the counter. She barely gasped, but it went off like a foghorn in my ears. "Lucy . . . you're . . ."

I opened my eyes at the last minute. Two pink lines.

"Pregnant."

And then I passed out.

The voices around me sounded like they were coming through a tunnel. They were all echoes. I wanted to open my eyes, but I couldn't. Not because they felt heavy, but more because they felt like they'd been taped closed. I wanted to escape the darkness, but I couldn't.

And then I heard a name. That was all I needed to kick through the darkness.

"We've got to call Jude," a familiar male voice said.

"Yeah. Yeah, okay. I'll get my phone."

This was the final push I needed to open my eyes.

"No," I said, my voice breaking. "Don't call him. I'm all right." I was laid out on the couch, and my head was propped up by a couple of pillows.

Holly and Thomas hovered above me, looking down at me like you'd imagine someone would look at a corpse.

"When did you get here, Thomas?" I tried sitting up, but my body wasn't having any of it.

"Just a couple of minutes ago. I was planning on walking Holly to work," he said, kneeling in front of me. "But it's a good thing I was early and I'm used to carrying you around, or else you'd be waking up on the cold bathroom floor right about now." A small smile formed, but it didn't touch his eyes.

"Do you know?" I whispered. I couldn't say the word. I wouldn't even let myself think it, but I could feel the word winding its way through my mind. That was all I saw when I thought about my future.

"Yeah, Lucy," he said, grabbing my hand. "I know. Holly didn't say anything, but it was kind of hard to ignore the positive pregnancy test on the sink."

I bit my lip, hard, hoping it would keep the tears contained. My tried-and-true method was failing me.

Holly knelt next to Thomas. Her eyes were as red as I guessed mine were. She held her phone up. Jude's number was on the screen, along with his picture. "You need to call Jude. He needs to know what's going on so he can be here with you."

"No," I said, shaking my head. "Not right now."

"Yes. Yes, right now," Holly said, holding the phone out to me. "Listen, Lucy, I know you're scared as shit and confused as all hell, but Jude will help you get through this. You *need* him to help you get through this. And I know from personal experience that Jude is a good person to lean on in this kind of a situation."

"What kind of a situation is this?" I said, twisting onto my side so I could look at her straight on. "The unplanned-pregnancy situation? Or the I'm-only-twenty-one situation? Maybe the I'm-not-married situation? And let's not forget the my-future-is-ruined situation." I'd been at a loss for words pre–passing out, but now I couldn't seem to say enough.

"Mom?" LJ stuck his head out of the bedroom. "Can I come out yet?"

"No!" Thomas and Holly answered at the same time.

"I'll go hang with the little man," Thomas said, giving my hand a squeeze before pressing a quick kiss to Holly's lips. "You girls don't need me here to offer my nonwisdom anyways."

"Aunt Luce? Are you all right?" LJ's sweet little face was creased with concern.

The answer to that was one I couldn't give a three-year-old, so I lied. "Yeah, LJ. I'm fine, buddy."

"Oh. Lucy?" Thomas stopped abruptly and snapped his fingers. "For what it's worth, I think you'd be one hell of a mom." That same small smile appeared again, but this time it reflected in his eyes as well. Before I could reply, he was ducking inside the bedroom to occupy LJ while Holly and I discussed whatever she was planning on discussing.

The thing was, I wasn't in a talking mood. I needed to process. I needed to think. And then maybe we could discuss.

"What's going on up there, Lucy Larson?" Holly asked, tapping my head.

"A whole lotta everything and a whole lotta nothing," I said, wondering whether, if I fell back to sleep, I could wake up and discover this was all one huge nightmare.

Holly sighed and plopped down on the floor next to the couch. "What are you going to do?"

I couldn't think about that right now. I didn't want to think about it ever. But I knew I'd have to not only face that question, but answer it.

"I don't know."

"And when are you going to tell Jude?" She started stroking the top of my head in a way that my mom used to when I was little and scared of the monsters I was convinced were lurking beneath my bed.

"I don't know."

Holly exhaled. "How do you feel?"

"I don't know." I was seeing a trend developing. I knew a whole lot of nothing. All I knew was that I felt confused and scared and lost.

"I know this is coming at you fast, Lucy, and I can see how terrified you are right now, but you're strong. You're stronger than I am, and I know this probably won't comfort you, and maybe I'm all kinds of stupid for even saying it, but if I can raise a child, I know you can, too. You've got Jude, and your family and friends, and—"

"And no future," I interrupted, seeing all those chapters I'd yet to experience in life go up in flames. How could I dance when I had a big round belly? How could I dance and travel the world with a baby on my hip? What had I worked my ass off for if, one year before I was set to graduate from a prestigious dance school, I wound up knocked up?

"How can you say you've got no future?" Holly said, looking insulted. "You've got the kind of future most people dream of."

"A future most people *used* to dream about."

"Wait. Are you saying that because you're going to have a baby, your entire life is ruined?"

It felt like that was what I was saying, but I was just too damned confused to be sure.

"Because, yeah, a baby's going to change things, but it's not going to end your life."

I wasn't sure I believed her.

"I love that you're here for me and are trying to make me feel better, Holly. I really do. But I kind of just need some time to be alone and sort some shit out," I said. "Okay?"

She looked like she wanted to argue with me but managed to hold herself back. "I'll have Thomas take LJ tonight so you can have some peace and quiet," she said. "And then tomorrow you and I are going to find a doctor and make an appointment, because we don't know if you're four weeks along or four months along." I about fainted again, thinking I could be four months pregnant. Surely life wouldn't be that cruel. I needed as much time as possible to wrap my mind around this grenade that had just gone off in my life, and five and a half months just wasn't going to cut it.

"And after that, we'll figure out a way to break the news to Jude and—"

"Holly." I grabbed her arm. "Too much, too fast. I need some breathing room."

"You're right," she said, raising her hands. "I'm just going to give you one giant hug"—she wrapped her arms around me and gave me one *ginormous* hug—"and then I'll round up the boys and we'll be out of here."

"Thanks, Holly," I said, curling deeper into the couch. "For everything."

"You know, Lucy, for what it's worth, I'm on the same page as Thomas," she said, heading down the hallway. "I know you'll be an awesome mom."

I tried to return her smile, but I couldn't do it.

All I could think about was shattered dreams. All I could see was Jude's shocked face when I told him I was pregnant.

I was sobbing silently into my pillow before the door had closed behind Holly, Thomas, and LJ.

I'd lived on saltines and lemon-lime soda for a week. My stomach was either unable or unwilling to keep anything else down. Those were the first things I asked for when I boarded the plane Sunday morning, and the flight attendant had given me a knowing smile, told me, "It gets better," and kept the crackers coming.

I'd made it through the entire flight having to take only one lavatory vomit break, and thankfully the driver who'd met me at the airport to drive me to Qualcomm Stadium kept a paper bag in the backseat for emergency purposes.

I'd had an emergency.

It was Jude's first game of the season, and back when he'd purchased the ticket for me, he'd wanted to make it for the entire weekend. But I thought I'd be dancing lead in a school production Saturday night, and I had class Monday morning, so I was doing a round trip from New York to San Diego and back in one day.

I hadn't danced lead last night. I hadn't even gone and cheered on the girl who'd been my understudy. I was in something of a "delicate" state.

After setting an appointment for me, driving me there, and basically pushing me into the waiting room, Holly made sure I saw an ob-gyn on Thursday. After some poking, prodding, and a quick ultrasound, she was able to determine how far along I was.

Almost four months to the day.

Just when I thought I didn't have any more tears left inside me, that day in the examination room I proved myself wrong. I still hadn't said anything to Jude. In fact, I'd been trying to avoid his calls all week. I just didn't trust that if he got me on the phone for very long, he wouldn't be able to figure out what was the matter with me. So we texted a lot, and the timing worked out well, because he was crazy-busy getting ready for his first big game.

That was how I'd convinced Holly to keep her mouth shut when we left my appointment on Thursday. She insisted Jude needed to know. Like, now. She said he'd need just as much time as I would to get used to the idea of being parents in less than six months. That had, of course, started a whole new batch of tears. I blamed my emotions on the hormones, but I knew they played only a very small role.

I told Holly I couldn't tell Jude a couple of days before he was playing his first game as starting quarterback in the NFL that I was pregnant. Talk about messing with a guy's game. Holly had seen the reason in that, but insisted I tell him the week after, or she threatened she would tell him herself.

I'd bought time, but not much. While I didn't want to mess with Jude's head right before the game, it was more a matter of not knowing what I'd say to him. A girl just didn't discover she was pregnant at twenty-one and get used to the idea in a few days' time. I'd gone through about every stage of coping: fear, anger, depression, uncertainty, and everything in between. Occasionally I'd have a twinge of excitement—I was having Jude's baby, after all—but then I'd have a reality check. I'd gone on an emotional roller-coaster ride in one week's time, and I was exhausted.

I was so tired, I passed out the second half of the ride to the stadium. The driver had to wake me up and remind me where I was. It was official. I was a wreck.

As I was making my way through the gates, I got a text from Jude. ARE YOU HERE YET?

Following the usher to wherever they stuffed the wives

and girlfriends of the players, I texted him back. JUST GOT HERE. U NERVOUS?

I smiled when I got his reply. NOT ANYMORE.

Following the usher into an elevator, I punched in my reply. SO PROUD OF YOU, BABE. KICK SOME ASS OUT THERE.

His response came instantly. RIGHT BACK AT YOU. WILL DO. LOVE YA, JUDE.

LOVE YA, LUCE.

I didn't know how he had time to be texting when the game was set to start in a few minutes, but I'd known from the beginning that Jude did what Jude wanted to.

It felt good to have a smile on my face. A real one. It might not have won any blue ribbons for biggest or best, but it was a genuine one. That smile ran away the moment the usher walked me into a big room lined with windows. The football field seemed like it was a mile below us.

Had I mistaken a nightclub for a football stadium?

Most of the same women I'd been hanging with on and off all summer, and a few new faces, were milling about the room, drinking their champagne or sparkling water, wearing dresses and heels. They had on their fancy jewelry and their evening makeup.

I was sporting my standard-issue game-day gear: black leggings, riding boots, and a jersey with Jude's name and number on the back. I looked like a country bumpkin in comparison to these Rodeo Drive glamazons.

After the initial glances over, no one noticed me as I walked across the room. Well, they noticed me, but they tried to keep the curled noses and *what the hell?* faces to themselves.

All I wanted to do was watch a football game, cheer Jude on, and forget about my life for a couple hours. I wanted to fade into the crowd.

Fading wasn't in the cards when you showed up looking like you were headed to a slumber party when everyone else was heading to a Miss January party at the Playboy Mansion. I grabbed a bottle of water from the end of the table that was lined with food and drinks, and beelined to the end chair in the corner.

I made myself forget about the room and everyone in it and focused on the game. I picked out Jude immediately. It was funny how he finally blended in more with the players. In high school, he'd looked like a hybrid giant on the field. In college, he'd still had a few inches and a good twenty pounds on a lot of the players, but now, out there with the best in the nation, he was about par for the course. I almost stood up and started cheering my head off, but caught myself. No one in here was cheering. No one was even watching. Sure, kickoff hadn't happened yet, but a survey of the stands proved that people were hooting and hollering, because that was just what you did at a football game—from the time you entered the stadium till the time you left it.

I knew we were supposed to have the nicest seats in the house up here, but I was jealous of even the fans in the nosebleed section. I'd have to talk with Jude and see if he could score me some tickets out in the stands. I missed my front-and-center seat, where I could scream his name and pretend that he heard me. I missed seeing his ass in spandex from up close, and I knew I'd miss our post-touchdown kiss even more.

A minute or so before kickoff, the door burst open and a familiar face waltzed in. "What's up, bitches?" Sybill said, filling the room with her voice and energy. I was able to release the breath I'd been holding for I didn't know how long. Greeting a few of the girls as she headed to the food table, she stopped when she saw me.

I waved.

"What the hell are you doing stuffed in the corner, Lucy?" she said, snatching a cola from the table as she crossed the room toward me. Another smile, a real one, blossomed when I checked out her wardrobe: jeans, sneakers, and a jersey. "These bitches put you in a time-out for your fashion offenses?" She winked as she took a seat next to me. "I mean, come on. What are you thinking, showing up to a football game without your Saturday-night streetwalking finest?"

Was that a laugh I just heard? Coming from me?

Couldn't be. I hadn't been in a laughing mood all week.

"Yeah. My bad. I think next time I'll be banished to the stands with the rest of the fashion-impaired." That sounded like even a bit of wit. Was the Lucy Larson snarkiness making a comeback?

I wanted to get up and dance.

And then I remembered I had to take it easy. Because I was pregnant. Doctor's orders.

A smile and the snark had never disappeared so quickly.

I swore I could feel my belly growing whenever I remembered there was something inside there.

"Are you excited?" Sybill asked, nudging me as she cracked open her cola.

"Yeah. Excited, nervous, you name it," I said.

"Yeah, it's always us who worry our heads off. The guys are cool as cucumbers out there," she said. "But don't worry. I watched Jude's warm-up, and that boy is primed and ready to get us to one and zero tonight."

"You got to watch him warm up?"

"The kids and me always show up an hour before the game to watch the players get ready."

"You brought the kids?" I turned in my seat, looking for a handful of munchkins. "Where are they?"

"God willing, they're still in their seats listening to my

mama," she said. "But they're most likely about to jump down on the field and ask their dad to sing them 'We Are the Champions.'" She took another sip of her soda. "Not that that happened last season . . ."

"Wait"—I grabbed her arm—"you sit down in the stands?"

"Front row, baby," she said proudly.

"By choice?"

"Mostly. But it would be so damn funny to see the look on these broads' faces if I ever dragged my four little twerps up here, I might just give it a go for fun," she said, glancing at a few of the girls and shaking her head. "This is all a little too Emerald City for me, you know? I'm more a jeans-and-hot-dog kind of girl."

"Sybill, I know this might seem forward, given that I've met you all of a handful of times in my life, but I love you," I confessed. "Would you mind if I sat with you at future games?"

"I'd love a little company that isn't my mama or a spawn of mine."

"Sweet. I'll talk to Jude about scoring me some tickets with you, because I don't think I can handle this Barbie brigade for the rest of the season."

"I'm sure he won't have a problem getting you a ticket. Deon started me out up here, too." She laughed, looking

lost in a memory. "Lord knows I love that man, but sometimes he's just too damn overprotective."

"I know the feeling."

"Jude said you've been real busy this week, being back to
school and all. How have you been holding up?"

The waterworks were twisting on. That one question
could reduce me to a near blubbering mess was further evi-
dence that I was an emotional, hormonal wreck.

"Not bad," I said, looking away.

"But not so great either, eh?" Sybill asked.

I'd gone from being happy at seeing her to wishing she'd
leave in the span of a couple questions.

"Not so great, either," I admitted.

"So . . ." She twisted in her seat to face me. Her eyes
dropped to my stomach. "How far along are you, sweetie?"

I wasn't sure if my mouth or my tears dropped first.

"It's all right, baby," she said, reaching for my hand.

"How did you know?" I asked, peering around the room.
No one was paying us any attention. I doubted they'd pay us
any attention if I got naked and started doing jumping jacks.

"I've been pregnant so many times in my life, Lucy, I can
tell when a woman's pregnant before she can."

I stared at my stomach. I wasn't showing. Yet. But I would
be soon. The doctor had said I could expect a bump to start
popping through in the next month. Even if I wanted to, I

wouldn't be able to keep it a secret any longer.

"So?" she asked when I stayed quiet.

"I'm almost four months," I said, feeling lighter just having admitted it to someone.

"And I take it that since Jude wasn't bragging and going on about this precious little baby earlier, he doesn't know yet?"

I shook my head. "Does that make me a horrible person?"

"Oh, Lucy, of course it doesn't, sweetie." Sybill draped her arm around my shoulders and tucked my head beneath her chin. She couldn't have been more than ten years older than me, but the gesture was so nurturing, it was clear she'd been a mom for a while. "It makes you a scared person. A worried person. But not a horrible one. Not even close."

"Then why do I feel like a horrible person?" I said, choking on a sob.

"Do you feel that way because you're pregnant or because you haven't told Jude yet?" She continued to hold me close and wouldn't let me pull away. I stopped trying.

"Both," I admitted.

"Can I ask why you haven't told Jude yet?"

"I don't really know," I said. "I'm scared to tell him, I guess. I'm scared of what his reaction will be. I'm scared that his feelings might change. I'm scared that he might not be ready to be a dad yet. I'm scared he won't want some fat college dropout when he's . . ." I waved down at the field, where kickoff was getting under way. "Everything he is."

Sybill sighed while I shed a few tears. When we should have been on our feet cheering, we were curled around each other, one trying to hold the other together.

"I know what it's like to be scared, Lucy. God knows I know," she said, watching the field with me. "I'm going to tell you a story. It's no fairy tale, but it has a happy ending. And I'm something of an expert on it, since it's my story." She paused and took a sip of her soda. "Deon and I met when we were in college. Lord, I loved that man the moment I saw him, but . . . he didn't exactly see me. Not at first, anyways," she said, laughing to herself. "One night we were both at the same party and, thanks to my cousin lending me a teeny little dress and showing me what mascara was, Deon and I wound up dancing. After a few dances, we were kissing. And after what felt like a few hours of kissing, we were losing clothes and looking for an empty bedroom. We had sex that night. It was my first time, and I was kind of horrified the next morning that it had been with some guy I barely knew during a drunken, wild party."

She was right: This definitely wasn't sounding like a fairy tale, but I loved it. I loved her story. I loved the way her voice was all soft when she told it.

"I made it my mission to avoid Deon at all costs after I

woke up that morning. And it worked. For all of a day." She laughed. "That boy went on a crusade asking anyone in passing if they knew the girl he'd been with the night before. Of course, very few in his inner circle did, because I was a loser to their elite status. He'd surreptitiously "run into" my cousin at the cafeteria that night, and she gave him my phone number, what dorm I lived in, my birthday. Hell, practically everything but my social security number. So he shows up at my door, flowers in hand, with those huge puppy-dog eyes of his, begging me to let him take me out on a date. A *real* date."

I was starting to smile at this point. God, this story was different from, yet the same as, mine and Jude's.

"So we went out on that first date, and a second and a third. We started spending every free minute we had together. It was something I knew was special, something I knew was meant to last forever. Two months later Deon got drafted. We were ecstatic, and he proposed to me that same day. I was living every girl's dream, as far as I was concerned, and then I found out I was pregnant."

Yep. This was *very* similar to Jude's and my story. So much so that I almost pinched myself to make sure I wasn't dreaming.

"I was sure Deon was going to leave me. Why would he want to be strapped to a quirky pregnant girl when he'd just signed a huge NFL contract? I didn't tell him at first. I didn't want the fairy tale to end. I didn't tell him until I started to show. I remember being so scared I almost passed out." A few more tears leaked out of my eyes. "I told him the night after his first game. I even had a good-bye all ready to go. And you know what he said right after I told him? What the first words out of his mouth were when I told him his nineteen-year-old girlfriend he'd been with for five months was pregnant?" Sybill must have started crying along the way, too, because I felt a tear land on my forehead. "He said, 'I always wanted a big family. I guess it's a good thing we got started early.'" She shook her head and laughed. "Then he told me he loved me and we got married a whole month later. And, ten years and four kids later, the rest is history," she said, sweeping her hand down at the field.

"Did you have to drop out of school?" I asked, realizing Sybill was the best possible person I could turn to for advice.

"I dropped out of school because I wanted to be with Deon and spend time with the baby. But I was able to take online courses and managed to get my degree along the way."

"Do you ever regret it?" I whispered. "Getting pregnant? Dropping out? Giving up on your dreams?"

"Not one single day," she said. "I've never regretted any of it. I don't live with regret, Lucy. It's poison. Did I mourn for certain things I felt I missed out on? Hell yes, I did. But if I stacked up everything I feel I missed out on and compared it to everything I gained along the way, there's a teeny-tiny pile of what-could-have-been standing in the shadow of a never-ending tower of what-has-beens."

I was no longer crying an occasional tear. I was a sobbing, hot mess.

"Yes, I've missed out on things. But that's life, Lucy. It's what I *haven't* missed out on that counts in my book. When I look at my family's faces, I know I wouldn't change a damn thing if I had the choice."

"So you're saying I should keep the baby, tell Jude, and we should raise it together?" I asked in between sobs. I wasn't sure if anyone had noticed the bawling girl in the corner, and I wouldn't have cared at this point.

"No, I'm not saying that. You're the only one who can make those decisions," she said, "but I know when you're ready to make them, you'll make the right decisions for you."

I didn't know who or which divine entity had brought Sybill up to the skybox tonight, but I was thanking whatever it was. I felt about a million times better and a thousand pounds lighter. I didn't have the answers yet, but I wasn't terrified of them anymore.

"Thank you, Sybill," I said, wiping my eyes with the

back of my arm. "I mentioned I loved you earlier, right?"

"You're welcome, baby girl," she said, giving my shoulders one more squeeze before rising. "And I'm sending a whole lot of love right back at you. Now I really got to get to my mama before she has a nervous breakdown, but if you ever want to talk, just give me a ring, okay?"

I nodded. "Okay."

"You good?" she said, looking around the room. The game had started, and still no one was watching. The mercy was that no one was watching me either.

"Yeah, I'm good." For the first time this week, it was the only time I'd answered this question without lying.

"I expect to see you down with us at the next game. You got it?" she said, grabbing another cola as she headed for the door. "I need all the help I can get."

"I'll be there," I said, "and I'm pretty darn good with kiddos."

Sybill gave me a knowing smile. "I can picture that, Lucy Larson. I can picture that." She flashed a wave before heading out.

Everyone was still busy talking about whatever was so important that they couldn't interrupt themselves to watch the football game, and, while they were all clustered around the food table, no one was eating anything.

My stomach rumbled. Crackers and soda were not an

especially filling diet. For the first time this week, I had a craving when my eyes landed on the fruit bowl. I knew I might regret it, but I wanted an apple. Popping up, I weaved through a few bodies to get to my coveted apple. I made my way back to my seat just as Jude was taking the field.

I forgot about the apple. I forgot about everything but him crouching into position. It didn't seem possible that four years ago he'd been a reluctant walk-on high school player, and here he was, about to make his first play in the big league.

I reminded myself to breathe.

The center hiked; Jude caught it effortlessly and stalled for a couple seconds, giving his receivers time to get into position. His arm snapped back and when he released that ball, I started shouting. Cheering my head off. It had a good few seconds of hang time, but I knew it would land right where Jude intended it to land. I'd watched enough games of his to know he rarely, if ever, missed his mark.

When the ball landed in the receiver's arms at the twenty, I cheered louder still. I was the only one cheering—I was the only one making loud noise—but I wasn't worried about it. Jude had just thrown his first pass in the NFL—a guy who had goals only of staying out of prison back in high school, and here he was now, living the dream, being watched and celebrated by millions around the country.

Another tear dripped from my eye. While he'd turned into a football god, I'd turned into an emotional sap.

When I stopped cheering long enough to catch my breath, I felt all the eyes in the room on me. "Did you see that?" I asked the collective bunch, waving at the field.

I didn't wait for an answer. I had a game to watch.

I didn't stop cheering, because I knew I'd never conform to whatever this Emerald City standard was, and what mattered more to me was that I never wanted to.

EIGHTEEN

I was sitting next to the most talked-about man in the country tonight. After completing four touchdown passes, not throwing a single interception during the entire game, and leading his team to a win that the analysts said would take a miracle of the raising-the-dead quality, Jude Ryder had proven himself ten times over in his first NFL game. He'd become a national hero today, yet he still draped his arm over me as we headed to the airport in his POS truck like he was the same old bad boy of Southpointe High.

I was exhausted, but it had been so worth it to make the grueling one-day journey, and I knew it meant a lot to Jude. Mainly because he hadn't stopped telling me it had.

"Did I tell you yet how proud I am of you?" I said, wishing all those lights in the near distance weren't the airport.

"Only five minutes ago." His arm tightened around me. "Thanks for coming. It's just not the same when you're not there to watch me play, Luce."

"It means a lot to me, too."

"Are you still on for two weeks from now? We've got a bye-week next weekend, but we've got another home game the following."

"I'll be there," I said, thinking this would be the opportunity I'd use to tell Jude about being pregnant. I didn't want to do it over the phone, and I wasn't quite ready to tell him today. Even if I was ready, there was literally no time. When we pulled into the airport, I'd be lucky to have a whole ten minutes before I had to start making my way to my gate. This was news I didn't want to rush. I didn't want to feel like I was racing the clock to get it out. I wanted a whole day if we needed it, to talk things out, or to say nothing at all and just be with each other while we processed the detour our lives were taking.

"And you'll be able to be here for the whole weekend, right?"

"The whole weekend," I said, as Jude pulled into the parking garage.

"I'm so sick of saying good-bye to you, Luce," he said, thumping his palm on the steering wheel. "I'm sick of crawling into a cold bed, and I'm sick of texting you more than talking with you. I miss you."

I was exhausted, and pregnant. And emotional.

His words made me weepy instantly.

"I'm sick of it, too," I said, keeping my head tucked against his shoulder so he wouldn't see my tears.

"I've got a solution to that, you know. To both of us being sick of being apart," he said, sounding hesitant.

"What? Me pick up and move out here with you and get hitched?" I said, not really having to guess this was where his mind was at.

He nodded against my head. "I'd do it for you if I could." And now his voice sounded sad.

"But I'd never ask you to," I replied. "You've got commitments and I've got commitments. It just sucks that our commitments have to be on opposite sides of the country."

His face nudged mine. He wanted me to look at him, but I couldn't. I had to put a stopper on these damn tears before he saw them. "My number-one commitment is you, Luce."

"I know," I said, wiping my eyes with my arm. "What are you asking me to do, Jude? I get that I'm your number-one priority, but I also get that you signed a contract with a little franchise called the San Diego Chargers."

"That's right, I do have a contract. For three years. If at the end of that, you want me to quit so we can spend the next thirty moving from one dance mecca to the next, that's what I'll do."

I blew out a slow breath. "You'd do that? Give up your dream so I could have mine?"

"Baby, football isn't my dream," he said, kissing my forehead. "*You* are."

Uh-oh. Choking sobs on the horizon.

"Don't get me wrong; I love football. A lot. But I can't even compare it to you, because there's nothing to compare. I signed the contract because I'm good at it, and I'll make so much damn money in three years we'll be set for life, and you can dance across any and every stage you want and not have to ever worry about money."

I knew I should get going, but I couldn't leave. I was tired of leaving him. "Three years of football. Then three years of dance. So on and so forth. Is that what you're proposing?"

"I'm proposing three years of football and you can have the rest of our years together dancing if that's what you want," he said.

"What if we want to start a family sometime along the way?" I asked, seeing my segue and taking it for a spin. "How does a baby factor into our three-years-on, three-years-off schedule?"

His body relaxed against me. "I can't wait for the day we

have kids, Luce, because you're going to make me the most beautiful little babies ever, but we're still so young." The smile that was forming on my face faltered. "We're barely twenty-one. We've got a whole decade ahead of us before we need to start worrying about popping a couple kiddos out. We've got time, so let's use it," he said, trying to turn his face so he could see mine. "Okay?"

I answered him with a nod, because I didn't trust myself to talk.

"Luce?" he said with concern when he caught a glimpse of my face. "Are you all right?" He twisted in his seat and held my face so I couldn't turn it away.

"Yeah," I said, sounding as upset as I thought I would. "I'm just tired."

"Then why does it look like you're crying?" he asked, sliding his thumb over my cheek.

"Because I get all teary when I'm tired."

He made a face. "Since when?"

"Since now," I said, needing out of this truck, and not just because I had to get to my flight. I knew that if Jude didn't back down and kept up with the grand inquisition, I was going to cave and tell him the big news. The big news he'd just admitted to not being ready for and not wanting for another ten years. How could I tell a man who thought he'd have a solid decade to get used to the idea of fathering a child that we were about to have one in a little less than six months?

The answer was, I couldn't tell him. Not right now. Not with those words so fresh in my mind.

"What's the matter?" Jude's face shadowed as he watched me. "Talk to me, Luce."

I looked down, unable to stare at those tortured eyes any longer. "I can't. Not right now," I said. "Soon."

He huffed. "I've been hearing that word *soon* from you for three years now. I think your definition and mine are different."

I didn't have three years. I didn't even have three months. My *soon*, in this case, would be his soon.

"Soon," I said. "I promise."

"I won't hold my breath," he said with a sigh.

I bit my lip. "I've got to get going."

"Yeah, yeah, I know. It's the story of our lives," he said, studying me like he was trying to see inside me. "I know you're tired and need to catch your flight and don't want to talk about whatever's bothering you, but after a good night's sleep you'll feel better. I want you to call me anytime, Luce, anytime. I don't care if I'm in the middle of practice or asleep or in the shower; I'll answer. Just call me. Tomorrow, or the next day, or the day after that, whenever you're feeling better, and we'll talk this over. We'll work this out the way we always do." He paused and waited.

"Okay, Luce? We'll work this out. Everything will be fine," he said, pulling me back into his arms. "Just call me and we'll figure this thing out together."

I hugged him back—I couldn't seem to hold him hard enough—but I never made that call the next day, or the day after that, or even the day after that.

Another week down, one week closer to D-day, as Holly and I had deemed it. Jude and I had talked every day, but we never had "the talk." I pretended everything was fine and dodged his probing questions, but I knew I hadn't fooled him. I was even avoiding my parents' calls, because how could I talk about school and dance when I was keeping the secret that I was in my second trimester from them?

So when Anton asked if I'd be able to work Saturday, I'd said yes without a second thought. When I was at school or work, my mind was distracted just enough for me to pretend my life wasn't spiraling out of control. Anton had found a new full-time admin once I'd gone back to school, but I still worked a Saturday or Sunday most weekends. There was always some report that needed to be filled out or completed or started. There was always a presentation that needed to be put together, and Anton not only didn't have a problem with letting me work a flexible schedule, he encouraged it. It didn't matter if I showed up early or late, Saturday or Sunday, the guy was always there. I was starting to wonder if he lived at the office.

Today, Thomas had been free to watch LJ while Holly was at work, so I'd showed up at Xavier Industries at eight a.m. I hadn't lifted my head from the computer once when Anton stepped out of his office later that afternoon.

"Thanks again for helping today, Lucy," he said, dropping a bottle of water on my desk. "It's amazing how much more I can get done when I don't have someone ducking their head in my office every two seconds."

"No problem," I said, saving the report I'd been working on the past couple hours before powering off my computer. It was getting late, and I'd promised to pick up dinner for everyone tonight.

"How have you been lately?" Anton asked with a serious expression. "India tells me you've been missing a lot of class."

Traitor. No dessert for her next Friday night.

"I'm good," I said with a shrug. "Just going through a bit of a life funk."

"Is Jude responsible for this funk?" he said, leaning into my desk.

A flash of anger. It had been so long since I'd felt it, I welcomed it. Like a long-lost friend coming home for a visit.

"Let me respond to that with a two-part answer," I said, crossing my arms. "None of your business. And none of your business." Jumping up, I grabbed my purse and headed for the coatrack to grab my jacket. I wanted out of here before Anton got warmed up.

"I make you uncomfortable."

I huffed. "Doesn't exactly qualify as the revelation of the year."

Anton chuckled. Infuriating. "Well, maybe this will," he said, coming toward me. "I know why I make you uncomfortable."

"I know why, too," I said, looking him up and down. "Everything. The whole Anton Xavier package makes me uncomfortable."

Super. I'd just mentioned Anton and *package* in the same sentence, and the twisted SOB hadn't missed it either. One side of his mouth was already lifting.

"I make you uncomfortable because some part of you likes me. Some part of you is attracted to me and that pisses you off. Some part of you knows that if you weren't with him, you and I would be together." He said this all without a bit of remorse, not even shame.

I was getting upset. More upset. I wasn't sure if it was because of how wrong he was or how right he was. It was all very confusing.

"Maybe," I said with a lazy shrug. "But that's the answer to every question in the universe. Maybe. Maybe you and I might have hooked up in some alternate reality where there was no Jude, but that's not the case. There is a Jude. And I'm in love with him." I was getting worked up, just shy of a shout. I held up my left hand, flashing the ring in front of him. "And we're getting married."

Anton stuffed his hands in his pockets. "When?"

"Soon." I grimaced at my word choice. He noticed that too.

"How long have you been engaged?" Still the picture of calm.

"Three years."

He took a step toward me; I took a step back. "What are you waiting for?"

Why hadn't I stuck with the whole none-of-your-business approach? "To graduate college."

"No, I don't think that's it," he said confidently. "I think you're waiting because you're unsure. Something's telling you this man is not the right one for you, and you can't kill that voice."

"Wow, good one," I said, clapping my hands. "And the Delusional Award goes to . . ." I stopped clapping to sweep my hands dramatically at him.

The more I got worked up, the cooler he seemed. Nothing

I said or did could tip his calm scale.

"You say we could never be together, but that's just because you've never even opened yourself up to the idea." He took another step toward me and this time, when I took a step back, I was up against a wall.

Fitting.

"I don't want to open myself up to that idea," I said, warning him with my eyes. Warning him not to take another step closer.

He didn't heed that warning. "Then I'm going to help you."

Before I had time to process his intention, his lips were on mine, his hands following. Though his mouth was unyielding, his hands dropped gently to my waist and stayed there.

I tried shoving him away immediately. It was a useless endeavor with Jude, but I at least managed to budge Anton, though not enough. His lips continued their assault on mine, like they were a drowning man begging for a lifeline, but I'd tossed my lifeline out a long time ago—to a different guy, and I'd never asked for or wanted it back. I knew that what Anton had said was partly true. The two of us very well could have ended up together had the world been Jude Ryder—less. But it wasn't. Anton was the understudy to

Jude. Anton was my what-might-have-been, but Jude was my was, is, and will be forever.

"Anton, stop," I protested against his unrelenting lips.

Either he'd gone deaf or he was ignoring me. Neither would work for me.

Raising my hand, I slapped it hard across his cheek. "Stop it!"

The slap got his attention. Good thing, because my next move would have been a sharp knee to the groin.

When Anton loosened his grip on me just enough, I gave him another hard shove, pushing him back a few feet. "You're an asshole. How's that for an answer as to why we're not together?" Shoving him in passing just because he deserved it, I marched toward the door. "And one more thing. I quit!"

I didn't wait for a reply. I ran for the elevator, hoping I'd make it to the car before the last two minutes had caught up with me. As it was, I felt like I was hyperventilating.

What Anton had said might have been true, but none of it mattered. I was with Jude. I wanted Jude. There was no Anton and Lucy when I'd given my heart to Jude Ryder four years ago.

I had no doubts that if you plugged Anton and me into a compatibility computer, we'd come out on the other end together. I knew that, but it didn't change anything. His rubbing that in my face when my fiancé was across the country, while I was an emotional, hormonal wreck, was not what I needed right now.

As soon as the elevator doors opened, I ran through the lobby, shoved through the revolving door, and continued my sprint to the Mazda. I was pulling my phone from my purse before I knew I'd gone searching for it. As if my fingers had a mind of their own, they punched in a number as I crawled into the car.

Jude answered on the first ring. "Hey, Luce."

Just hearing his voice unleashed the flood of emotions I'd been trying to hold back. I started sobbing. Hard-core, rocking, choking sobs. The kind I'd experienced only in the days after my brother's murder.

"What's the matter, Luce?" Jude's voice was tight with worry. "Shit. Are you all right? Where are you?" He was frantic, and it sounded like he was running.

I inhaled and counted to five, trying to compose myself enough to reassure him I wasn't dying in some back alley. "I need you, Jude," I sobbed. "I'm sorry. I know it's late and I know you've got practice in the morning"—it was next to impossible to get words out, and each one felt like a victory—"but I need you."

I heard him curse under his breath. I don't know if my

idea of composing myself had calmed him or made him more panicked. "I'm coming, baby. I'm coming," he said, definitely running now, because I could hear the air cutting through the phone. "I'll be there as soon as I can."

I hated feeling so weak, like I needed someone else to hold me together, but I tried not to focus on that. I tried to focus on how lucky I was to have someone to call when I needed to be held together.

"Thank you," I whispered as I tried to start the car. My hands were shaking, making it difficult.

"Are you safe, Luce?" he asked. "Are you hurt?"

I knew he was talking about the physical safe and hurt, so that was why I replied, "Yes, I'm safe, and no, I'm not hurt."

"Where are you?" he asked, before talking in a clipped tone to someone. A taxi driver, maybe?

"I'm in my car. I'm heading back to the apartment."

"Are you okay to drive?"

I took a few more deep breaths until my shaking stopped. "Yeah, I'll be fine."

"Okay, Luce. Wait for me at the apartment. I'm on my way, baby."

"Thank you." There was nothing else I could say.

"I love you, Luce." His voice was still anxious, but it soothed me.

"I know, Jude," I said. "I know."

I hoped he would feel the same way once I told him everything I'd been keeping from him.

After a teary drive home, I found Holly waiting for me. Thomas and LJ were gone.

"Did you get off work early?" I asked, faking a smile.

"Jude called me," she said, pulling me into her arms. "He was freaking out and asked me to meet you here until he flew in."

"I'm sorry you had to leave work early," I said, melting into her arms.

"That's not what I'm worried about," she said, steering me toward the couch. "I'm worried about you. What happened?" She inspected me as she sat me down. "Jude said you'd told him you were okay, but he wasn't so convinced."

"I'm okay in the way he was worried about," I said, as she slid my heels off.

"Jude's worried about you being okay in all the ways you can be, Lucy," she said, grabbing the pillow and blanket over on the chair.

"I know he is. And I guess I'm both okay and not okay. If that's even possible." I let Holly ease me down on the couch until my head crashed into the pillow.

"What happened?" she asked as she layered the blanket over me.

Suddenly, just having my feet up and my head on a

pillow, I felt exhausted. Utterly spent from the month, the day, and the past hour. It had all caught up with me, and my body was going to revolt if I didn't let it shut down for a while.

"I'll tell you later, Holly," I said, yawning as I closed my eyes. "Will you wake me when Jude gets here?"

"Of course, Lucy," she said. "Sleep tight." She pressed a kiss to my temple, and then I was asleep.

NINETEEN

"*H*ow long has she been out?" Jude's voice broke through my dreams, but didn't fully free me from them. Dreams that had been more dark than light, more nightmare than dream.

"Since she basically walked through the door," Holly replied, sounding far-off.

"What's going on, Hol?" His fingers started stroking my hair.

"She wouldn't say, but I've got a few ideas."

"What ideas?" His voice was so tight with worry, and something else. Exhaustion, maybe?

"Nope, not my place to say. Lucy can tell you what's going on when she wakes up."

Jude's mouth pressed into my temple and stayed there for a beat, like he was trying to breathe me in. "I was so worried, Hol. So fucking worried."

"It's going to be all right, Jude. Whatever Lucy needed you for, you two will work out."

"Yeah," he said against my skin, "I know."

It might have been his lips, or it might have been his words, but one of the two freed me at last from the curtain of dreamland.

"Luce?" Jude's face was blurry as my eyes adjusted. "Baby? Are you all right?"

"You made it," I said, smiling up at him. I already felt ten times better just having him close.

"I told you I would."

"I know," I said, shifting below him. "What time is it?"

"A little before midnight."

"How did you get here so fast?"

His fingers continued running through my hair, soothing me. "I chartered a plane," he answered. "A fast one."

This time, the price tag didn't bother me. He was here in less than eight hours' time. "Thank you," I said, knowing two words were inadequate, but not being able to offer him anything else right now.

Jude smiled his reply. He was so close I could smell the scent of his favorite soap. Having him here, his presence, his smile, his scent . . . I was home.

"I know I should probably let you wake up and give you

a minute, but I'm dying here, Luce. I've been dying since I got your call." His voice got tight again. "What's the matter? What happened?"

For one of the few times in my life, he looked scared. Scared of the questions and scared of the answers.

"First things first." Holly appeared behind Jude holding a cup of orange juice and a handful of crackers. "You haven't eaten anything for hours, Lucy. Eat this. Drink this. Or else." She winked as she waited for me to sit up.

I twisted around so I could face Jude and took the OJ and crackers. "Thanks, Holly." Again, there was so much I owed her for, but two words of gratitude were all I had right now.

Jude waited for me to take a sip and get down half a saltine cracker, but I could tell the waiting game was killing him. How could I break what happened to me this afternoon to him gently? If there was a way to ease the blow that the man Jude had been so certain had a thing for me had just plastered his lips to mine, I wasn't finding one.

Segue . . . ease him into it with a segue.

"Anton kissed me."

Segues, apparently, in my book, sucked.

The worry lines of Jude's face deepened, until each wrinkle was its own canyon. "When?" His voice was so rough it scared me.

"Right before I called you." I took another sip of my juice and waited.

"Where?" His jaw was locked and his shoulders were tensing.

"At the office."

And now the veins in his neck were popping against his skin. We'd hit rage liftoff.

"Where is he now?"

"I don't know," I said. "And I don't care."

"Well, I care, and I'm about to find out." He pulled his phone from his pocket and started searching through his contact list. I knew who he'd call first on this Anton manhunt.

"No," I said, wanting to grab the phone out of his hands and toss it out the window. But then he'd just go find mine. "You're not going to go find him so you can teach him a lesson and kick his ass."

"That's exactly what I'm going to do," he said instantly, stopping when he got to the *I*'s in his phone.

"No, you're not," I said firmly, setting my juice and crackers down. My attention and hands were needed elsewhere. "I don't need you, or anyone else, to prove to some other guy that I belong to you."

"He kissed you, Luce," Jude said, his eyes immediately

narrowing. "It appears you do need me to do just that."

I gently traced the scar I'd memorized years ago. "It doesn't matter how many guys want to, try to, or actually succeed before they feel the slap of my hand on their cheek," I said, forcing him to look me in the eyes. "Because the only one of them I want to kiss is you. And that's what matters."

To prove it, I lowered my face until our mouths were just a hair apart. Our lips hadn't touched and already electricity was bouncing between us. When my lips did cover his, that electricity became something else entirely. Our lips played together, smoothing and sucking, until my breath started hitching in my lungs. Jude's hand held my face carefully, but there was an undercurrent of strength in that touch.

I ended our kiss by running my tongue along the seam of his lips before pressing a featherlight kiss to the corner of his mouth.

"That's who I want to kiss, and how I want him to kiss me, until the day I can't kiss anymore," I said, staring into his eyes. The darkness in them was gone. "So don't feel like you need to kick Anton into next week to defend my honor. I can defend my own honor. Just stay here. With me," I said, patting the couch. "Kissing me would be an added bonus."

He sat beside me and grabbed my hand. "You know it might kill me not to give that little jerk-off a piece of my boot, right?"

I nodded. In fact, I was surprised he was still here, relatively calm, and talking in his normal Jude voice again. That kiss must have worked a miracle, because the Jude I'd known would have already tracked the guy down and broken his nose.

"But I want you happy. Nothing's more important to me than that," he said, sighing. "So I'll resist every instinct and not hang him over the edge of the Empire State Building." Another sigh, this one longer. "Happy now?"

"You have no idea," I said, running my fingers through my hair. It was a mess, tear- and snot-coated, topped off by hours of twisting it into a pillow.

"I've got a quick solution to that," Jude said, patting my leg as he stood up. "I'll hunt down one of those ponytail-holder thingies you leave all over the place."

"Bathroom's a good starting point," I called after him. I smiled. Jude had gone from hard-core Hulk to my ponytail-holder-thingy hunter in under a minute. Plus, he was here. I didn't care why or what events had led up to his chartering a plane and flying across the country. Because he was here.

"Impressive," Holly muttered to me from the kitchen, sipping a cup of tea. "I thought I was going to be sweeping up glass for weeks from that special shade of pissed he turned."

Before I had a chance to reply, I heard a drawer slam before

Jude came stomping out of the bathroom. "Goddammit, Hol," he said, clutching something in his fist. "Did you go and get yourself knocked up again?"

Holly's face did the confusion thing before she noticed what was in Jude's hand. Then her face fell.

"What the fuck?" he said, holding up the pregnancy test in front of her. The pregnancy test I'd stuffed in the top drawer where I kept my toothpaste, ChapStick, and ponytail-holder thingies. Shit.

"Jude," I said, but he didn't hear me.

"How the hell are you going to take care of two kids on your own, Hol?" he said, sounding truly upset.

"Jude," I said again, this time louder.

Holly was glancing between me and Jude, not saying a thing. She couldn't lie, but she didn't want to rat me out.

"Say something," Jude said, waving the test.

"Jude!" There. I'd gotten as loud as he had.

"What?" he shouted, spinning around. His face softened just a bit when he realized he'd snapped at me.

"The test isn't Holly's," I said, unconsciously draping my hands over my stomach. "It's mine."

It didn't register right away. It took a minute. But as Jude's face changed from red to white, I knew my words were settling in.

"It's mine," I repeated, looking at the test.

344

"Wait . . ." He shook his head, glancing at the test, then back to me. *"What?"*

I prayed he wasn't going into shock, because I'd never seen this pale, clammy look on his face, and it sure as hell looked like shock to me. "The pregnancy test is mine." He actually went a degree whiter at the word *pregnancy.*

"Don't play games with me, Luce," he said, frozen in place.

"I'm not," I said, my voice quiet. "I'm pregnant."

He wavered but caught himself. Oh, God. He spread his hands over his face, leaving them there. "When did you find out?"

He'd accepted that I was, indeed, pregnant. We were making progress, although this was hardly the response I was looking for. I knew he wouldn't be jumping for joy, but I'd hoped for a hug and a *We'll get through this together* reassurance.

"Two weeks ago."

His hands fell from his face. "Why didn't you tell me?"

That was the million-dollar question.

"For a lot of reasons," I answered. "A lot of reasons that don't matter anymore."

He stared down at the test in his hand. "They matter to me."

Okay, I could do this. "I was scared."

"Of what?" he asked, not able to take his eyes from those two pink lines.

"Everything," I answered, because it was true.

"Of me?" His voice and the expression on his face broke me. I'd hurt him. The one thing I never wanted to do but could never seem to escape from doing. It was my damn Achilles' heel: hurting Jude.

"Yes." I swallowed back the lump forming in my throat.

He flinched. "Afraid that I was going to turn out to be some piece-of-shit father like mine was?"

This time I flinched. That thought had never once entered my mind. I'd had a lot of anxious thoughts, enough worries to fill a person's entire lifetime, but that had not been one of them.

"No, Jude," I said, wanting to sit up and go to him, but I wasn't sure my legs would work at this point in the conversation. "That never crossed my mind."

"Then why were you hiding the fact you were pregnant from me for two weeks? Two goddamned weeks!"

He looked lost. And the kind of lost where he wasn't hoping to be found.

"Because of this," I said, motioning at him, feeling my temper boiling to the surface. "Because I was scared of what your reaction would be."

He cracked his neck and looked away from me. "Yeah, well, you were right to be."

"Obviously," I replied, wondering if I could rewind to two minutes ago and tell Jude myself that I was pregnant before he found the test stick.

"Is it mine?"

Now it was my turn for a blow of his to take a while to settle in. Sure I'd heard him wrong, I said, "What?"

"Is. It. Mine?"

Nope, I hadn't heard him wrong.

"Jude," Holly hissed from the kitchen, marching toward him like she was going to punch him in the stomach.

"What?" he said, his eyes crazy. "If she hides the fact that she's pregnant, who's to know what else she's hiding from me?"

Those words, that insinuation, cut me like nothing had before. Jude implying I could have been, or had been, unfaithful to him . . . this was the kind of cut that would never heal.

"Get out," I whispered, staring into my lap. "Just get the hell out."

When he didn't move, I shot up from my seat and pointed at the door while I glared at him with fire shooting from my eyes. "Get the hell out!"

I saw his eyes flash before he turned away, but I couldn't tell if it'd been a flash of anger or hurt. But I was too hurt myself to find out.

Jude stormed down the hall and slammed the door so damn hard, I thought it was going to fall from its hinges.

Before I collapsed back onto the couch, I heard a string of curses, then what sounded like a fist going through a sheet of drywall.

TWENTY

*S*chool, dance, marriage, career . . . *Jude*. My entire life felt like it was hanging in the balance. There wasn't one thing I was certain about anymore. Well, save for one: I was certain I still loved Jude. I wanted to be with him, marry him, live and die with him. When life throws you a curveball like it had thrown me, you realize exactly what is important and what isn't.

Jude, and now our baby, were at the top of that list.

After Jude had stormed out last Saturday, I hadn't seen or heard from him since. Four and a half days I'd gone without knowing what he was thinking or where his head was or if we were going to make up, or if he even still wanted to marry me. If I hadn't developed an ulcer yet, I was close.

When I'd shouted at Anton, "I quit!" last Saturday, I'd

meant it. He'd sent a bouquet of flowers and a note to apologize, but I was one forced-upon kiss past forgiving and forgetting right now. One day, maybe, but not a few days later. Anton had crossed a line and proved that he couldn't take no for an answer. It was obvious we couldn't just be friends, so I made an executive decision and cut off all contact. Even Indie had my back. When she found out he'd kissed me, she went ballistic.

After I skipped class again, Holly and Thomas basically dragged me to the studio Tuesday morning. That didn't last long, though, because as soon as I slipped into my dance leotard I could see the slightest of bumps stretching the fabric above my belly. This brought me close to a meltdown. It wasn't just the baby bump; it was everything that had piled up in the days before.

A box of tissues later, Thomas walked me over to my academic adviser and informed her of my "fragile" condition while I went through another box of tissues. By the end of the day, we'd been able to work out a modified schedule that would allow me to continue the semester without having to adhere to a rigorous dance course load. I'd never checked before, because I didn't want to do anything but dance, but it turned out there were quite a few theory courses I could take that would count toward my degree.

Since the baby was due sometime in February, I wasn't

sure what I'd be able to do about my last semester, but that was okay. I couldn't think that far ahead. I still hadn't wrapped my mind around having a child growing inside me, or that, once I pushed it out, I might be raising it alone.

Holly and I had discussed the double *A*s, as she called them: abortion and adoption. I wasn't going to judge what was right for someone else, but abortion just wasn't an option for me. I couldn't do it, simple as that. We'd talked back and forth about adoption, until I realized that this, too, just wasn't an option for me. I hadn't planned for it, I hadn't seen it, didn't even know what I was having, but it was *my* baby. And Jude's baby. I couldn't give it to someone else. I knew it was upending my life, in a present and future tense, but that wasn't the baby's fault. So I was going to have it and raise it. Hopefully with Jude, but alone if that was my only option.

So even though my life felt like it was one giant question mark, I attacked those few little things I could put a period after. I read a couple of books about the whole pregnancy and birthing process; one had pictures, *detailed* pictures, of the actual birth, which still haunted me. I made sure I got enough sleep, which was easy enough, considering my body felt tired twenty-four-seven. I took my prenatal vitamins, I walked and did my stretches, and I drank so much water I was making bathroom visits every half hour. I was moving forward.

The whole concept of having a baby growing inside me had set in. Finally. And I was going to do everything in my power to make sure it was healthy. There were moments in the night when I'd wake up and a flicker of excitement would flash through me. Then I'd find the spot beside me empty and I'd check my phone and find no missed calls or texts, and that spark of happiness would fizzle.

No matter what happened, no matter what Jude did or didn't do, I knew one thing: I was going to be the best damn mom I could be. I doubted a lot of things, but this was one thing I knew for sure. And I wouldn't be alone. I had Holly, who had plenty of firsthand experience to help me. I had India and Thomas to encourage me along the way, pat my back when I needed to cry, or tell me to suck it up when I needed to. Even though I hadn't told them about the baby yet, I had Dad and Mom, too, and I knew they'd be there for me. They'd be as shocked as I'd been at first, but they'd come around just like I had, and help me find my way on this scary road.

I focused on the pieces of my life I could control and tried not to fixate on the ones I couldn't. I lived life one hour at a time, because if I looked even one day into the future, I felt the stirrings of a panic attack.

This afternoon was the day of my first ultrasound. I could find out the gender of the baby if I wanted to know. I felt like I'd just woken up yesterday, learning I was pregnant, and today I'd know if I'd be buying blue or pink onesies. Like so much of my life, it was all too surreal.

Up until last night, I hadn't attempted to call Jude since he'd stormed out. I couldn't remember how many times my finger hovered over the call button before I chickened out, but the fear of my call going to voice mail, or of never hearing back from him again, was too much to contemplate. But letting him know about the ultrasound was the right decision. I at least had to give him the option to show up, because even if he didn't want anything to do with me anymore, I hoped he wouldn't feel the same about the baby. I should have told him the minute I found out I was pregnant; I got that. I got why he was so upset. But he should have called me the minute after he realized what an ass he'd been that day. I was still waiting for him to "get" that. The longer I waited, the angrier I got. But most of all, the sadder I got.

After an hour of going back and forth, I settled for a brief text. I let him know the address of where the ultrasound was taking place, and the time, and, against my better judgment, ended it with an I'M SORRY. I LOVE YOU, and hit send before I could agonize over the message for another hour.

I never got a reply, but even as I checked my phone when I sat filling out paperwork in the waiting room five minutes before my appointment, I hadn't stopped hoping. Both

Holly and India had offered to come for moral support, but I'd made up half a dozen excuses about why I wanted to be alone today.

I'd been filling out so much paperwork my hand was starting to go numb when I got to the last section: "Paternal Support." The first question was easy, although Jude's biting words rang in my ears as I checked the yes box: "Do you know who the baby's father is?" The second and third weren't so easy. "Is the father planning on playing an active role in the baby's life?" and "Is the father supportive?" As soon as I was about to mark yes for both, I convinced myself the answer was no. After finding myself stuck on the same two questions when the ultrasound tech called my name, I created my own box of "I don't know" for both.

"Hi, Lucy," the young tech greeted me. She didn't look too much older than me. "I'm Amy. Right this way."

I followed her down the antiseptic-smelling hall, feeling like I was in a dream. Or a movie. My life no longer felt like my own, but like I was a passive spectator observing it, unable to control it.

"How are you doing?" she asked as she opened a door. The room inside was dark.

I was ready to answer with my standard as-of-late reply of *fine* when I stopped myself.

"I'm scared shitless," I said, flashing her an apologetic smile.

Amy laughed. "At least you're honest," she said, motioning me toward the vinyl-covered bed. "I think that might qualify as the best answer I've heard all week." She sat down on a rolling chair beside the bed and began tapping on a computer. "Go ahead and get comfortable and we'll get started."

I inhaled and tried to make myself comfortable as I reclined. Nothing was really comfortable about it, though. The room was too cold, the pillow was stiff, the paper covering the bed crackled loudly as I moved against it, and there was something so final about finding out if I was having a boy or a girl. I also knew I couldn't get comfortable because Jude wasn't here with me.

"Go ahead and roll up your shirt," she said, grabbing a tube from her cart. "And you'll be happy to know that some genius invented a warmer for this belly lube gunk, so you won't hit the ceiling when I squirt some on your tummy."

I almost smiled as I pulled my shirt up. "Belly lube gunk? Is that the technical term for it?"

Amy shook the tube and squeezed a good-size blob just above my belly button. "As technical as I'll ever get," she said, grabbing the ultrasound reader and lowering it to my stomach. "I'm going to take a quick look at your baby's lungs, heart, and spine, and then we can determine the gender if you like."

"I want to know," I said, as she distributed the blob around.

Amy pressed a button on a remote and the TV in front of me clicked on. It was nothing but a bunch of darkish static, until all of a sudden a white little bean-shaped thing with arms and legs showed up on the screen.

"There's your little peanut," she said, rolling the instrument to give a different view.

I choked on a sob that came out of nowhere. It was primal—everything about my reaction to watching the baby inside me on a TV. Amy handed me a couple of tissues right before my first tears fell. She was an old pro.

These tears had nothing to do with hormones or me being one giant hot mess for the better part of a month. These tears were the kind that came from deep within your soul. They were the tears when life was created or taken away, and I wasn't sure if they'd ever let up.

"This is one healthy little baby you've got cooking in here, Lucy," Amy said after a while. "Everything looks great."

Another assault of tears.

"You ready to find out if it's a boy or girl?" she asked,

shifting the view yet again. I nodded, because I was past words.

The door creaked open, filling the room with a ray of sharp white light as a body slid inside.

"Am I too late?" Jude asked, closing the door.

"No," Amy answered, "you're just in time."

"Luce?" he said, coming toward me. "Am I too late?" he repeated with a whole lot of meaning between his words.

It took a moment for my eyes to readjust, but when they did and I saw the expression on his face, my heart kind of broke and burst at the same instant. He'd made it. He hadn't let me down. He was here for me when I needed him most, looking tortured and anxious and as scared shitless as I was.

It was the most beautiful sight I'd ever seen.

"No, Jude," I said, extending my hand toward him. "You're not too late."

He took my hand and knelt down beside me. "I'm so sorry, Luce," he said, wrapping his other hand around mine. "I love you so damn much. And I love that baby in your belly so damn much." He paused, biting the inside of his cheek. Seeming at a loss for words, he leaned his forehead into our entwined hands and closed his eyes. "I had so much else I wanted to say, but I'm sorry, and I love you . . . *both* pretty much sums it all up."

I was convinced that this past month my tear ducts had taken it upon themselves to revolt and catch up on eight years of trying not to cry. "I'm sorry, and I love you, too," I said. He was right: Those two sentences really did say it all.

"I take it you're the father?" Amy said, fighting a smile as she watched us.

Jude's eyes opened. He lifted his shoulders. "Yeah. I'm the father."

"Well, then, Daddy," Amy said, glancing at her computer screen. "You ready to know what you're having?"

Jude's gaze shifted to the TV and his face went blank. Blank with awe. He'd been too caught up in our sorry-love makeup that he hadn't noticed the baby on the screen. But he did now. And he couldn't look away.

He could barely blink.

"Look at that," Amy said, shaking her head. "Baby's awake now. She must like her daddy's voice."

My head whipped to the side. "She?"

"You're having a little girl," Amy said, winking at me before glancing at Jude.

He was still transfixed, totally enamored as he watched our baby girl's arms and legs move. Then a tear bubbled in the corner of his eye, before it fell down his cheek.

It was the first tear I'd seen Jude shed.

"How are you?" I asked softly.

"Speechless," he breathed, studying the screen like it wasn't real.

"That's the first tear I've seen you cry," I said, skimming my thumb down the moist trail it had left down his face.

"That's *the* first tear I have ever cried," he said, clearing his throat. "I can't imagine a better time to let one fall than finding out I'm going to have a little girl with you, Luce."

"Yeah," I said, "I can't either."

"Well, we're all done here," Amy said. "But I'll print you out some photos to put on your fridge and show off to all your friends, that kind of thing. So, say bye-bye, Mommy and Daddy."

"Bye, baby," I whispered, watching the screen. She was still moving around, almost dancing. She really was my daughter.

"Bye, baby girl," Jude said, before the screen went black.

"You two can have a few moments in here," Amy said, wiping my belly off with some tissues before standing up. "And here are your first baby pictures." She handed me a strand of six photos taken from different angles. All of them brought a smile to my face.

This was our baby. Our baby girl. *Surreal* was the word of the day.

"Do you have some scissors in here?" Jude said, wiping his eyes with the back of his hand. "I want to put one in my wallet."

Amy smiled at him and pulled a pair from her cart. Cutting the top one free, she handed it to him. "I don't need long to know when a baby's going to be well loved and cared for," she said, handing the picture to Jude before heading for the door. "I didn't need more than a few seconds with the two of you to know your little girl is one lucky baby." She smiled and started closing the door. "Take your time."

Jude carefully folded his photo before sliding it into his wallet, his expression peaceful.

"I'm so sorry I didn't tell you right away, Jude," I said, swinging my legs around as I sat up. "I never wanted to—"

"Luce, you don't have anything to apologize for," he said, staring at my stomach before meeting my eyes. "But I do. I behaved like an asshole. I *was* an asshole."

I held up my hand, because I wasn't going to let him take all the blame like he always did. "Lord knows I love you for saying that, but I've plenty to apologize for. So please let me. Okay?"

He took a seat next to me on the edge of the bed and nodded.

"I should have told you the minute after I found out I was pregnant," I began, running my hands down my legs. "But

I was scared. Terrified. I couldn't wrap my mind around the fact that I was pregnant, and I assured myself I'd tell you as soon as I'd gotten used to the idea. I think I've figured out that you don't get 'used' to the idea of being pregnant when you're an unmarried twenty-one-year-old trying to finish school."

Maybe no one, no matter what their age or place in life, got used to the idea, because it was something so beyond comprehension. Something epic. Creating life. Sustaining life. Giving life. It wasn't a concept that was easy to wrap any mind around.

"After a week passed and I wasn't feeling any better, I knew I needed to tell you, but I didn't want it to be on the phone, and I didn't want it to be something I had to rush when I flew in for your first game. I wanted there to be a perfect time and place to tell you, so we could figure this curveball out together, but I should have remembered I'm a walking experiment in imperfect timing."

Jude reached for my hand and weaved his fingers through mine.

"I should have told you sooner. I'm sorry I didn't. And I'm really sorry you found out the way you did." I squeezed his hand. "But I'm so, so happy you're here with me now."

"Me too," he said, lifting my hand to his lips. "Are you done now? With your apology?" His lips grazed along my knuckles, heating the skin along the way. "Because I've got something of a monumental apology to make, too."

"You've got the floor, Mr. Ryder," I said ceremoniously.

Pressing one final kiss to my knuckles, he lowered our hands to his lap. "I walked out on you Saturday night because I was scared, too, Luce," he said. "I was scared of the reasons you'd kept it from me in the first place. I was scared that you would forever resent me for getting you pregnant. I was scared that I didn't have what it takes to be a father. I was scared of so much, but what I was mostly scared of was losing you." His voice was tight as his eyes lowered to my stomach. "And losing our baby.

"I ran that night because I was scared, and the fact that I ran away when you needed me most made me even more scared. So that's what I've been thinking about nonstop, all day, every day, since Saturday night. And you want to know what I came up with?" he asked, leaning his forehead into mine. At this proximity, his eyes took up my whole field of vision.

"What?" I said, almost kissing him because our mouths were that close.

"That it doesn't matter why I ran," he said, staring at me without blinking, "because I came back. I'll always come back, Luce. No matter how many rip-roaring fights we have and no matter how many miscommunications we have. I'll always come back because *you're* where I belong."

"That's quite the revelation there, Ryder," I said. "You have a lot of those, don't you?"

"I didn't get this far with you without having a good epiphany knock me over the head once in a while."

"So," I said, "anything else or can we just kiss and make up now?"

His forehead left mine. "One more thing," he said, as his face wrinkled. "Are you worried I'm going to be the kind of dad mine was?" I could tell he was trying not to show how hard these words were to get out, but I'd seen this man through four years of life's highs and lows.

"I meant what I said Saturday, Jude," I said, trying to erase the worry lines from his face with my fingers. "That has never been one of my concerns. Ever, and you want to know why?" I fed him back his line.

"Why?"

"Because you're aware of it, because you're worried about it. That fear of becoming your father will drive you to be the best father you can be," I said, watching the first batch of wrinkles vanish from his face. "You know what would worry me, though? If you were overwhelmingly confident you could never become him. If you were so positive you could never in a million years be like him, I'd be worried that kind of confidence would make you lazy. Make it that

much easier to fall into the traps when the hard times came."
I stopped to take a breath. I was really on a roll, but I had a
lot to say. "But that's not how you are, and that's why I'm
not worried. And, Jude? I wouldn't pick another man if I
had the whole entire world to choose from to be the father
of my baby."

The last remaining wrinkles ironed out. "Dammit,
woman," he said, "you keep saying that kind of stuff and I'm
going to shed another tear." Leaning in, he kissed me again,
but this one lasted longer than the last, although it was still
too short for my liking.

"So we're good now? Everything off our chests that
needs to be off them?"

Like the twisted guy he was, his eyes drifted to my chest.
A wide smile appeared.

I shoved him in reply.

"So maybe I've got one more thing to get off my chest."

"There's always one more thing with you and me."

"Yeah, but this will tide me over for a while if you agree
to it," he said, rubbing the back of his neck.

"Are you nervous?" I said, shocked. The last time I could
remember him visibly nervous had been on the fifty-yard
line, when he'd asked me to . . .

"Marry me, Luce," he started, blowing out a breath. "I

need to do what I can to make this whole thing right, and the way I know how is to make us a family."

"We are a family, baby," I said, wondering if he was going to rub the skin raw on that neck of his.

"I know we are, but I want to be the kind that can frame their wedding certificate and hang it above the fireplace," he said. "I want our little girl to have a mom and a dad who are committed to each other, *married* to each other. I want her to have the stable, nurturing environment I didn't have. I want you to be my wife and me to be your husband for our little girl, Luce, but I'd be lying if I didn't admit I have selfish reasons for wanting to tie the knot with you."

"You have a right to be selfish," I said, grabbing his hand and pulling it away from his neck. "You've been a patient man with me for three years while I kept up the whole 'soon' thing."

"Yeah, I don't think your idea of 'soon' is going to work, Luce. I don't want our daughter to be old enough to get hitched before we do." His nose wrinkled. "Wait. What the hell am I saying? Our daughter is never going to get married. She's never going to date. In fact, she's never going to know what a boy even is, because I'd lose it if she brought home a guy like me."

I was laughing. The good, real kind that rocked your whole body. I hadn't laughed like that in a while. I smiled up at him. "I'd be thrilled if she brought home a boy like you one day," I said. "She'd make her mama proud."

"I don't think so. The whole piece-of-shit-attraction thing ends with you. Nothing but the best for my daughter."

"Okay, okay," I said, holding up my hands in surrender, because this was a topic Jude and I could go 'round and 'round on for days and no one would ever be declared a winner. "So when are we getting married?"

Jude's eyebrows went sky-high. "Wait . . . are you saying you're ready? Like to set a date and send the invites?"

"I'm ready," I said, trying not to laugh at his expression. He'd almost looked as surprised when he'd found out I was pregnant.

"What are you thinking? Weeks? Months?" He was wringing his hands, he was getting so excited.

"We're at a hospital, aren't we?" I said, shrugging. "There's got to be a chaplain or a minister or someone who can make us official."

That look of shock that had been on Jude's face a few seconds ago? Yeah, it had nothing to do with the new one he had on right now.

He opened his mouth, but nothing came out. Giving his

head a rough shake, he tried again. "Are you saying what I think you're saying?"

I knew I was crazy, and friends and family would hit the ceiling when they found out, but I'd blame it on the hormones and the way Jude's eyes were looking at me now.

Life was about compromise. It was give and take, and with Jude and me, I'd been more take than give in our relationship. He'd given me everything and would do it all over again. It was my turn to step up to the give plate. Whether I married him today or ten years from now, I was marrying Jude Ryder. It was time for me to let go of my baseless fears and doubts and grab onto what was guaranteed: Jude.

"If it involves you and me saying 'I do' this afternoon, then yeah, I'm saying what you think I am."

I'd never seen him beam the way he was now. "Just when I think I can't possibly love you more . . ."

"I go and propose a shotgun wedding at a hospital chapel when I'm knocked up and wearing a T-shirt and plaid skirt?"

His smile stretched higher. "Exactly." Then, before I knew what had happened, Jude had me in his arms and was rushing out the door.

When we hit the hall, he started running. The heads of

nurses and doctors and patients were whipping around to take in the pair of us, laughing and sprinting our way to the chapel.

"We're getting married!" Jude shouted in between his laugher. "Holy shit!"

Jude hadn't set me down until we'd made it to the hospital's chapel on the first floor. He dropped me off at the gift shop, giving me a nice long kiss that made my toes curl in my flats, before jogging off to find the minister. Or the pastor. Or the priest. Or whoever had the ability to marry us. We didn't care.

I walked up to the gift shop counter, hoping they'd have something that would work as a temporary wedding ring until I could find a suitable one. My prayers were answered.

There were several brushed-titanium bands in the display case. Perfect. I asked the woman behind the counter if I could see one, and, after trying three of them on my finger to compare, I was fairly sure I'd found the one that would fit Jude.

It was a whopping thirty dollars, and after assuring the saleslady I didn't need it gift-wrapped because it would be sliding onto a finger in hopefully less than ten minutes, I rushed to the chapel.

I scanned up and down the hall, but didn't see Jude, so

I shoved through the door and found who I'd been looking for.

Standing in front of an altar. There was a smile on his
face that made me think things that could probably get me
struck down by lightning for having them in a church. He'd
tucked in his white undershirt, but that was as formal as the
occasion got. I was no better. I hadn't even made a stop in
the women's restroom to run a comb through my hair or dot
on a bit of lip gloss.

That was part of the beauty of today. Part of the beauty
of Jude and me. We came as we were, minus the frills and
the fluff, accepting each other as-is.

"Hello, my beautiful, blushing bride," Jude said, nodding
his head behind him. "I wrangled us up a priest." An elderly
man wearing his white collar and a smile stood behind what
looked to be more a podium than an altar. "And a witness."
He motioned to a middle-aged man sporting scrubs sitting
in the front-row pew. "Did you find a ring?"

I held up my thumb, where the band dangled from it.

"All that's left is a couple of signatures and 'I do's, then,"
Jude said, inclining his head, encouraging me to walk up
the aisle.

Throwing my shoulders back and putting on a dramatic
face, I held an imaginary bouquet of flowers in front of me
and started my left-together, right-together march down

toward the man I was about to promise forever to.

"Baaa-bum-ba-bum," Jude sang in a low voice, "Ba-bum-ba-bummm."

Even at a slow walk, I was in front of him before he'd finished singing.

"Didn't I tell you, Father Joe?" Jude said, fitting his hand against my cheek. "Isn't she the most beautiful thing you've ever seen?"

Father Joe's warm smile grew. "I'd say you're a very lucky young man."

"Hell yes, I am . . ." Jude's voice trailed off as he gave the priest a sheepish smile. "Sorry."

Father Joe just chuckled and folded his hands in front of him. "Shall we get started?"

"Hel—" Jude caught himself this time. "You bet."

"Thank you for marrying us," I said. "I bet you don't get too many shotgun weddings in a place like this."

Father Joe leaned in like he was telling me a secret. "You'd be surprised."

"This is your last chance to run away screaming, Luce," Jude said, holding his hands out for mine.

I studied the door before turning to him. I grabbed his hands. "How about once we're done here, we run away together?"

"Deal," he answered, nodding his head at Father Joe.

"Mr. Ryder said he'd like to keep the vows brief," Father Joe started.

I chuckled. "Of course he did."

"If that's all right with you, Miss Larson."

"Whoa." Jude's eyes widened. "Do you realize that's the last time you're going to be Miss Larson?"

"Yeah, that's kinda the reason I'm standing here," I said, laughing at the irony that our wedding was just as unconventional as our entire relationship. "And yes, Father Joe, I'm just fine with keeping things brief."

"Something tells me the two of you have quite the dynamic relationship," Father Joe said, his eyes sparkling.

Jude and I looked at each other and smiled. "You have no idea," we said in unison.

Father Joe cleared his throat and angled himself toward Jude. "Son, repeat after me—"

"Oh, I'm good, Father," Jude said, raising his hand. "I memorized the vows a while back."

"What?" I shouldn't have been surprised.

"I never knew when I was going to finally wear you down, and had to be ready for whenever that moment occurred," he said.

I stood up on my toes and planted a kiss on his lips. "Just

when I think I can't fall any more in love with you."

He winked and blew a slow rush of air out of his mouth. "I, Jude Ryder Jamieson, take you, Luce Roslyn Larson"—I bit my lip to keep from smiling—"to be my wife, to have and to hold from this day forward, for better or for worse, for richer, for poorer, in sickness and in health, to love and to cherish—until death do us part." He blew out another long breath. "How was that?"

"Pretty much the most romantic thing you've ever said to me," I replied.

"Very well done, son," Father Joe said before angling in my direction. "Lucy, would you like to repeat after me, or did you memorize the vows as well?"

"I've got this, Father," I said, squeezing Jude's hands. Amazingly, neither of our hands were clammy. Neither one of us was nervous about making promises of forever to the other. "I, Luce Roslyn Larson"—now it was Jude's turn to keep from smiling—"take you, Jude Ryder Jamieson, to be my husband, to have and to hold from this day forward, for better or worse, for richer, for poorer, in sickness and in health, to love and to cherish—until death do us part."

As I finished my vows, I wondered what had taken me so long to get here. What had I been so worried about waiting for? Jude was just as much mine now as he had been then. A simple exchange of vows shouldn't change anything. But as

I stood here before him now after exchanging our vows, it kind of changed everything, too.

"I understand you have rings you'd like to use?"

"We do," Jude answered, slipping something from his pocket. It was a tiny silver band. A wedding band with three alternating gemstones. It looked like he'd been hoping for this moment when he got dressed today.

Holding my left hand in his, he positioned the finger above my ring finger. "These stones represent you and me, Luce, and our little girl," he said. "Emerald for your birthday, ruby for mine, and amethyst for the month she's supposed to be born. I wanted it to be special, you know?"

He'd put a serious amount of thought into this one ring. "I know," I said, fighting the lump in my throat. "It's beautiful, Jude."

He slid the ring down my finger. "With this ring, I thee wed."

The wedding band with the three members of my family's birthstones sparkled above the engagement ring I'd worn solo for three years. It was happy to have its mate.

I had to wipe my eyes before I grabbed his left hand. "Mine's not nearly as thoughtful, but it'll work. For now."

"It'll work for*ever*," he said, admiring the band.

As I slid the ring down his finger, I realized it would work forever. It suited him. "With this ring, I thee wed."

Father Joe looked between us. "And now, by the power vested in me, I hereby declare you husband and wife. You may—"

"Yeah, Father," Jude said, wrapping his arms around me and pulling me close. "I memorized this part, too." His mouth covered mine, and he kissed me. It was a bit like our first kiss, timid and hungry, and a little like it would be our last kiss, slow and consuming.

My first kiss as a married woman was pretty damn amazing.

Only when we had to surface for air did Jude's lips leave mine. He sighed. "Finally."

"Yeah," I said, kissing his scar. "Finally."

"Congratulations," Father Joe said, his eyes still sparkling. "Be good to each other." Giving us one last smile, he backed away from the podium and headed out of the chapel, along with our silent witness.

"What now?" I asked, tugging him toward the door. "Now that you've made an honest woman out of me, what have you got in mind next?"

"We should probably get that official wedding license thing so I can hang it on the wall," he said, grinning ear to ear.

"We're as official as you and me need to be," I said, "but

a framed wedding certificate would be a nice touch to the Ryder family home." Wherever that home would be. We were in something of a TBD state in the home department. "But when I asked 'what now' I was referring to the next few *hours* future, not the next few *days* future."

"In that case . . . how about a nice dinner? Candles? A bottle of champagne," he said, catching himself. "Or a bottle of sparkling water?"

Shoving through the door, I pulled him along. "Dinner sounds good," I said, pulling him faster down the hall, until we'd passed the elevators and nurses' desk. "But I've got a better idea." Pausing at the last door at the end of the hall, I slid inside and gave it a quick once-over. It was empty, and had a lock on the door and a freshly made hospital bed against the window.

"I'm all for better ideas, Luce," Jude said as I pulled him inside, "but what does sneaking into a hospital room have to do with it?"

Locking the door behind us, I shoved him up against the wall.

"This," I said, kissing him. Hard.

"Better idea," he said in between my frantic lips. My hands grabbed the hem of my shirt and tugged it over my head. "Much better idea."

His shirt was the next one off, and then his fingers were releasing my bra. His hands skimmed around the front, covering my breasts.

"Shit, Luce." Jude pulled away from me, and his eyes dropped to where his hands had just been. They widened. "What the hell?"

"Being pregnant has its advantages," I said, glancing down where my baby Cs had blossomed into full-on Ds in the wake of baby making.

"Hell yes, it does," he said, lifting his hands back into position.

"Plus, I've got increased sex drive," I added with a wink. "We're talking crazed, panting, do-me-in-the-morning-afternoon-and-evening kind of increased sex drive."

"If I don't get inside you soon, I'm going to bust something," he said, lifting me up and beelining for the bed. "Your huge tits and your dirty mouth are doing a number on me."

"Well, you'd better hurry then," I said, kissing his neck as my hand slid inside the front of his pants.

"Shit, baby, I'm serious." He groaned when my hand tightened around him.

"So am I," I replied, gliding my hand down him.

Then he had me on the bed and was crawling into the

space between my legs. His face took on a serious expression all of a sudden.

"Can we be doing this?" he said, still breathing heavily. "With you being pregnant and all?"

If we didn't do this I was fairly sure I'd burst into flames. I grabbed the top button of his jeans and tugged it free. "Does it seem weird to you that you want to abstain from the act that made the baby because of the baby?" I made quick work of his zipper.

"You're talking over my head again," he said.

"Then why don't you just shut up and make love to your wife already?" Grabbing the waist of his jeans, I tugged them down.

"Okay." His fingers slid inside my panties and he pulled them down my legs. The skirt would have to stay, because I couldn't wait any longer. "Let's see how Mrs. Ryder is in bed."

Hovering over me, Jude braced his arms around me and lowered his chest until it smashed against mine. A stupid little grin formed on his face.

"I think I can get used to these things, Luce."

I lifted my hips until I could feel him hard against me. "Enough talking. Not enough screwing."

His dopey smile morphed into something else when he

pushed himself inside me. I'd been so ready for him he sank all the way in. His mouth dropped to my neck, sucking the sensitive skin into his mouth, torturing me with each slow kiss as he stayed unmoving.

"Be nice," I said, trying to flex my hips against his, but he had me pinned. I was at his mercy. "I'm your wife, after all."

Jude gave my neck one final nip before his face moved above mine. "When you put it that way," he said, staring hard into my eyes as he slid back—and, just when I thought he was pulling out all the way, he thrust back inside.

My arm flailed to the side, winding around the metal bedrail for support. It appeared that along with increased sex drive came a decreased thrust count until orgasm.

My other hand dug into his backside, curling into his flesh as he pulsed in and out of me.

"I can't wait, baby." I moaned as he rocked inside me again, already feeling my climax coming on.

"I can't either," he panted, picking up his pace until my moans came at the same time as his low groan. His fingers wove through mine on the bedrail as I pulsed around him.

Wrapping his arms around me, Jude rolled over and cradled me to him. His breathing was just as labored as mine as our chests rose and fell to the same count.

"I love you, Luce Ryder," he breathed, running his

fingers up and down my back.

"I love you, Jude Ryder." I looked up at him. "So . . . how was Mrs. Ryder in bed?"

That same stupid smile broke over his face. "Fucking fantastic."

I chuckled into the crook of his arm. "Good thing. Since you're going to be stuck making love to her until you shrivel up and die."

"Good thing," he said, sounding happy, satisfied, and tired. That was a powerful combo.

"So, Mr. Jude Ryder." I lifted my head from his chest and pretended to talk into a microphone ceremoniously. "You just got hitched at the age of twenty-one, will be changing your baby's diapers before you turn twenty-two, and just had your honeymoon on a hospital bed." I held out the imaginary mike. "How do you feel?"

"Like the luckiest damn bastard in the world."

I could relate.

"Well put," I said. "Very convincing."

He ran his fingers through my hair and stared at me like I was the most special thing in the world to him. "I must be convincing. I got you to say yes a few minutes ago, didn't I?"

I thought of all the ways he'd gotten me to a yes. That first day at the beach, when I'd known he wasn't good for me but couldn't stay away. That morning at my locker, when he'd gotten me to say yes to going to Homecoming with him. His proposal at the fifty-yard line in front of fifty thousand fans. And finally, at the altar becoming his wife, when I couldn't say yes fast enough.

"Yeah, Jude," I said. "You sure did."

EPILOGUE

*J*ude was at the fifty-yard line again, being cheered on by tens of thousands of fans, but this time it was a few games into his second season playing for the Chargers.

I was still in the front-and-center seat, cheering along with the rest of the fans.

But this time our wiggling, cooing six-month-old baby girl was on my lap. No surprise she'd had her own agenda when it came to what day she wanted to come out and meet the big world. Jude and I were her parents, after all. She was born three weeks early, and I don't know if Jude breathed the entire twelve hours of my delivery. But he never left my side. When she finally came out, Jude could barely look away from her long enough to cut the cord. He'd cried his second tear that day. And his third, and maybe even a fourth when the doctor said our girl was perfectly healthy.

After fall semester, I moved out to San Diego to be with Jude. To have our baby and figure out our future. After she was born, life had been crazy, but I'd just enrolled in a few courses at a local college that would count toward my degree, so, slowly but surely, I'd get it done. Finishing my degree was more a matter of pride and stubborn resolve.

We'd named our little girl Annalise Marie Ryder. It wasn't a family name; nor had we agonized over selecting just the right meaning. Jude had fallen in love with the name one night when we'd been scanning baby-name books, like, *really* fallen in love with it. I knew he would have backed down if I said I didn't like it or wanted a different name, but Jude had a grand total of zero blood relatives in his life anymore. He'd earned the right to name the little girl who was half his DNA and would be forever in his life.

So Annalise Marie it was. She looked like me, but had her daddy's gray eyes, and could form expressions at six months that were eerily identical to Jude's.

Speaking of a certain Mr. Ryder . . . Jude got into position, ready for the hike. I was about to pop up and jump and cheer with a fifteen-pound Annalise bundle when someone tapped me from the side.

"Can I hold her, Aunt Luce?"

LJ had grown into a not-so-little man in a year's time.

He and Holly still lived in the old apartment back in White Plains, but now Thomas lived there, too. He'd proposed last month and they were tying the knot this winter. We didn't get to see them as often as I'd have liked, but they made it out a few times a year to come to one of Jude's games or to play at the beach, and we did our best to make it back east.

"Sure, LJ," I said, setting Annalise on his lap, but keeping my hands close by. "She's a little mover and shaker, so hang on tight."

"I will," he said, winding both arms tight around her middle. Of course, she calmed down almost right away now that cousin LJ had her.

The stadium was loud from the start to the end of the game. To help muffle some of that noise on baby ears, Annalise had her own special knit beanie she wore to every game. Unlike Jude's, hers was pink, and she had a handful of Chargers outfits she rocked along with the jersey I wore.

I stayed seated next to LJ just in case Annalise decided to take a flying leap from his arms, and waved down the row at Sybill, who was wrestling her own four kiddos.

"I gotta tell you, Lucy," Holly said, elbowing me from the other side, "that little beach house Jude got you for a wedding present is pretty fantastic. Just so you know, LJ, Thomas, and I are considering making the second floor our winter home. You guys wouldn't mind, right?"

Since we were playing the elbowing game, I gave her one of mine. "No, we wouldn't mind. As long as LJ doesn't pee on all of my plants and Thomas picks up his dirty underwear."

"Yeah, I don't see that ever happening," she said. "Darn, I guess it will just be me!"

I laughed, knowing she was partly serious—not about leaving LJ and Thomas, but about moving. They always stayed with us whenever they flew out, since we had the room, and the beach for our backyard, and when it came to Holly, Thomas, and LJ, it was truly the more, the merrier. Dad and Mom made it down to see us a bunch, too. Something about having a baby in the family was especially motivating. As a wedding present, Jude had surprised me with the keys to that beach house I'd wanted to rent for the holidays. Except instead of renting, we owned.

So we got to stay in it for the holidays last year, and we'll get to stay in it every holiday after that. Jude had even sold his souped-up truck and had his old piecer totally rebuilt. I couldn't call it a POS anymore, because it was gorgeous.

"How's the dance studio coming along?" Holly asked as she watched the field.

Jude had called a last-minute time-out and was deep in a huddle with his teammates.

"Great. The dance floor goes in this week and then it's pretty much done," I said, rummaging through the diaper bag for Annalise's teething giraffe she liked to gnaw on. "I've already got a list of dancers enrolled."

"Those poor kids are going to go home crying after spending an hour in class with you as their teacher," she said, smirking over at me.

"Why don't you enroll in my adult class and I'll make sure I send you home crying," I replied, mirroring her smirk.

"Nah," she said, nudging Thomas beside her. "Tights and ballet shoes are for men."

"Damn straight, baby," he said, pulling her close and kissing her full on the lips.

I laughed, and checked the field. They were out of the huddle and getting back into position. As yet another wedding present, Jude had purchased an old, run-down building in an artsy part of the city. He put me in charge of the design and renovation for its transformation. While I was finishing up fall semester, the dance studio came together. I'd made some solid progress with my money-issues thing. Jude had promised me that the money and the fame wouldn't change him, and he'd been right. He still swaggered around in his Cons and Levi's and drank cheap beer, but, most important, he still looked at me like I was his whole world. His eyes still went soft when he said, "I love you," and he didn't hesitate to help change a tire for some stranger stranded on the side of the road. So Jude was still Jude, I was still me, and we were still us. About the only thing that had changed was our bank account, just like he'd promised.

In between rooting for my favorite football team and changing diapers, I was still hell-bent on working in some sort of capacity, but I'd come to realize I wanted to work not so much because I needed to make my own money, but because I wanted to make a difference. Pairing that desire with my obsession for dance . . . well, the dance studio was the result. The knowledge that one day I could possibly influence a young girl the way Madame Fontaine had influenced me felt like it was the cherry on top of a very fulfilling sundae.

"Go, Uncle Jude," LJ said, careful not to shout with Annalise in his arms.

"Here, buddy," I said, reaching for her. "Let me take her so you can get up and bounce and scream for Uncle Jude. You know he can hear you out there, right?"

"I know," LJ said importantly, letting me take Annalise.

"Come here, sweet girl. Let's cheer for your daddy." Kissing Annalise's head, I stood up just as the center hiked the ball.

Jude didn't even fake a pass; he just cradled that ball against himself and sprinted for the end zone.

I held my breath as everyone around the arena exploded.

When he'd hit the ten I let myself exhale. He was going to do it.

When his foot landed in the end zone, the roof felt like it was going to blow off the place from the noise. I just stood there and grinned down at him. He was still a show-off.

Dropping the ball, he turned and jogged down the sidelines.

He high-fived a few of his teammates in passing, but he couldn't be stopped. Coming to a pause in front of us, he grinned up.

"That one was for my girls," he said, sliding his helmet off.

"And consider your girls sufficiently impressed," I shouted, leaning forward. Annalise was really wriggling now that she'd caught sight of her daddy. She was smiling and making spit bubbles from her excitement.

"Come here, baby girl," he said, lifting his arms. I surrendered her to his strong hands. "You want to see the best seat in the house?"

Annalise jolted, shaking her baby arms. She was such a daddy's girl.

"Okay, okay." He laughed, tucking her close to him. "But first I got to get a little something-something from your mama."

Smiling that smile of his that made my stomach drop, he tilted his head up at me.

Leaning down, I kissed him and, no different from the first time we'd done this, the rest of the world faded away. It was just Jude and me and our little girl.

It was what you'd call something of a full-circle moment.

"Love you, Luce," he said, after Annalise's little hand had poked up between our mouths. She'd grabbed onto Jude's lower lip and wasn't letting go.

"Love you, Jude."

Turning around, Jude carried Annalise out onto the field. He didn't stop until he came to the middle of the fifty-yard line. Cradling her in his arms, he did a slow spin. Cameras were flashing, fans were screaming, and it was controlled anarchy, but I knew there was no one else but Jude and his little girl out there right now to him.

As I watched them, I felt the same thing. We were in our own bubble, and it was a good one. My life wasn't how I planned it would be. It wasn't even close.

It was a thousand times better.

Sybill had been right: The few things I'd sacrificed, or put on hold, to be with my husband and baby were worth it. That broken boy on the beach seemed like a lifetime ago. Years had passed, college and the NFL, marriage and a baby, but every once in a while, when Jude looked over at me and gave me that slow, knowing smile of his, I was that girl in a black string bikini all over again, longing for a boy I never thought could be mine.